For Lizzie

Perhaps being old is having lighted rooms
Inside your head, and people in them, acting
People you know, yet can't quite name; each looms
Like a deep loss restored, from known doors turning,
Setting down a lamp, smiling from a stair, extracting
A known book from the shelves; or sometimes only
The rooms themselves, chairs and a fire burning,
The blown bush at the window, or the sun's
Faint friendliness on the wall some lonely
Rain-ceased midsummer evening. That is where they live:
Not here and now, but where all happened once.

—Philip Larkin, "The Old Fools"

Influential Figurative Painter Oscar Feldman Dies at 78

By GINA TSARKIS

Oscar Feldman, whose bold and innovative female nudes are among the most admired and influential artworks of recent years, died of a heart attack August 7 in the Riverside Drive apartment where he'd lived with his wife and son for many decades. He was 78.

Until the end of his life, Mr. Feldman was a dedicated and accomplished artist, and his paintings are often shown in museums and galleries. For decades, he worked every day in his studio on the Bowery. Mr. Feldman was admired both for his prodigious output and the steadfastness of his artistic aims. Throughout his artistic career, his primary, indeed only, subject was the female nude.

"The female body is the ultimate expression of truth and beauty," he wrote. "I mean truth in all its ramifications: terror included, and death. Beauty likewise: There is a dead stinking creature in every perfect shell on the sand, and in many ways that is the whole point."

Oscar Avram Feldman was born April 5, 1923, in New York City. The son of an Orthodox Jewish butcher, he grew up on Ludlow Street on the Lower East Side. He attended P.S. 137 and 65, then Seward High School. Mr. Feldman was a Brooklyn College student in the early 1940s, when Jackson Pollock and other artists created the stylistic revolution that came to be known as Abstract Expressionism. After graduating with a

degree in art history in 1945, Mr. Feldman briefly attended the Art Students League, but dropped out halfway through his first year to work as a taxi driver and paint on his own. He rented a loft on the Bowery, which he kept as his studio when he married Abigail Rebecca Lebowitz in 1955 and moved to Riverside Drive. Their son and only child, Ethan Saul Feldman, was born in 1959 and was diagnosed with severe autism at the age of three.

Largely self-taught, Mr. Feldman chose deliberately not to follow the Abstract Expressionists' path, preferring instead to work in the figurative vein that characterized his work until the end of his life. Mr. Feldman expressed admiration for Philip Guston alone of his near contemporaries. Mr. Guston abruptly abandoned abstraction for the cartoonlike, strangely passionate, rough drawings that shocked the art world in the 1960s.

Mr. Feldman's nudes are characterized by the boldness of his brush strokes and palette. He painted women as complex and earthy, never idealized or purely sexualized. His treatment of skin in particular, or "flesh," as he liked to call it, was notable for its range of colors and textures. "The flesh, not the eye," he wrote, "is the portal to the soul."

"Oscar Feldman's work was bold and original and gives definition to those two words," said Earl A. Powell, director of the National Gallery of Art. "His work was exciting, determined, and passionate. He made a huge contribution to postwar art."

Hilton Kramer, the idiosyncratic and often lacerating art critic and editor of "The New Criterion," has described Mr. Feldman's work as "ballsy almost to the point of testicular obnoxiousness, going up to but never crossing that line."

If not widely known to the general public, his paintings are prized by collectors and are housed in many leading museums, including the National Gallery of Art, the Hirshhorn Museum, the Museum of Modern Art, and the Whitney Museum of American Art. His full-size paintings routinely sell for more than $1 million.

Mr. Feldman led a life of relative isolation from the rest of the art world by choice. He also disavowed politics and any connection with the antiwar movement. In 1987, when he was honored by the Guggenheim Museum, he came to the reception wearing a guayabera shirt and work trousers spattered with paint. He was a larger-than-life figure, by all accounts opinionated, occasionally boisterous, visceral, with insatiable appetites of many kinds.

In 1976, he was inducted into the American Academy of Arts and Letters, and he received a National Medal of Arts from the National Endowment for the Arts in 1986.

"When I think of art, I think of women," he wrote, riffing on Agnes Martin's famous lines. "Women are the mystery of life."

He leaves behind his wife, Abigail, their son, Ethan, and his sister, the well-known abstract painter Maxine Elizabeth Feldman.

PART ONE

One

"It's amazing how well you can live on very little money," said Teddy St. Cloud to Henry Burke over her shoulder as she strode into the kitchen of her Brooklyn row house. She hoped he was noticing that her hips and waist were still girlishly slender, her step youthful, and that he'd describe her accurately instead of saying she was "gaunt but chipper," like that sour-faced squaw with the crooked teeth from *The New Yorker* who'd written the profile of Oscar a few years ago. "I hope you're a Reform Jew," she added. "I got prosciutto."

"I'm not Jewish," he said after a second of displacement. They stood somewhat awkwardly together in the kitchen, not sure suddenly where to go now that their short walk down the hall had disgorged them into their destination. "But people often think—"

"Burke," she said. "That's not the Ellis Islandization of Berkowitz?"

"No," said Henry. "It's English."

She leaned against the counter, her eyes fixed on some middle distance in her mind. She suspected that she looked much older in person than Henry had expected, but then, of course, she was seventy-four, and the person he'd no doubt been expecting, unconsciously, to meet was the young woman Oscar had fallen in love with. But she was proud of the fact that as old as she was, she still resembled her younger self. Her oval, narrow face had aged markedly, with shallow grooves running along both sides of her nose, slight hoods over her eyes, a subtle lengthening of the earlobes, a thinning of the lips, a network of extremely fine wrinkles around her eyes. But she held her small, well-shaped head very high, with the self-aware edge of mischief and manipulation Oscar had loved, eyes glittering foxily, as if she were about to snap out of her feigned concentration and laugh at her observer for being fooled into thinking she hadn't been watching him all along. This air of expressive, confident intelligence, Oscar had told her, was one of the sexiest qualities about her, the electric flame that ran almost visibly soft and licking over her skin, hinting at interesting flare-ups. Then he had added that having incredible boobs didn't hurt.

"Please sit down," said Teddy; she intended it as a command. She wasn't impressed by Henry. She guessed that he was forty or thereabouts. He looked like a lightweight, the kind of young man you saw everywhere these days, gutless and bland. He wore soft cotton clothing, a little rumpled from the heat and long drive in the car—she would have bet it was a Volvo. She could smell domesticity on him, the technologically up-to-date apartment on the Upper West Side, the ambitious, hard-edged wife—women were the hard ones at that age. Men turned sheepish and eager to please after about forty. Oscar had been the same way; he'd turned into a bit of a hangdog at around forty and hadn't fully regained his chutzpah until he'd hit fifty or so, but even then, she had never lost interest in him, and she was still interested in him now, even though he was gone.

Henry chose a chair facing her and sat at the table.

"Look at this melon," she said. "I asked my grocer to give it to me half price by letting him think it was a little soft. Well, it is, but just in one small spot."

She began slicing the cantaloupe in half on a cutting board, holding the knife in her small square hand. Her kitchen was a long, narrow galley-shaped room with glass-fronted cupboards and an old-fashioned stove and refrigerator, a deep cast-iron sink. The room, like the rest of the house, felt as if she were only temporarily inhabiting it. It had no particular odor. Most old houses were clogged with the olfactory remnants of years of living, the memories of long-ago meals, hidden mold, the strong scent of people. This wasn't the house she had lived in when she and Oscar were together, but the one she'd bought after his death five years ago, after selling the other one. This one had lost its history when the family who'd owned it for decades had moved out with all their stuff and Teddy had moved in with hers. Somehow, during the transfer, everything had discharged its freight of sediment, the walls of the house, her furniture and belongings, and now it all just smelled clean and impersonal. None of Oscar's paintings hung on these walls: Oscar had never given her one.

"So," she said abruptly from the sideboard. "What can I tell you about the great man?"

"Well," said Henry, caught slightly off guard. "I was thinking we would start at the beginning. For now, just talk about him. We'll get down to the nitty-gritty of dates and times later. Maybe start with how you met him, how the two of you fell in love—"

"Wine?" she said with a glint of aggression. She reached into the refrigerator, the corkscrew already in her other hand. "It's a Sancerre, but not as expensive as it tastes, by far." She wrested the cork from its hole with a faintly savage twist of her wrist. She had been expecting someone Jewish like Oscar, someone ballsy, someone fun to banter and flirt with, not this twerp in rumpled khakis.

"Sure," he said with a puzzled sidelong look up at her.

"Henry," she said as she set his glass down with a snap in front of him, "let's establish one thing right now. This discussion is nonnegotiable. If you won't listen to what I have to say, you can drink your wine and eat a little melon and then you get up and leave. You've clearly arrived with some preconceived notions, and if you can't shake them loose out of your head like a lot of . . . moths, then I have nothing to say to you."

Henry blinked. "I have no preconceived notions," he said. "I'm here to listen."

"I want to see a flock of moths rising from your head," she said. "I'm going to roll the melon with prosciutto now, and when I next turn around, I want to see white fluttery little things rising from your hair and flying out the window."

She flung open the casement window over the sink and the room was immediately crowded with the sounds of tree leaves, birdsong, and the shouts of kids in a nearby backyard. Her back was turned to him. She could feel her body quivering like an arrow aimed at someone's heart as she worked.

"You're right about this wine," he said. "It's delicious."

"No man should ever use the word *delicious*," she said.

"Teddy," he said clearly.

She turned slowly to stare at him. Had he actually just called her by her nickname? They looked at each other blank-faced for an instant, and she imagined that he was also wondering this same thing.

"Claire," they both corrected at once.

"Yes?" she said.

"Talk to me about Oscar," he said. He took another taste of wine.

"The great man," said Teddy with a private inner smile, "was the biggest human baby in all of history. That's no secret: We all know how his women propped him up, me and his wife, Abigail, and sister, Maxine, and our daughters, not to mention every woman he met at an opening or on a train. He couldn't live without a woman around to look at and probe, by which I mean fuck but also investigate thoroughly."

Henry picked up his pen and glanced at his notebook but didn't write anything down.

"He couldn't live without a woman around," she repeated. She knew he wanted dates, knew his monomaniacal, orderly biographer's mind was lying in wait, biding its time, until it could spring forth like an anteater's tongue and cleanly extract the facts of her history with Oscar like a swath of ants from an anthill. She felt herself resist this with everything she had. No fact, no date—"Oscar Feldman first met Claire St. Cloud on October 7, 1958," for example—could convey anything of what had really gone on between them. "He saw women as the most powerful beings on earth. You can see it in his portrait of our daughter Ruby as a baby, the girl child with the knowing eyes of a brutal queen. He could catch that complex expression in a baby girl without undercutting her cuteness, without forgetting she was just a baby. But he wasn't Picasso."

She looked at him for a reaction. He smiled a little.

"Well, obviously no one is Picasso," she went on. "That's not what I meant. My point is, Oscar had no fear of women's power; he thrived on it. He got off on how strong the women in his life all were; it turned him on; he sucked on the nipples of all of us. That's where his strength came from. He went right to the source, and it always flowed. His electricity outlets. I think we all liked Oscar, really *liked* him, not only loved him—all of us in our own different ways, even his sister, Maxine, with whom he never got on at all. I think she secretly liked him, too."

"What's the difference?" he interjected. "Love, like."

"I imagine," she went on as if he hadn't interrupted, "that Picasso was erotic catnip, with his fear and arrogance and his cold sexual eye. But he didn't really like women, and I don't imagine women really liked him, although they may have felt no end of passion for him, the feckless need to conquer or submit. Oscar was needy and soulful, and he liked women without fear. He respected us; he let us be as powerful as we were capable of being. But he wasn't pussy-whipped, as the excellent expression goes, not by me, not by his wife, not by his mother when she was alive, although he adored her, too. He was fully independent of us. He came and went as he pleased and didn't let us control him. . . . No, he was an appreciator. I liked him right back, more than I've ever liked anyone else, my own children included."

She stopped for a moment to think. This time, Henry didn't interrupt her. "Well, we women don't always like our children, not always; we love them with that primal mother instinct, and we love our power to take care of them, but sometimes we don't like them somewhere deep inside. I sometimes felt it toward my twin girls— I couldn't help it—maybe because I had them both at once, so it was intensified, and of course their father was no help whatsoever; I did it all alone. Which is completely preferable, please don't misunderstand me. I didn't want any help from Oscar. This way, I had all the power; I was in control. It was a fair trade-off, I thought. You haven't written anything down yet."

"Some women go off the opposite edge," said Henry. "My wife adores our baby son beyond all reason. I worry sometimes that she'll eat him alive. This morning, she kissed him with the predatory zeal of a succubus."

Teddy smiled at him, appreciating the phrase. "We all adore our babies beyond reason; it's the way we're made. And I didn't say I thought *all* women harbor a small amount of dislike for their children; obviously, I couldn't possibly know that."

"Abigail Feldman talked at length to me a few days ago about Ethan," he said. "How it feels to love someone who can't express love back . . . She talked about how pure her love for him has always been, untainted by resentment of any kind."

"That's love, Henry. You're not making the distinction. He's so deeply autistic he's locked up in his own mind; it's impossible to dislike someone who isn't fully there. Dislike requires presence."

"She was very open with me. You are, too. I appreciate that. I had expected it to be much harder to get you all talking."

"Then you didn't know Oscar. He always got us all to spill everything, hold nothing back, so we're well trained."

"In that case," said Henry gingerly but with a daring expression, as if he thought he was about to cross a line, "since the subject has been brought up, Maxine suggested to me that the reason Oscar stayed with you was that he felt displaced. That when Ethan was born, of course all Abigail's energy and time went to her son. Maxine suggested that Oscar replaced her with you."

"Did she say that?" asked Teddy, hoping she sounded calm; she'd never liked Oscar's sister one bit, and knew it had always been mutual. It enraged her that this version of her affair with Oscar might make it into Henry's book in any form. "I'm not surprised that Maxine would draw such a crude, wrongheaded, idiotic conclusion about why Oscar loved me."

"It's understandable that someone might draw such a conclusion. . . . It seems like elementary psychology, doesn't it?"

"I was right," Teddy snapped. "Those moths are eating into your brain. Burrowing into the wet gray folds and gouging tunnels." She stopped and looked hard at him, something working in her expression. "I bet," she said, "you're one of those failed painters who think they can redeem themselves if they pay homage to Saint Oscar. And I bet you're projecting your own sexual frustration onto Oscar."

Henry coughed, probably with surprise.

"Here, have some melon," she said. "Trust me, the prosciutto is some of the best in Brooklyn."

"You were right about the wine, I'll give you that," he said.

"I'm always right," she said. "It would be much easier for both of us if you just accepted that now and proceeded accordingly. Oscar came to me, in short, because I was exciting. I always liked Abigail, by the way, when I met her at openings and so forth, but I never thought she had much juice. Oscar married her to please his family. He took up with me to please himself."

"Fair enough," said Henry.

She imagined he was probably thinking he should appease her, or else he was feeling sorry for her for just being Oscar's mistress all those years, and never his wife.

"Fair enough," he repeated.

Nettled, she turned to the window to look out at the pale blue Brooklyn sky, crisscrossed by wires and leaf-filled branches.

"This prosciutto is perfect," Henry blurted through a mouthful of cantaloupe. "I was going to say 'delicious,' but I was afraid you'd stab me."

"It's such a precious word," said Teddy. "No one should use it to refer to anything but food, and even then, with caution. My dearest, oldest friend uses it to describe her grandchildren, the summer morning, a cello sonata on 'Evening Music,' and the way her bare feet feel on the sands of Shelter Island. I can't believe she's still my friend, but we were college roommates, and then we raised our children together."

"Lila Scofield," said Henry, taking another piece of melon.

Teddy laughed. "You are diligent," she said. She stood there, her hands on her hips, looking at him. She wore a straight ankle-length off-white skirt, a long-sleeved white crew-necked T-shirt, and white sneakers without socks. In these plain and timeless clothes, she had a fresh, oddly modern angularity, a wiry strength. Her bones, revealed now by the paring down age seemed to confer on some women, were long and elegant, her chin-length hair shot through with a glinting silver that only heightened her aura of indestructible glamour.

She sat opposite him with her own glass of wine. "Finally you're writing something. Let's hear what you've got."

He covered his writing with his hand as if it were his naked crotch. "I'm not a failed anything, by the way," he said in a clipped voice. "I have a B.A. in English from UC Berkeley. I got my M.F.A. from UC Irvine. To make a living, if you can call it that, I teach creative writing at Columbia. A few years ago, I published my first novel with Random House. It sank to the bottom of the pond without a trace, but I'll write more of them, and at least it saw the light of print. I've also published another biography, of Greta Church, an obscure but very brilliant poet no one's ever heard of but who should be in every canonical anthology. She died a penniless morphine addict in Chicago in 1932 at the age of sixty, living in a rented room with a hot plate."

"She died like a male artist, then," said Teddy. "How's her work?"

Henry quoted raptly, looking down at the table, " 'The light of winter stands/ On the silent road, waiting to kill me/ With a cold shot to the heart,/ Tapping its booted foot/ Its gray gun aimed and cocked,/ And I am pierced to the utter root.' "

"Good Lord," said Teddy, laughing. " 'The utter root.' Almost as bad as *delicious*."

"You were a secretary for how many years?" Henry asked tightly.

"Oh, you think I make fun of these so-called great artists because I'm a never-was? Maybe I could never take myself seriously enough to muster the kind of ego and sense of self-mystique you need to write 'the utter root' with a straight face. Come to think of it, that didn't help her either at the end, did it? At least I have a house and I'm not a junkie."

"She uses the word *utter* complexly," Henry said. "She's talking about her own writing. Her 'utter root' is her tongue. The winter light is the clarity of self-knowledge that comes with age. She could hardly write at the end; she was too beaten down by poverty and addiction and the inescapable knowledge that it was all her own fault. Read my book; you'll see what she meant. I defy you to read my biography of her and then laugh at that line."

"You're a romantic," she said. "Aren't you? You love artists; you think they're better than the rest of humanity. Like modern-day saints. So my reference to Saint Oscar wasn't far from the mark. They suffer for humanity. They absorb our failings and weaknesses, transmogrify them, reflect them back to us in the light of truth and beauty."

"Why are you psychoanalyzing me? I'm here to interview you about Oscar."

"You can't 'interview' me 'about Oscar,' " she said. "I can tell the truth about Oscar and tell you my incidental observations about you. Take it or leave it. And my guess—not that you asked, but you deserve it after that crack about my being nothing but a secretary and therefore unqualified to criticize Great Art—is that your wife is very distant now that she's in thrall to new motherhood. I'm guessing that her interest in sex is next to nothing, and who can blame her? And I can tell you what you're doing wrong and how to get her to want you again, but you have to listen to what I say and not interrupt, and, most of all, not come back at me with your starry-eyed wishful thinking about what was going on. Oscar was the furthest thing from a genius I ever knew. He was a very good painter with a shtick and a way with women. He knew how to stir up a scene, how to create a buzz before anyone ever heard of buzz. But you should go back to his paintings and really look at them. Really look. What you see through all those moths' wings is a slap-dash crudeness in his brush strokes, a boyish swagger in his adulterous success. If you look at him clearly without needing to see him a certain way, you'll see that he was like a grocery man with three barrels of pickles, an apron, a roll of waxed paper, and a nose for excellent meat. He painted like a grocer; fucked like a grocer; lived and died like a grocer. No more and no less. The art of the delicatessen."

There was a brief silence, during which Teddy ran a hand through her hair and Henry somewhat peevishly turned the stem of his wineglass between forefinger and thumb slowly against the tabletop.

"Which is a worthy art," Teddy said, "do not misunderstand me, but it doesn't qualify one for sainthood. Women were his real obsession, more than painting. Painting was just an outlet for him, like the store is for the deli man. He saw women, he *knew* women, the way a deli man knows smoked meats: He knew how to pick them, weigh and touch and price and display them. His brush strokes were crude and he painted too many paintings and he cheated on his wife for more than forty years with me but couldn't leave her and couldn't give me up, not that I ever wanted him to do either. He waffled between two women and two families, the good Jewish wife with the damaged son and the bad shiksa mistress with the perfect daughters. He was a deli man at his utter root."

"I can't believe you're debunking him," said Henry.

"I knew you'd be a calf-eyed hero worshiper," she said. "When oh when is Oscar going to get a real biographer?"

"You are not always right, Teddy. In fact, at the moment you're wrong on all counts. Not only am I not sexually frustrated at all, but my wife will not stop hounding me for sex. She complains that now that I'm past forty, I can't keep getting it up all night long anymore. We've been married eight years and she's just getting hungrier." His nostrils flared defiantly with the force of this wishful fantasy. "Twice in one night should satisfy any human. She's a she-wolf." He took a deep breath. "She's a witch," he added.

"She's human all right," said Teddy. "She's forty?"

"Forty-two."

"She's how you were at eighteen."

"That's what she tries to tell me. But when I was eighteen, I didn't have a girlfriend. I had no outlet for my horniness, and even if I'd had, I would have had no perspective on it. Women are lucky: They get it when they can use it. Men get it when they're dumb as sheep. And then it ebbs away."

"Nature is very cruel," said Teddy. "Women get it when they're on the edge of irrelevancy, sociobiologically speaking. One last great burst of white light and you're a dwarf star, humpbacked and withered. Although women don't wither anymore like they used to. But I bet Greta Church was withered. Morphine addicts always are."

"She was a skeleton, actually."

"And pierced to the utter root. I know what the utter root is, and it's not the tongue, Henry. And incidentally, I think it's all hogwash, every word you just said about your marriage. Maybe before the kid was born she wanted sex all the time, but I will bet you anything that she doesn't anymore; she's got a new newborn helpless love, and you're feeling very left out."

His eyes shifted briefly to the floor. "Spoken like someone who knows from experience," he said.

"Meaning what, exactly?"

"Meaning that maybe Maxine's theory about you and Oscar is true."

She cast him a sharp look from the corners of her eyes. "In time, if you pay attention, you will learn that it's not."

"Do you live here alone?"

"Alone as a stone. My daughters call and visit, of course, but it's complicated. Ruby loved her father. She looks like him. She reminds me of him. I think there's a part of her that can't forgive me for not making him marry me and be a real father to the girls and live with us instead of coming and going at odd hours, so that she hardly ever got to see him, and when she did, it was never on holidays, rarely on her birthdays. Of course she blames me for this, not him. Samantha was always my baby; she's loyal to me. She looks like me. It's funny how Oscar and I had twins, one in each of our images. It's so fitting, somehow, and that they're both girls, given his passion for women. Interesting, too, that his only male offspring is emotionally unknowable, a cipher, when all of Oscar's women are outspoken as hell. Anyway, Samantha adores me, but she needs to keep some distance from me, too. . . . I imagine she's unconsciously resentful at some perceived neglect on my part; she has accused me, on several occasions, of loving Oscar more than I loved her and Ruby. That isn't true at all, although I certainly liked him more."

"Liked Oscar more than your children," Henry repeated.

"He was a man," Teddy said, "and they were little girls. I always knew the difference. I never let my children dominate my life the way you parents do now with your children; they take over your lives!"

"My kid has not taken over my life," said Henry.

"It's all wrong," she said. "I set limits; I had my own life. I wanted them to learn that even if you have children, you can have a life that doesn't include them. I think therapists now are encouraging adult children to view this sort of old-fashioned parenting as neglectful, which makes them into victims of their parents and martyrs to their children. Kids need to know their place in the scheme of things, like dogs. And children, of course, leave you in the end. . . . It's your contemporaries who stay, spouses and old friends. That's who you have in your later years. Oscar's death was the hardest thing I've ever gone through. My friend Lila of the delicious grandchildren is my most loyal and stalwart companion here at the withered root. She lives nearby. We know each other better than anyone else alive. Of course I can hardly bear her."

"I don't believe you."

"You are half right."

"I'm always half right," he said, and caught her glance. They smiled at each other, suddenly battle-weary. A silence fell between them. They felt they'd earned it, and settled simultaneously into their chairs. Teddy drank some wine; Henry ate another chunk of sweet melon wrapped in salty prosciutto. The sounds of the backyards and streets mingled peacefully, the late summer afternoon, the humid air.

Henry swallowed his mouthful and yawned, rubbed his eyes. He'd drunk two large glasses of wine without knowing it. He hadn't had a good night's sleep in two months.

"You can nap on the couch," said Teddy. "I'll wake you when the meal is ready and you can ask me your questions over supper. I know you have a whole numbered and annotated list of them. Questions, subquestions, a, b, c, asterisks and arrows. You strike me as that sort of person."

"Actually, I am that sort of person, but I wouldn't mind a nap," he said.

"There's a very comfortable old couch in the living room," she said, gesturing toward the front of the house. "Supper should take about half an hour."

Henry lay fully stretched out, shoes off, on Teddy's long green velvet couch, which smelled of dust and years-old incense. When he awoke half an hour later, the hot early-evening sunlight slanted along the hallway from the kitchen. He heard a pot lid clanking and water running in the kitchen and smelled something cooking.

He found Teddy in the kitchen, stirring a pot on the stove. "It's almost ready," she said without turning around. "You can wash up in the lav; the door's just to my left."

The "lav," like the rest of the house, was in a comfortable state of semicleanliness, with deft cartoon faces drawn on cardboard glued to the wall in haphazard rows.

"I set a table in back, on the patio," said Teddy when he emerged. She was dishing something onto plates: stewed chicken over couscous. On the counter was a salad made of only some sort of strange purple lettuce, nothing else.

"Did Oscar draw those faces in the bathroom?" Henry asked.

"No," said Teddy. "I'm sorry, it was the former owner of this house. Good, aren't they?"

He helped her carry things out to the patio, the two plates laden with steaming food, the salad bowl, another bottle of cold Sancerre. The evening sunlight in the yard was so intense, it was almost surreal. It was an odd little garden, a jumble of flowering bushes and wild grasses crowded together in a lush tangle that seemed to grow as it liked, without human interference, yet there seemed to be an original organizing principle behind the riot, God's or Teddy's or someone else's.

Henry sat at the old enameled metal table on Teddy's tiny bluestone terrace and picked up his fork. "This looks"—he cleared his throat—"delicious, but now I can't say it."

Their eyes met.

"A pernicious word," she said with smug satisfaction.

"Only because you made it into one. It was a fine word before I got here."

"I only pointed out what ought to be clear to everyone."

"A habit of yours."

"Henry," she said, pouring the wine, "eat your supper."

He augmented his plate with things from the bowls Teddy had already set out: toasted sliced almonds, homemade apricot chutney, fried banana-pepper rings, minced raw red onion, matchstick-size pieces of fresh jicama, wedges of lime.

The food, which looked bland and unprepossessing, was subtle and amazing. The couscous tasted nutty and buttery. The rich chicken stew was laced with hints of saffron, cinnamon, cayenne, lemon zest, and something else, unfamiliar and exotic, but these things announced themselves very faintly, so he had to concentrate to taste them through the perfectly cooked meat and grain.

"Teddy, this food is brilliant."

"Why, thank you," said Teddy. She let the nickname pass this time. Her mood had changed entirely; now she felt mellow, almost flirtatious. This was due in part to the wine; Sancerre was in a class by itself; it could hardly be called by the same name as Chardonnay or Chablis. It had some other dimension other whites lacked.

"You accept the word *brilliant* but not the word *delicious*?"

"You parse it out, Henry. You're a bright specimen. But while you do, I must be permitted to boast about the provenance of my chicken. It's the very best chicken money can buy, the sort of bird who ran free and ate food of a higher quality than that of most of the people in the world. But I didn't have to pay for it. . . . I bartered for it with flowers from this very garden. I'm single-handedly bringing the art of village subsistence living into an urban setting."

Henry nodded, swallowing, clearly not fully listening. "How do you feel about the fact that Oscar left everything to Abigail? You don't even own a single one of his paintings."

"He never promised me a thing. He loved me for my self-sufficiency, and as you see, it was no act on my part. I am quite poor, monetarily, but I get by very well on my wits and charm." She laughed. "You can write that down; it's a tailor-made quote for your book, but you won't be able to convey the irony with which I said it, will you? I know people in this neighborhood; I have lived around here for decades. Not in this house, of course."

"Of course," he said. "After Oscar died, you sold the Calyer Street house to a young couple with three children. I went there. They let me go in and look around, but of course they've completely renovated it."

"Don't tell me," she said, closing her eyes. "I don't even walk on that street anymore if I can help it."

"He could have left you a painting or two," Henry prompted.

"Oscar owed her," said Teddy. "It was as simple as that."

"I wonder," said Henry. "I wonder if it's really that simple in your heart of hearts. But I can't really ask you that. . . ."

"Listen, Henry," she said. "Oscar was my beloved mate. I never had any other or wanted one. But after forty-odd years, the word *beloved* takes on some fairly perverse complexities. You're probably too young still to know. To be truly loved is to be . . . known, of course, which also implies despised and even hated. I'm trusting you to see the love in everything I'm saying, including the deli-man comparison. I let you into my house, fed you, gave you a nap, and told you the truth. I have no idea whether or not this was a colossal mistake. But I can't do otherwise. You have a lot of power."

"It isn't a mistake to tell me these things," Henry assured her. He took some salad and forked a slippery dressing-coated burgundy lettuce leaf into his mouth. Fresh lemon juice, coarse black pepper, and olive oil mingled on his tongue. He stared at the salad on his plate.

"I grow it myself," said Teddy, who had been watching him closely. "Not directly in Greenpoint soil, don't worry; that's so contaminated, it would make you grow another head. Look, over there in tubs by that corner near the fence, an unusual and rare lettuce most people haven't heard of: Les Oreilles du Diable, ears of the devil. It's excellent, isn't it? Nutty and robust. I bought the seeds for the name. I always splurge on interesting-sounding seeds. Thank God I'm healthy. . . . Most people my age spend everything on medications; I buy good wine and rare seeds. Something symbolic there . . . maybe out of Greek mythology, seeds and wine . . ." She took a dreamy sip of wine, a bite of lettuce. Alcohol softened her. It blurred her edges, smoothed her face.

Henry watched her without self-consciousness, half-drunk himself.

They finished their salads, drank more wine. With warm peach crumble and vanilla ice cream, Teddy served espresso and little thimbles of *poire* liqueur. The sky darkened; the sounds of children in the streets tapered off as they were all called inside. Henry leaned back a little tipsily in his chair. They had talked about a lot of things, but he'd written very little in his notebook.

"Okay," he said. "Tell me."

"Tell you what?"

"What I'm doing wrong. With my wife. Tell me how to get her to . . ."

She didn't laugh; she understood immediately what he was getting at. "Have an affair," she replied gently. "A passionate affair. It doesn't even have to be literally sexual. An affair of the heart, it could be. Daydream about someone else obsessively."

He didn't laugh. "That's how to make my wife want me again? Sleep with someone else?"

"Or just think about sleeping with her. But really think about it."

"I should get going," he said.

"You really should," she told him. "It's getting late; your wife will be annoyed. Even if she takes care of the baby, she still wants you home."

"I help," he said.

"Where did you park?"

"Right out front."

"Well, you're not driving home to—where do you live, Westchester or Connecticut?"

"Astoria," he said. "In a tacky little frame house with aluminum siding."

"Sounds just like mine," she said. "Well, you're not driving home tonight. I'll call you a cab."

"I can drive after a few glasses of wine."

At the door, she handed him a container. "The leftovers," she said. "For your wife. So she won't be upset that you're so late. Or less upset, anyway."

He took the package from her and went into the night. Teddy stepped out onto her front stoop and watched him get into his car, which was indeed a Volvo, but an old one. She waved as he drove off, watched his taillights disappear.

Two

Teddy and her friend Lila had a standing breakfast date: every Saturday morning at eight. Today they were at Lila's. On the way over, Teddy had stopped at the little Mexican market that lay between their houses and bought four of the fresh buns they always had on the counter in a plastic box, not too sweet, not too soft, four for a dollar. Lila had heated them up and served them with blackberry jam, butter, Jarlsberg, fruit salad, and coffee. They were sitting on Lila's shaded back deck, looking at her yard. A large-leafed vine sprawled on a trellis, heavy with the kind of perfectly shaped, cascading bunches of purple grapes Teddy had always associated with the Calvinist Dutch masters: symbols of bacchanalian wantonness and drunkenness. Lilac bushes, tea roses, rhododendrons, and hydrangeas, in splotches of purples, reds, pinks, and oranges, grew against the back brick wall. On the cartoonishly green lawn, under a little pergola, were a white wrought-iron table and matching chairs. Two docile little pear trees rose near the house, thoughtfully blossoming in the spring and bearing fruit in the fall. An equally thoughtful pine tree provided shade in one corner of the yard, under which Lila had had built a playhouse for visiting grandchildren.

Teddy had not been born to end up in a neighborhood like Greenpoint: She had chosen to live here. In 1952, during her sophomore year at Vassar, her English expatriate financier father, Herbert Groverton St. Cloud, the untitled younger son of a nobleman, had lost everything all at once on a bad investment, a South African diamond mine swindle he should have been too shrewd to fall for. He'd sold his Fifth Avenue town house and all his various possessions to pay his debts, and his only child had had to leave college abruptly. Almost penniless, Teddy had camped out with her father at an old family friend's house and enrolled in a secretarial course, then found work as a secretary for an entertainment law firm and got herself an apartment. Her father, her only family, had died shortly afterward of a heart attack, leaving her almost nothing. She'd zealously reinvented herself as a working girl, settling in Greenpoint in the late 1950s. Originally a nineteenth-century rough-and-tumble riverfront shipbuilding town at the northernmost tip of Brooklyn, just across the river from midtown Manhattan, it had been populated largely by immigrants, Italians and Irish first, then Poles.

Lila also lived here by choice. In 1985, shortly after Sam Scofield, her first husband, had died of colon cancer, she had sold the apartment in Gramercy Park they'd owned since 1968 and bought an old Queen Anne brownstone on stately, tree-lined Noble Street, just a five-minute walk from Teddy's smallish old brick house with its tiny back garden on the more heavily trafficked, down-at-the-heels Calyer Street. Back then, this neighborhood had been seedy, run-down, so the house was a bargain, and after Lila had had it refurbished and reappointed, it was as elegant as any house, anywhere.

Teddy had always liked coming to Lila's house, which was the sort of place she'd been born to inhabit, the life she'd lost. Coming here always reminded her how much happier she was as a "single working mother," lackadaisical housekeeper, and server-forth of imaginative cookery on mismatched chipped dishes than she would have been as the inhabitant of such a house, with its daily maid, grand piano, heirloom dishes, groomed back garden, and state-of-the-art appliances. She loved Lila's house both because it was comfortable and luxurious and because it reassured her that she didn't regret her fate.

Teddy had put the Calyer Street house on the market immediately after Oscar's death; she'd found the house on India Street that same afternoon at the Realtor's office. The unmarried old owner, Homer Meehan, the last surviving descendant of the family who'd bought it when it was built in the 1870s, had become too crippled to live alone and so was headed for an old-age home and was selling his family house. He left behind odd touches, like the Chinese-cardboard cartoon faces in the lav, ballpoint pen—scrawled maunderings upstairs on the wall of the smaller of the two bedrooms (her favorite: "It's useless to give up and useless to persevere, so take the path of least resistance with your eyes and mouth shut"), and photos of wild animals mating or about to mate, cut from *National Geographic*s and pasted in a free-form collage on the wall of the tiny boot room leading out to the backyard. Teddy had left all this handiwork untouched, partly out of her heartbroken reluctance to start over in a new place, partly out of an appreciation for weirdo eccentrics.

"He seemed too earnest at first," Teddy said to Lila, slathering her second bun with jam.

"Earnest isn't bad," said Lila. She rightly suspected that Teddy sometimes secretly chafed at her own earnestness.

"Not bad," Teddy said. "Just a little boring."

There was a brief, pointed silence. Lila nibbled her roll, then set it carefully back down on the plate. She was a large woman, but she still felt and behaved like the sylph she had once been. Her gestures were miniature, girlish; she wore a gauzy dress that reminded Teddy a little of the "frocks" they had affected when they were freshmen and sophomores at Vassar and had worshiped the campus phantom of the young Edna St. Vincent Millay. Now (more than half a century later) she wore a blue shawl and house slippers with her gauzy dress, but she still looked girlish. Tendrils of her curly pure white neck-length hair stuck to her cheeks and neck in the humidity. Her dress had long, filmy sleeves; Teddy knew she was embarrassed by her arms, which were more sagging and wrinkled than the rest of her skin, which had aged very little. She also knew that Lila took special pains to appear young whenever one of her sons was coming over with the grandchildren; Joe was coming today, her baby, her favorite. Teddy also did the same with her daughters, tried to seem young and alive when she saw them, tried to hide the signs of age as best she could; as mothers, they didn't want their children to think of them as decrepit, needy, without the ability to help them. But Lila didn't have to worry. At the moment, she looked like a fat, hot, beautiful baby.

Lila Emerson had been a scholarship girl from a rural Maine family, the youngest daughter of a Presbyterian minister, thirsting to soak up every drop of academic bohemia she could absorb. She'd been instantly intrigued by her roommate, Claire St. Cloud, whose father was rich and English and whose mother had died when Claire was a small child, like the parents of certain heroines of James, Austen, and Brontë, not to mention Frances Hodgson Burnett, Lila's favorite writer as a girl. Claire was outspoken, extremely smart without being an egghead, confident, unapologetically sexual. Lila was shy, bookish, reserved, and alight with the desire to flee her cage, itching for mischief. She had seduced Claire into being her friend by letting her glimpse hints of the person Lila might become and tempting her with the power to coax that person into being. It was Lila who had given Teddy her nickname; Teddy was half girl, half boy, Lila liked to say, so the androgynous toy-bear name suited her. In homage to Millay, Lila had sewn them both dresses in shades of fawn, ecru, pastel yellow—sleeveless for spring and long-sleeved for winter—which they'd worn with ballet slippers or Greek goddess sandals, bead necklaces or arm bracelets, depending on the season. They had danced on the lawn in them, burbled off to classes, run up the stairs of their dormitory to their room, and, a few times, stripped them off each other.

Teddy had matter-of-factly, with frank lust, initiated these occasional trysts, and Lila was too hot with her own need for subversiveness to resist, or to pay full attention to what her body was doing. Although it wasn't really so subversive when you thought about it; women's schools had always been full of affairs between girls who went on to have husbands and children. But at the time, it had seemed to Lila's puritanical New England soul like the wickedest of transgressions. And their schoolgirl sex, innocent and laughing as it was, had cemented her undying passion for Teddy. When Teddy had to leave Vassar in the winter of their sophomore year, Lila had suffered a mild nervous breakdown and almost had to take a semester off.

"More coffee?" asked Lila.

"But then in the end," said Teddy, "I found him . . . sympathetic. I don't know why. Maybe because he lives in Queens. . . ."

Lila refilled Teddy's coffee cup. Teddy was such a reverse snob; she wasn't going to touch that comment about Queens.

"The funniest thing, though—I had a call two days ago from another would-be Oscar biographer. Henry has a rival, unbeknownst to him, I'm sure."

"*Another* biographer called you?" Lila asked, instantly jealous in spite of herself. She reached into her fruit-salad bowl and pulverized half a cherry with her molars.

"He's coming over for lunch today. Why would two people want to write a biography of Oscar?"

"I can imagine that a lot of people might!" said Lila.

Lila had been flabbergasted and hurt that Teddy hadn't seemed even remotely put out when she'd had to drop out of college. Instead, she'd seemed galvanized, even excited, by her sudden reversal of fortune. Lila had had to admit to herself that being a secretary had agreed with Teddy in a way student life hadn't; she had drifted through her three semesters at Vassar without much ambition, but over the years, then the decades, she'd stayed at the same law firm, working for a succession of lawyers she bossed around and whose schedules, kids' birthdays, file contents, and correspondence intricacies she knew better than they did. They trusted her completely to run their lives. When one retired, the lawyer who got her next felt honored with a great treasure. She had retired at sixty-five, to much fanfare; she'd become a legend at the firm, a force to reckon with. "You'll have to get past Mrs. St. Cloud," people said when they wanted a favor from her boss (that

Mrs. was nothing but camouflage, an honorarium of sorts, of course). Or, if they were in with Teddy, they showed off their right to call her by her nickname. After work, she went home on the subway to her Calyer Street house, where she was likewise ruler of the roost. She cooked excellent meals and was generous and loving in her way, but she raised her girls firmly and without sentiment, and whenever Oscar came around, she sent them off to bed so she could take care of the insatiable, all-consuming needs of the great artist with undivided, clear-eyed attention. She argued with him, laughed at him. She lit fires and made midnight suppers and entertained him with stories about the lawyers she worked for, one of whom represented him, and their clients, some of whom were his fellow artists, many of whom were famous. He ate and laughed and drank and smoked and opined and argued and listened; then he took Teddy off to bed and left before the girls awoke.

Whenever, during the sixties and seventies, Lila had managed to sneak away from husband and children and have an evening or afternoon to herself, it was Teddy's house she went to, Teddy's life they talked about—Oscar, his tantrums, his other women, the hilarious poetic notes he left on his pillow for Teddy in the mornings. Lila always felt both revitalized and soothed after a visit to the Calyer Street house, with its crazy old icebox and funky furniture, Oscar's sketches pinned up haphazardly over the fireplace, filled year-round with the ashes left over from their firelit dinners. She breathed easier there, spoke more loudly, smoked cigarettes and took a snort or two of whiskey, listened to whatever records Oscar had brought over—Miles, Mingus, Monk, Sun Ra, Coltrane, Louis Prima, Harry Partch—as she ate the food Teddy cooked and put in her two cents if Oscar was around and there was an argument afoot. At the parties they gave, Teddy competed with Oscar for the limelight, teased him in front of people, disagreed openly with his pronouncements about his rival painters. Oscar seemed to get a huge kick out of Teddy's jabs and jousts and never seemed to notice that Lila drank in everything he said and yearned to lick him all over like a big lollipop. If he ever looked Lila's way at all, he treated her like a lesser adjunct of Teddy, like Teddy's dimmer domesticated sister.

While Teddy, without having graduated from college, lived out Lila's youthful dream of hobnobbing with artists and living an unconventional life, Lila had capitulated to her own tame destiny, which even her Vassar degree hadn't altered. She had planned to be a novelist, and had moved to Manhattan to pursue this plan, but then she promptly acquiesced to her parents' unspoken but ironclad expectations and married Sam Scofield, a young English professor at NYU, at twenty-two. By thirty, she'd found herself the mother of three small boys. Until recently, she had been "nothing but" a wife and mother, and now she was "nothing but" a twice-widowed grandmother. She had always, through all those years, tried very hard not to compare exciting, sexy Oscar to faithful, gentle Sam, who stayed up late grading papers, who had tenure and was good at what he did but was never ambitious enough to publish, network, push himself out of his comfortable groove. She sustained and tortured herself with her own suppressed ambition, the idea that someday she would write the novels she'd been born to write.

But shortly after Sam's funeral, she'd been introduced by mutual friends to a wealthy retired engineer whose wife had also died recently, the kindly but not-quite-there Peter Williams, and a little later on Lila had married him, almost out of the habit of having a man around. He had lasted ten years with her before he, too, gave out, and during their marriage she had found that he, like Sam and the kids before him, took up all her time. Now that everyone was gone, she kept trying to start a novel, but no matter how many times she tried to get a narrative going, she discovered that the fire of inspiration she'd tried to keep burning in the pit of her stomach through decades of ministering to others seemed to have gone completely out.

"Well, if either of these biographers wants to talk to you, are you available?" Teddy said, throwing Lila a bone; of course she knew Lila had always secretly lusted after Oscar and also secretly judged Teddy for being what Lila perceived as rough on him. But neither of them wanted the slightest crack of a schism between them or could afford one; even though they both had children and grandchildren and other friends, in a nearby daily sense, as someone to count on, Lila was Teddy's mainstay, and vice versa.

"Of course," said Lila, seeing right through her ploy and accepting it as the small peace offering it was. "Anyway, who's this new one?"

"His name's Ralph Washington," said Teddy. "Sounded wet-lipped on the phone."

"What did you think of the first one, besides the fact that he was earnest?"

"Henry Burke? In the end, I liked him. He was insulted at first that I'd made him a tan-colored mush; then he took a couple of bites." She paused a moment to remember something, smiled inwardly, and added dryly, "I think he fell a little in love with me, actually."

"Really?" said Lila. "How old is he?"

"I would say forty, maybe a little older."

"A boy," said Lila.

Teddy said with a gleam in her eyes, "I bet I could have seduced him."

"How would you know? I'm not sure I would be able to tell such a thing at my age."

"He was . . . ripe for the taking, in a general sense, and he was surprised by his attraction to me, which is always an advantage in seduction. When a man is tipped off balance, there's nothing easier than knocking him over." Teddy flicked the air with her index finger.

"Did you *want* to?"

"Only to prove I could. And at my age, that's not enough of a reason."

"At your age, I'd say that's a great reason."

"So I could tell you all about it over breakfast today?"

"Of course," said Lila.

"I bet you can't wait to get these biographers to yourself."

"Oh, come on, Teddy."

"Actually, Henry didn't care for my lack of proper humble womanly devotion to Oscar any more than you ever did; it almost scotched the whole deal. But once we got off the topic of Oscar and onto the topic of his sex life, he was all mine, although he may not have realized it."

"His *sex* life?" Lila sputtered with laughter. "What did he say?"

"That he's married to a forty-two-year-old woman in love with her newborn baby boy. I bet they tried and tried and tried, and Henry mistook this bonanza of sex for lust for him, and once she got what she wanted, wham-o, no more blow jobs to get him hard and afternoon quickies and hot couplings at the kitchen sink. He's shunted aside, useless, the cast-off male. . . ." She stopped, went off into some private reverie again. "I know, let's make a bet. Let's see who can fuck a biographer first."

Lila waved her away. "What are you going to cook for this second one?"

Teddy cocked her eye at Lila. "No bet?"

"No, no, I'll just live vicariously through you," said Lila, trying for light teasing, but dismayed by the edge in her voice.

"You're right," said Teddy, not missing a beat. "The whole idea is ridiculous."

"Besides," said Lila after a silent deep breath, "it doesn't seem right, an old woman with a much younger man. Remember that movie *Harold and Maude*? That wrinkled crone with a teenage boy. I never understood why so many people loved it."

"Me, neither." Teddy laughed. "But I wouldn't mind seeing my old carcass in bed with a nubile forty-year-old body. . . . For him, no doubt, it would be terrifying and distasteful, but for me it would be glorious. All the men our age are so . . . old, aren't they? They have ear hair, their teats droop, and they look cadaverous. Not for me, thanks. I'll take a sapling."

"Speaking of which . . ." said Lila coyly.

"Speaking of what? You're simpering. Cough it up."

"I am not *simpering*! No one simpers anymore."

"Well what?"

"I met a nice man. . . . There he was with his big black dog up on Manhattan Avenue, and I stopped to pet him, the dog, and we started talking, the man and I. His name is Rex. He lives way over on Devoe Street. He asked me to dinner."

Teddy said through a flash of something she hoped wasn't envy, "When are you going?"

"Tonight," said Lila with apprehension.

"And you're just telling me this now?"

"It didn't seem as important as all these biographers."

"Rex . . . he's Italian?"

"No, he's not any ethnicity I could guess. He's a graphic artist."

"How old is he?"

"I would guess early to mid-sixties," said Lila.

"A nubile young thing . . ."

"He's actually pretty youthful, come to think of it. I don't know why he's single. He has the look of a confirmed bachelor, though—you know what I mean, the collector type with stuff like boxes of valuable old blues records or a model train with a whole town built around it."

"Still," said Teddy. "A nice, eligible, interesting younger man. So? Is he picking you up, or are you meeting him somewhere?"

"He's coming by to get me at seven. . . . I'm a little nervous. What will I wear? What will I do when he eventually catches sight of my fat old naked body? He won't want me; he can't possibly . . ."

"Lila, you're hyperventilating. It'll be okay. . . ."

"I am not hyperventilating. God, you make me sound like a swooning old maid. I've had two husbands, Teddy. I know how to—"

"Take a deep breath."

Lila sighed deeply, then asked, "Do you have spider veins on your thighs?"

"Of course I have spider veins on my thighs; I'm seventy-four years old."

"But, Teddy . . . are you getting bald . . . down there?"

"We all are. Stop obsessing. He won't be looking at every detail; men never do. All they see are lips, boobs, and cunt. As long as there aren't too many negatives, you're fine."

"A balding snatch isn't a negative?"

"A balding snatch could be a fetish."

They both laughed.

"Honestly, Teddy, tell me you wouldn't be nervous, too."

"Have a couple of drinks before he picks you up. Two glasses of sherry and you'll be relaxed and confident as a twenty-year-old."

"God, if only I still were."

"We were so incredibly beautiful," said Teddy. "Well, at least we knew it. At least we enjoyed ourselves."

"That gets me through many a night."

Teddy leaned back in her chair and looked out at her friend's yard. "The male cardinal is back," she said. "That's good luck. Where's his mate?"

"She's around here somewhere. She likes to keep a low profile, unlike him."

"Like me and Oscar. Anyway, I made a soup for Ralph Washington. Something to disappoint him initially and woo him eventually. Like the saffron chicken stew I made for Henry. What a funny question about the spider veins. Haven't you had them for decades now?"

"I only got them recently."

"Your skin is so much younger than mine."

"That's because I'm fat," said Lila. "All that adipose is holding my face up."

"My wrinkles used to bother me in my early fifties," said Teddy, "but I don't mind them anymore now that I've had time to get used to them. Now I feel like a well-worn old leather handbag with all sorts of intriguing bobby pins and sticks of gum in my crevices. No telling what you'll find if you go digging around."

Lila laughed. "What kind of soup?"

"Lentil, a very good gourmet one. I pulled out all the stops from my spice rack and added some beautiful-smelling merguez and chopped grilled artichoke hearts I couldn't really afford. I'll serve it with cheese biscuits made with some of that cheddar—you know, the very inexpensive cheddar that tastes so good baked in things . . . Cracker Barrel. And of course a devil's-ear salad. And Sancerre."

"What will you serve for nibblies?"

"For appetizers," said Teddy, cringing silently at "nibblies," "I got some simple antipasti from that hippie-dippy place on Manhattan Avenue, stuffed grape leaves, grilled peppers, goat cheese, olives, babaganoush. . . . Where are you and Rex going for dinner?"

"I hope he doesn't take me to one of those places all the kids go. I'd hate to walk into one of those dark, noisy hot spots looking like someone's grandma, which I am, but you know, it's like being a humpback with two heads around here. I hope he takes me to that mafioso seafood place near the river. Even though the food is mediocre, I wouldn't feel out of place there. But I have a sinking feeling. . . . He has that confirmed-bachelor air about him—the kind of ex-hippie who still lives like he's thirty and has a budget to match. . . ."

"I know exactly what you mean."

"I guess I could offer to pay for dinner, of course. What pride does anyone have about such things at our age, really?"

"He might surprise you. Maybe he's more mature than he looked."

"He was wearing a T-shirt and jeans."

"What kind of shoes?"

"Black loafers."

"Could go either way. Old-man shoes are very in right now. Was there anything written on the T-shirt?"

"No, it was plain. Blue."

"Besides, so what if he still lives like he's thirty? Maybe that means he can still get it up."

"Maybe. It's been so long, you know. I don't know what they're using nowadays, how they get around that. Well, Viagra, but isn't there a new thing that makes them hard for four days? I hope he doesn't have that."

"So where's he been all this time?"

"He was living in Amsterdam last winter, designing a catalog for a Dutch furniture company."

Teddy rubbed her eyes and swallowed a sleepy yawn. While Lila was being fed bits of lobster by this youthful, successful graphic designer who could probably still muster an erection, she would be drumming up old stories about Oscar and serving forth a meal for some wet-lipped Oscar worshiper who would of course take no romantic interest in her whatsoever, all her earlier braggadocio aside. She had been yearning lately for male attention and companionship, although sex would have been nice, too.

"An employed graphic designer; that means he'll probably be able to afford a nice dinner," she said.

"Maybe," said Lila, obviously comforted.

"What are you going to wear?" Teddy asked, stifling another yawn. She hadn't slept well the past few nights. All the wine and reviving old memories with Henry had kept her awake after he'd left; then she had dreamed vividly about Oscar during the short time she'd been able to fall into a trance deep enough to be called sleep. The past few nights had followed a similar pattern.

"Oh God," said Lila. "Clothes . . . I need help here, Teddy. I don't think I have anything. . . . It's been so long."

"Let's go in and see what you've got."

"I'm telling you, nothing."

"Come on."

Upstairs in Lila's bedroom, Teddy rifled through her closet.

"Maybe I don't want to wear a dress," said Lila. "I don't want to seem old. Aren't dresses sort of old-seeming?"

"Look," said Teddy. "I can't believe you've still got this." She pulled out a bottle green granny dress with an embroidered bodice. Lila had worn it all weekend once at a rock festival in the late sixties. She and Teddy had taken the kids, all five of them. Lila's three boys were older than Teddy's twin girls, so they couldn't all play together in one satisfying clump; they had to be monitored in two distinct groups. Lila and Teddy, with the help of Lila's boys, had pitched two big tents side by side in a field, spent the entire weekend soaked with rain, marshaling their offspring to and from makeshift outhouses, feeding everyone peanut butter sandwiches, making sure no one drowned in the creek, while all around them, people not much younger than they were, tripping on acid, danced to meandering guitar solos in the downpour, flowers in their hair and beads around their necks. Still, it was a weekend they'd looked back on together through the years with a sense that it had been memorable and amazing in some way they couldn't quite identify; the memory of it made them both nostalgic for something, although they weren't sure what or why.

Lila and Teddy looked together at the dress for a moment; then Teddy put it back into the closet. "I don't think dresses per se are old-looking," she said. "Look, what about this one? This one is beautiful and youthful and I think it's very sexy on you."

Lila took the dress Teddy handed her, a deep blue sundress with fitted bodice and full skirt. She held it against herself and looked down, patting the dress against her stomach. "You think this is all right? My arm dingle-dangle won't gross him out?"

"He'll fall at your feet," said Teddy.

Lila laid the dress on her bed and wandered out of the bedroom and down the curved staircase. Teddy quickly cased the boudoir, pretending to be a potential suitor, looking for any telltale old-lady signs. Nothing but a pill bottle, which she knew contained Lila's hormone-replacement therapy, which she'd told her for years not to take because it probably caused cancer (although really, what didn't these days?), and a threadbare flannel nightgown that very well might have hailed from Lila's first marriage. She scooped up both and hid them in Lila's underwear drawer, then went out to the landing and called, "Where did you go?"

"What are you doing up there?" called Lila, who was tidying the living room with exactly the same thing in mind as Teddy, hiding her copies of *Active Senior* magazine and the special pillow that allowed her to sit without bothering her occasional hemorrhoids.

"Hiding your grandma nightie and your hormone pills in your underwear drawer," called Teddy on her way downstairs.

"Come in here, Teddy," Lila said in a different tone. "Look what I found."

When Teddy came into the living room, Lila handed her an envelope. "It was on the floor by the front door. I must have missed it when the mail came yesterday. Look, it's from Oscar's sister."

"Maxine? Why is she writing to you?" Teddy opened the envelope and slid out a piece of paper carefully folded into thirds. On it was a brief handwritten note. " 'Dear Lila,' " Teddy read out loud. "'I don't know whether you know about Oscar's two new biographers. Their names are Henry Burke and Ralph Washington, and they're both nosing around Oscar's family and friends this summer in hopes of getting information about him for their respective books. I imagine they'll contact you, as the best friend of Oscar's mistress. If they do, please notify me before you speak to either one of them. There are a few things I'd like to discuss. Thank you. Sincerely, Maxine Feldman,' and then she wrote her phone number."

"You call her," said Lila. "She's got nothing to do with me."

"You're scared of her."

"She's some kind of fanged beast."

" 'Oscar's mistress'?" Teddy repeated. "Good God."

"What do you think she wants?"

"I think she just wants . . . power. What she always wanted. I'm sure it's about that bet with Oscar. I'll call her, don't worry. I'd better go, Lila. I have so much to do in the backyard, and I have to get ready for this guy, what's his name, Ralph Washington."

"Don't go yet," said Lila. "Have some more coffee."

"It'll be fine, Lila," said Teddy, following Lila into her kitchen and somewhat reluctantly accepting another cup of coffee. "Do you want to come and have lunch with us? The kids are supposed to come over, but I know Samantha will cancel at the last minute, and anyway, there's plenty of food."

"Why would she do that?"

"Because she doesn't want anything to do with Oscar or his biography. She's mad at him; Ruby's mad at me. So complicated with kids, even when they're almost forty. Jesus, if I'd known, I might have opted out of the whole circus."

"No, you wouldn't have, Teddy."

They went back out to the porch and sat down again and looked out over the garden. Teddy noticed that Lila's hyacinths were flourishing; last summer they had moped and drooped.

" 'They call me the hyacinth girl . . .' " Teddy recited dreamily.

"I know, aren't they thriving this year? So mysterious, plants . . ." Lila replied just as dreamily.

"You know what I miss the most?" said Teddy with a sudden jolt of erotic nostalgia. "Being in a man's house, a man you're about to fuck for the first time. Looking at the things he has, his masculine things . . . God, that was exciting. Having him make you a drink, put on music that he's chosen, a man you really want with all of yourself. Oscar had a hot plate, a small refrigerator, a mattress on the floor. He had an old record player and a portable radio. . . . Everything was spattered with paint. Such a cliché of an artist's studio. I remember teasing him about it, accusing him of spattering everything with paint so women would swoon over him. God, Oscar . . . I felt like I was going to throw up if he didn't touch me. He played the radio, but I was sick to my stomach with sexual excitement—remember that feeling?—so I don't recall a single song, but I remember the sound of Billie Holliday's voice, which I'd never liked much, but it didn't matter. It was early fall and the windows were open, and we sat facing each other on his mattress and ate the spaghetti with canned sardines he'd made and drank warm vodka, passing the bottle back and forth between us. That was the best meal I've ever had in my life. . . . We got drunk, but we weren't drunk. . . . It was the way he smelled, the look in his eye, the way he asked me questions and paid attention to my answers, really looking at me. We knew we were going to devour each other the minute we'd wiped the sardine juice from our chins, and it made the meal taste so good and last forever. . . . I seriously thought I was going to explode with hot juice and electricity." She stopped. "But why me? Of all the women who wanted him. He was married, famous; I was his lawyer's secretary . . . nobody."

Lila considered this question. Her date with Rex seemed anemic in comparison. What did they have to offer each other that was in any way biography-worthy?

"Of course you," she said.

"I never asked him for anything," said Teddy. "Never asked him to leave Abigail, never asked him for a cent. When I was sick, I told him not to come around. When I gave birth, you brought flowers, not Oscar."

"And you never resented it," Lila prompted.

"I preferred it that way. I wasn't pretending. I loved Oscar. I loved who he was. I wouldn't have changed a thing about him, and I saw him so clearly. . . . That's why he came back to me, even with all the girls and models and married women who chased him. He always came back to me, and he told me everything. I wasn't being a martyr. . . . I was never jealous. I always felt a man was lucky to have me and if he was smart, he'd see that, and if he didn't, he was an idiot. Arrogance, I guess it is. It served me well, though, because my lack of jealousy was another thing that kept him interested. And I knew him better than he knew himself. He was such a pathological narcissist. Telling him what he was thinking was the equivalent of a blow job for him. He made me feel brilliant for understanding him, made me feel as if I were a genius."

She laughed and looked out at the yard. Lila kept quiet. Teddy had never talked like this before about Oscar.

"I can't bear that he's gone sometimes," Teddy said. "I sometimes literally feel that I can't bear that I'll never see him again. Am I romanticizing Oscar?" Her voice was high.

"Not at all," said Lila.

Teddy reached over and took Lila's hand. Lila started a little; Teddy wasn't the touchy type. She rarely hugged anyone, and although they always exchanged a mutual peck on the cheek to say hello or good-bye, it was generally more out of form than feeling. Their brief sexual past was there between them, of course, but it was light-years away from where they were now. Teddy's hand tightened around Lila's.

"Isn't it strange," she said, "to be at the end of your life, to feel you have so much more life in you. . . . But you won't get it. The body gives out. I feel as if I were ready to start all over with someone, all of a sudden after missing Oscar for so long. . . . This feeling reminds me of youth. But youth is gone."

"What about your old boss Lewis?" asked Lila.

"Lewis," said Teddy. "What about him?"

"He's been in love with you for decades. He's rich and handsome and intelligent and so nice. And he's not married to anyone else."

Teddy waved the thought away, looking inscrutably amused. "I'm so happy you have a date with a nice suitable man."

"What's gotten into you?" Lila said warmly. "This isn't like you at all. You're usually so stoic. . . . It's good to hear you talk like this."

"It's these biographers," said Teddy. "Stirring the pot."

"You know," said Lila, "you never really grieved for Oscar; you just went on after he died. It's good you're saying all this now."

"You mean I didn't grieve publicly. How could I? I wasn't his wife."

"You were. You were his true wife."

"Well, I was certainly faithful to him. One narcissistic baby-man was enough. And I could share Oscar, but he couldn't share me. That was the deal." Teddy and Lila both laughed.

As Teddy was leaving Lila's house, she heard the phone ring, heard Lila answer it and cry, "Ben!" Her eldest son, who called her every day. Lila's three sons all loved their mother uncomplicatedly. They had always felt sure of her devotion to them and returned it in kind. It served Teddy right: She had girls, twin girls, difficult, complicated, mercurial girls who felt for their mother a strong tumult of love and hate and many other things. Teddy had had Oscar, Lila Sam, but Lila had had sons, Teddy daughters; Teddy had had independence, Lila security. It was always a trade-off, no way around it. If you were a woman, you could never have everything.

Three

When Teddy got home, she spent an hour or so in the backyard pruning her gnarled wayward rosebushes and rooting around in the tiny shed under the kitchen porch, sorting through packets of seeds and old plastic potting containers, trying to find the rosebush food she was sure she'd bought months ago but hadn't used yet, and it was already mid-July; the summer was half over. She had forgotten how nice it could be back here, despite the limp rows of the neighbors' laundry overhead and rank sewagey breezes that blew up from the Newtown Creek a few blocks away. The heat of the day hadn't yet penetrated the deep shade of the giant old fir tree in the yard next door. The shadowy air had the feel of a grotto, somewhere underground and undisturbed. The back wall of the house undulated with a lapping underwater green, sunlight refracting off the spreading trees. She cut an armload of the salmon-colored roses planted long ago by some member of the Meehan clan, big loose blooms, and carried them into the kitchen. Her bare arms prickled with scratches.

She laid the roses on the counter and stood on the threshold between kitchen and dining room, listening with her whole body to the silence.

The telephone rang. She jumped at the sudden noise, then went into the kitchen and answered it. "Hello?"

"Teddy," said Lewis Strathairn, her old boss, Oscar's longtime lawyer. "It's me."

"Oh, hello, Lewis!" she said. "That's funny, Lila and I were just talking about you. How are you today?"

"I've got a touch of a summer cold," he said, "but other than that I'm all right."

The subject of Lewis's health was an old joke between them; Lewis was never sick, but he was constantly convinced that he was about to be.

"You don't sound like you have a cold," said Teddy.

"Just a tickle in the back of my throat. Teddy, I miss you."

"I miss you, too," she said, realizing that it was true as she said it, although she hadn't thought much about him since the last time she'd seen him, a couple of months before.

"Can you come into town today and have lunch with me? I can send Benny for you."

Lewis lived on East Seventy-seventh Street in an apartment Teddy found cluttered and antiseptic. Benny was the driver of his Town Car.

"I can't, Lewis," she said. "I'm sorry, I have Oscar's biographer, or one of them, coming for lunch."

"So Oscar's biography is finally getting written."

"Actually," she said, "there are two of them." She stretched the phone cord and went to the sink and filled a blue crackle-glazed vase with water, then put the roses into it. They looked pleasingly blowsy and decadent.

"Two," Lewis said.

Teddy had first gone to work for Lewis in 1957. Back then, he had been the balding, affably witty husband of a B-movie actress, who left him in 1979, predictably, for the director of a film she was starring in. Since then, he'd lived alone in his bachelor digs, his torch for Teddy burning bright. Teddy loved and respected Lewis and enjoyed his company tremendously, but his passionate adoration of her had always served, ironically, as a barrier to further intimacy; the strength of his desire created a hazy miragelike force field around him. She couldn't see him clearly enough to desire him.

"That's right," said Teddy.

"I'll call you again soon," said Lewis. "I do miss you."

"I'll be here," she said, and they rang off.

She set the vase of roses on the dining room table. Looking through the front window of the living room, she could see kids hanging out, half-grown pups of various shades of brown. Oscar had loved all the earlier incarnations of these kids. He'd been fascinated by their music, their clothes, their indeterminate ethnicities and aggressively fake Puerto Rican accents, fake because they'd all been born right here, which he knew because Oscar was what used to be called "a nosey parker." He had prowled the blocks around the Calyer Street house, befriending the Polish store clerks up on Manhattan Avenue, stopping to talk to young mothers, snooping around, eavesdropping. Teddy remembered how he'd perched on her living room couch, staring out in the window like a big cat, gossiping with Ruby about the passersby with the nicknames he'd invented for them. "There goes Melanie," he said about a young mother with melon-size breasts. "She's talking to Smoking Man. Hey, it looks like Bambi's pregnant. Did you know that? Wonder who the father is! Maybe it's Dingbat. Think Dingbat knocked up Bambi? I saw him sweet-talking her a while ago." Ruby had chimed in with whatever information she could muster up about the neighbors, beaming whenever he praised her for giving him something juicy.

It was quarter after one, and Ralph Washington was coming at 1:30. Teddy went back to the kitchen and put the pot of lentil soup on a low flame to warm, then set the table for four. She threw the cheese biscuits together fast, because they tasted better if they were made quickly and lightly, without any fuss about measuring, and put them in the oven, then washed fresh-picked devil's-ear lettuce. No point in trying to tidy up for Ralph if Henry had withstood this squalor; she wanted to be fair. And although her house was shabby and as neglected in its way as the potting shed, any attention she gave particular corners now would only make the general disheveledness that much more obvious. She lacked the energy to mop or dust or tie old magazines into recycling bundles on a regular basis anymore. Well, an artist's biographer would presumably expect his subject's mistress's house to be unconventional.

When the doorbell made its *blat-blat* sound, she was just pulling the biscuits out of the oven. She went to open the front door. The black man who stood on her front stoop sported a straw boater hat like a baritone in a barbershop quartet in the Roaring Twenties. He had on gold-rimmed glasses, black jeans, and a short-sleeved white button-down shirt. He carried a canvas shoulder bag so full, it bulged. His skin shone with blackness and a fine sheen of sweat.

"May I help you?" she said, cursing herself for not looking through the peephole first before opening the door. These fanatics came around sometimes. Oscar used to encourage them, argue with them, lead them on, but those days were over.

"I'm Ralph Washington," he said. His cheeks were high and applelike.

"Of course you are," Teddy said, flustered. "Come in."

"Thank you," he said, and stepped over the threshold. "You must be the famous Claire St. Cloud."

"Famous? I hardly think so."

"That's the province of the biographer," he said. "History, in other words, makes people, not vice versa."

"Quite a sense of purpose you've got," she replied. So mistaking him for a Jehovah's Witness hadn't been entirely her own fault.

"You could call it that," he said without smiling.

She gestured toward the sofa, for lack of anything better to do with him. He perched on the sofa and removed his hat, revealing a set of short, neat dreadlocks sprouting from his head like a multitude of little horns.

"May I?" he asked, placing his hat on the ottoman in front of him.

"By all means," she said with a deep foreboding at his courtly manners and overarticulated speech. She felt a disinclination to sit across from him in the cramped little living room. It was much too hot to keep up with this politeness much longer.

"I've been looking forward to meeting you for many years, Miss St. Cloud," Ralph said.

"Oh, call me Claire, please," she said. "The girls aren't here yet, but we can go ahead without them; they both said they weren't sure when they'd get here. Lunch is almost ready."

"Of course," he said, his face alight with an obvious desire to do and say the proper things.

"Why don't you have a seat at the table," she said. "Might as well get this show on the road. I have to do a few things, so please help yourself to wine and antipasti and make yourself at home in the meantime."

She went back to the kitchen, stirred the soup again, arranged the biscuits on a board, dressed and tossed the salad, filled the water glasses.

"Now," she said, going back into the dining room with a tray, "I imagine you'd like to get right down to business."

Ralph looked startled. He held an olive in midair. He looked at it as if he were trying to decide whether to put it back or eat it. He kept it suspended there and said, "We don't need to get to work right away, Miss—"

"Claire," she repeated, sitting down across from him. "So where would you like to begin?"

Ralph hesitated a moment, then set the olive on his appetizer plate and reached over and switched on the small tape recorder he had set on the table in front of him. "Well, one thing I'd really be interested to hear you talk about," Ralph said, "is where Oscar felt his work fit into the grand scheme. He wasn't friends with de Kooning, Guston, Pollock; he wasn't a joiner; he didn't fraternize. Do you think his insistence on the figurative, his obsession with the human form, his refusal to capitulate to the prevailing passion for abstraction, allowed him an independence at the same time as it isolated him? Which is not to say he was entirely isolated; look at

Lucien Freud, John Currin. . . . They're his artistic offspring, wouldn't you say? His figurative, if you'll pardon the pun, children."

"Are you taping this?"

"Do you mind?"

"Oscar always said," she told him, dishing out some soup into a bowl, "that Lucien Freud was a pompous, overrated no-talent without a smidgen of technical skill, and that his people all looked like badly made meat dolls. John Currin, he found a sensationalistic fool, a cold void. He hated Currin's women so much, he said he wanted to slash his canvases. This was, of course, when Oscar was an old man. But when he was younger, he was neither isolated nor independent; he always had plenty of people around him who believed in what he was doing. As for those 'New York boys,' as he called them, as if he didn't live here himself, he felt he didn't need them. Abstract Expressionism was a wet dream, embarrassing to look at, he always said: grown men spurting like virgin boys in their sleep. Guston, at least, had the sense to switch to those dreary little cartoons. Guston was the only one he had any respect for; we met him a few times, had dinner with him and his wife, Musa, once in the city, visited their place in Woodstock another time. I don't think Guston liked Oscar's work too terribly much, although they got on well enough, but Oscar respected Guston's later work. He liked the smoking kidney-shaped heads very much."

"Well, I know he hated Pollock," said Ralph.

"Pollock," said Teddy, smiling at Ralph's obvious anticipation of Oscar's reproduced diatribe. "Oscar almost had a stroke if anyone started praising Pollock. He thought Pollock was a retarded child who dribbled all over himself, who had no control of his bodily functions, all spray and spurt, like a bad dog."

Ralph laughed almost ferally, showing a lot of white teeth. He wasn't bad-looking really, although he wasn't her type. There was something a little moist about him; her impression of him as wet-lipped on the phone hadn't been too far off the mark. She wondered what steely depths of driven egomania undergirded his studious eagerness, the ghosts from the past he had to shove to the back of his mind as he got on with his mission.

She splayed one hand on the table and moved it up and down so it resembled a tarantula, the gesture Oscar had made when he was worked up. "The female figure was the only real subject as far as Oscar was concerned," she told Ralph. "Cheese and oysters and bottles of beer were all very well if you were a medieval Dutchman and they were imbued with morality and social context. Landscapes had their power, their beauty, of course they did. But the female body was the most beautiful thing on earth, the most powerful and mysterious of all subjects and objects, animate or inanimate, the most familiar, the most earthly, and the most sacred. He used to chant it: " 'mother, queen, goddess, bitch, whore, saint, virgin, milkmaid.' "

Teddy drank some wine, tried a bite of a cheese biscuit. She had bought the cheap cheddar at the C-Town, where she bought all her cheese now. She missed the exciting, expensive cheeses she'd hand-selected every week from her favorite Manhattan shop before her commute home on the subway, with its big cut wheels, its tangy smells of milk fat and good mold. But these biscuits weren't bad at all.

"And do you think," Ralph asked, the words surging forth as if they'd been dammed up for years in his head and were finally being released into the air, "that the reason he's not as famous as he should be is that he refused to 'join the gang,' so to speak? He didn't hobnob at the White Horse or the Cedar Tavern. He didn't go to their openings. He deliberately spurned their dealers and gallery owners. Clement Greenberg had a vendetta against him, and he didn't seem to care. He essentially sat out the dance after the abstract expressionists' big party."

"You're certainly obsessed with this so-called isolation. Oscar had a party of his own; who needed theirs?"

"That's true," said Ralph. "And now there's Lucien Freud and John Currin to prove it. Tell me Oscar didn't influence them both tremendously."

"Lucien Freud. Lucien Freud. Oscar couldn't wrap his mind around how that man avoided becoming a laughingstock. And he said he wouldn't touch one of John Currin's menopausal drones and booby freaks with a cattle prod. He called him 'the modern-day Antonio Villapardo.' "

"I'm not familiar with that name," said Ralph bemusedly, writing it down in his notebook to look up later.

"Exactly my point. That's what Oscar said people will say about Currin in a little while."

"Was he a Renaissance Florentine?" Ralph asked. "I thought I knew them all."

Teddy chewed an olive, shaking her head: Antonio Villapardo was Oscar's made-up scapegoat. This was her little private revenge on Ralph for talking about Oscar as if he were a maladjusted stick-in-the-mud. And for his stiff, academic diction, which had annoyed her since he'd arrived. She would have bet anything it was his adult overcompensation for having grown up a very bright but underprivileged and probably fatherless black kid uncomfortably out of place in the ghetto, then just as uncomfortably out of place at Harvard or wherever he'd gone to school on full scholarship. Actually, he struck Teddy as someone who wouldn't ever feel comfortable anywhere, and this made her more sympathetic to him, but it was too late to tell him the truth about Villapardo.

"In fact," she said instead, "toward the end of his life, when he had softened slightly, but only slightly, Oscar said he thought the only one around here with any balls was a girl, Cecily Brown. He thought she had a real knowledge of how to paint bodies, and technical mastery. But he also believed that a woman couldn't really paint another woman. She's too close to her subject. He thought only a man could paint a woman with the proper sense of awe, lust, the sense of otherness, the necessary distance."

"I see," said Ralph with a dubious look at Teddy through his rather long eyelashes. He had eyes like a deer's, far apart, elongated. Yet there was nothing deerlike about him. The animal he most resembled, to Teddy, was a dog: a hungry jaw full of strong teeth camouflaged by a domesticated, eager-to-please smile. Was that a racist thought? she wondered, then ceased to worry about it.

"I take it you're already familiar with Oscar's views on the subject of his fellow painters," she said, "and you disagree with them."

"Frankly," said Ralph. "I disagree with him on many points. It doesn't in any way lessen my reverence for his work."

"No doubt you think de Kooning is a great painter," Teddy said.

"Guilty as charged."

"You'll be taken out in the yard and kneecapped later," said Teddy. "I'm an excellent shot."

Ralph laughed with his whole head and torso, as if this were very funny.

She disliked overlaughter; it always irked her. "Actually," she said, "I disagreed with him for years about de Kooning and Pollock and much more. All my arguments never made a dent in his convictions."

"Of course not," said Ralph with an echo of fulsome laughter in his voice.

Not sure whether he was implying that Oscar was a stubborn old wing nut of a goat or that she was an uneducated nonartist unworthy of influencing a great painter, or both, Teddy smiled a secret smile and took a bite of her lentil soup. Limited access to the best ingredients, she thought, was a real test of any cook's mettle. This soup was rich and complex and full of *umami,* the meatiness and soul that undergirded all the other flavors, sweetness, sourness, bitterness, saltiness. The lentils had a satisfyingly mealy give between the teeth. A suggestion of cardamom in the broth hinted at duskiness. She had added the artichoke hearts because they had an enzyme that made everything taste sweeter, a different quality of sweetness from sugar, hitting a different part of the tongue. She had added the lamb sausage because it was so good.

The doorbell rang. Teddy got up and went to the front door. Peering through the peephole, she saw Ruby.

"Well," said Teddy, opening the door, "you're just in time to meet your father's biographer. He's in full interview mode."

Ruby kissed Teddy on her cheek, and Teddy put a hand against Ruby's cheek as she did so. It was their familiar, affectionate greeting. Teddy didn't sense any coolness in Ruby's manner, but she felt wary about expecting too much affection from her. She stood back and looked at her dauntingly voluptuous, nearly forty-year-old daughter. Ruby's face was wide and very pale; her mouth was red and full, and her naturally thick eyebrows had been plucked into fine arches over her smoky, slanted blue eyes, Oscar's Slavic eyes, black-lashed, heavy-lidded. Her dark curly hair was piled on her head. She looked so much like Oscar . . . and she was so young still. . . . It was very complicated, being such a mother of such a daughter. Ruby's nonidentical twin sister, Samantha, resembled Teddy; she was slinky and catlike, delicate and sensitive, whereas Ruby and Oscar were robust and sensual, blunt and unself-conscious. Because they were so much alike, mothering Samantha had been so easy, whereas Ruby, who loved her father more, had always been a challenge.

"We've been discussing the female form," Teddy said.

Ruby laughed. "What else?" she said. "Well, let's go in and offer our opinions and see where that gets us."

Ruby put her arm through Teddy's as they headed for the dining room. But Teddy couldn't fully give in to her warmth. She felt that somewhere, very early probably, she had lost Ruby, and she had never been sure how to win her back. This made her act overly sensitive and cautious with Ruby, and also caused her to think critical thoughts about her, which for the most part she kept entirely to herself.

Ruby sat down in the chair across from Ralph.

"I'm Ruby Feldman," she said.

"Ralph Washington," he responded. "Very glad to meet you." He had been looking over his notes.

Ruby helped herself to some wine. "I hear you've been talking about the female form. A subject my father would have been happy to expound on all day and night."

"Your mother was just telling me that she and he differed in opinion about de Kooning and Pollock."

"Oh, they argued all the time," said Ruby. "It was their hobby."

"Your father disliked the work of many of his contemporaries."

"His sister's most of all," said Ruby with a quick laughing glance at her mother.

"Oh, Ruby, he didn't dislike Maxine's work; he just thought it was too easy."

"Your aunt," Ralph said to Ruby, "is widely considered a great artist in her own right."

"She doesn't acknowledge herself as related to me," said Ruby, "but technically, I suppose, she's my aunt."

"Oscar would have thrown a fork at you if he'd heard you say Maxine was great," Teddy said, handing Ruby a bowl of soup. "In his opinion, she made black splotches bold enough to thrill the boys but not big enough to threaten them. Consummate game player. Not an artist at all. A politician, second-rate. Like a state representative."

"According to what my father told me about their arguments, Maxine always thought he was limited and stuck in his ways," said Ruby to Ralph. "You can imagine how amicable their relationship was. She got a show at Leo Castelli's gallery and Dad went ballistic and ranted all over our house, saying she wasn't any good and she was just making a fool of herself. Do you come from a family of artists, Ralph?"

"No," Ralph said, turning to Teddy, "my parents are both college professors, but I had the immense good fortune to be taken as a teenager by my uncle, who was a painter himself, to Oscar's retrospective in 1991 at the Jewish Museum. I knew nothing about women then, but I felt I did after I saw *Helena* and *Mercy*—the society girl and the nightclub singer."

"That retrospective was a strange time for Oscar," said Teddy, amused at the thought of the teenaged Ralph beholding it. "Exciting, of course, but a retrospective implies encroaching obsolescence."

"It was the contrast with *Mercy* that struck me at the time. That you could see into these two different women's souls, the trapped bird in the debutante's chest, the wild flame in the chanteuse's eye—I had never been so moved before by the presence of greatness. Now, of course, I have seen many of his paintings, and I am never disappointed, not even by the sixties subway nudes, which I venture to say are among his riskiest, most out-there work. . . . Anyway, that adolescent experience I had of *Mercy* and *Helena* . . ." Ralph closed his eyes. "I went to art school after I graduated from college and studied painting, partially in hopes of one day meeting Oscar and writing his life. Then he died before I had the chance to talk to him."

"I'm so sorry," said Teddy. "I hope we can re-create him for you."

Ralph blinked at her, flummoxed.

"This soup is incredible," Ruby told Teddy.

"Inedible?"

"No! Incredible," Ruby said, laughing. "Is there grated ginger in it?"

"Good guess, but no," said Teddy, looking pointedly at Ralph, who was eating slowly and offhandedly, without noticing a single flavor, she would have bet. He struck her as a man made more of spirit and mind than of flesh, someone for whom bodily pleasure was a sometimes guilty and generally abstracted afterthought. It had long been Teddy's theory that you could tell how someone was in bed by the way he or she ate; she was sure that Ralph would be ethereal and self-abnegating.

"A tiny bit of mace?" asked Ruby.

"Nope," said Teddy again. "You're way out on a limb." It was a game she'd taught her daughters to play as children: guess the ingredients. She'd always put one secret thing into a dish to test them. Whoever guessed it got the satisfaction of her mother's approbation.

The telephone rang. Ruby put her hand on Teddy's to keep her from getting up, then answered it herself in the front hall.

"It's me," her twin sister said. Ruby heard squalling in the background. "Buster's having a meltdown. I can't make it to Mom's. Can you tell her for me?"

"This is important," said Ruby. "Dad's biographer is here. Can't Ivan take the kids for a couple of hours?"

"Ivan had to go into the lab today. Please tell Mom I'm sorry."

"So bring the kids."

"Ivan's got the car," said Samantha.

"So I'll treat you to a cab."

"The car seats are in the car; Ivan would kill me if I went anywhere with the kids without them. And I wouldn't wish Buster on anyone right now. No one would get a word in."

Ruby happened to know that Buster, a three-year-old boy whose given name was Peter, behaved with admirable civility in the care of his aunt and grandmother. She suspected that Samantha exacerbated rather than soothed Buster's tantrums, and that, in fact, he threw these tantrums to distract Samantha's attention from her husband, then kept them up when he figured out that as long as he acted horribly, he had her undivided attention. If Samantha hadn't been so vapor-locked on Ivan, their son might have been calmer and better adjusted. But no one could tell Samantha anything: She often acted, Ruby thought, as if she were the first person on the planet to give birth to a human child, as if mothering were so sacred and rarefied, anyone who wasn't a mother couldn't possibly understand how profoundly it changed you. But Ruby guessed she had to act this way in order to make herself feel better about being in the thrall of a two-foot-tall manipulative, punitive tyrant and a small screaming bag of stinking humors who sucked her dry. Whenever Samantha described the amazingness of breast-feeding or the miracle of watching her child take his first shit on a potty, Ruby would think of the quiet little apartment she'd lived in alone for fifteen years. There was no greater joy she knew than going home alone to find everything as she'd left it, her bed, her books, her computer, her refrigerator, her bathtub, her solitary self.

"Sam," she said, "come on. It won't kill them to take a cab ride without car seats this one time."

"Buster," Samantha replied in a deadly, cold, even voice. "I think you need a time-out. Sorry, Rube, I gotta go. This little ape child needs to take some deep breaths."

Ruby returned to the dining room. "Samantha has bagged out," she said. "Peter's apparently being a monster."

"Peter," said Teddy, "is never a monster. I'm very disappointed she won't come."

"She apologized," said Ruby in a tone that conveyed what she thought of her sister's apology. "I think she's reluctant to talk to you, Ralph. She didn't get along with Dad. She's still mad at him."

"Ruby," said Teddy. Although she was older by only eight minutes, Ruby had always been much more assertive and mature, so naturally Teddy had been more protective of Samantha. As a mother, you played the cards you were dealt. "I don't think Samantha would appreciate your revealing that."

"Probably not," Ruby admitted. "But it's just so annoying."

"By the way, Ralph, did you know you had competition?" Teddy asked him point-blank.

He swallowed his mouthful and looked at her.

"It's true," she said. "Another biographer is writing a book about Oscar; he interviewed me several days ago. Has no one told you?"

"No," said Ralph. He lifted his napkin and wiped his lips.

"His name is Henry Burke. Maybe you know each other."

"I have never heard his name before now," said Ralph.

"Oh dear," said Teddy, who was enjoying this a little. "I can see that this is bad news, and I'm sorry to have to be the one to tell you. He interviewed me just this week."

"I haven't spoken to him yet," said Ruby. "Well, except on the phone. So I'm virgin territory, Ralph; he hasn't gotten to me yet."

Ralph tried to laugh through his consternation. "Does he . . . does he have a book contract, do you happen to know?"

"Yes," said Teddy. "With Yale University Press."

"My contract is with Norton," said Ralph. "Does he know about me?"

"I haven't told him," said Teddy.

"Me, neither, obviously," said Ruby. "But I bet Maxine will. She'll love playing you both off against each other."

"Oh, we all will," said Teddy, laughing. "Why not? Two young men vying for Oscar like vultures over a dead hyena—"

Ralph laughed ruefully. This time, his laughter suited the scale of the joke.

"All right," said Teddy, softening toward him a little now that she'd sprung bad news on him, "coffee, anyone? I've made a fresh blueberry cake. It's still warm, and there's ice cream."

"No coffee for me, thank you," said Ralph. "And I'm sorry to say no cake, either; I have to watch my sugar; diabetes runs in my family."

"Too bad for you," said Ruby. "My mother's blueberry cake could launch ships. I'll have his piece, too, Mom."

Teddy got up and went into the kitchen, laden with empty soup bowls and salad plates.

Ruby took a drink of wine, then looked hard at Ralph. "What's your grand theory about my father?" she asked. "I know you have one."

"My grand theory about Oscar?"

"Come on."

"He was a great painter."

"Obviously, you think that; otherwise, you wouldn't be going to all this trouble. I mean the guiding idea you're going to marshal these interviews and all your research around."

"What makes you think I have one?"

"I know you have one," she said. "Come on, what do you think of his work, honestly?"

There was a silence brimming with all sorts of thoughts in both their heads.

"My only *criticism* of Oscar's work," said Ralph slowly after a moment, "if that's what you're looking for, is that his adherence to figuratism made him great and original but paradoxically might have kept him from achieving his full potential. I say *might*—this is pure hypothetical speculation. *Maybe,* if he had allowed himself to flower into abstraction the way de Kooning did with his female nudes, he would have become both one of the foremost painters of his generation and one of the greatest. As it was, he was simply one of the greatest, which is nothing to sneeze at. But the way de Kooning stretched the female form, pushed it as far as it could go into abstraction without losing the integrity of the woman's individual self . . . His nudes are glorious and remarkable for their perfectly balanced tension between paint and flesh. Oscar's nudes, in light of de Kooning's, have a slight tendency to seem didactic and self-limiting, but only in their literalness, and only in that one respect."

"If my father had heard you say that, he would have socked you in the eye."

"No doubt."

"I grew up here in Greenpoint," said Ruby. "Where did you grow up, Ralph?"

"Born and raised in Fort Greene."

"So you know how, walking down the street, you see people in motion, on the fly, blurred. One face jumps out of the crowd at you. It's a blink, a glimpse, but you feel like you've really seen that person; then you're on to the next. . . . Growing up in the city, you are constantly seeing the faces of strangers, your eye taking them in so intimately, so briefly."

"Yes," he said, leaning forward, his eyes alight, narrowed.

"And you know how at the end of a day of being in the streets, walking to school, messing around with your friends, you lie in bed and you remember the faces sort of like afterimages right before you fall asleep? They collect in your retinas and play themselves back like a slide show on your eyelids, all these strangers your eyes collected through the day."

"Yes," he said again in a rapt voice. "I know exactly what you mean."

"Dad's paintings always bring back that feeling to me. Some more than others. The mystery of strangers. It's just stupid to think of his paintings as self-portraits."

His bedazzled expression turned immediately blank and inoffensive. "Oh, I never said—"

"I know you didn't, but a couple of clueless critics did, and it infuriated him. Nothing wrong with self-portraits, but it just completely missed the point. My father wasn't portraying his own psyche in female nudes; that's like saying he should have 'flowered into abstraction.' "

She shot a glance at Ralph, who had assumed a blank, pleasant, attentive expression.

"Of course he was monstrously self-involved, my father, but when he looked at you, he saw you and not himself. He had an appetite for other people's stories, their souls even. He was visceral, not reflective. . . . His paintings are about seeing people, not paint, not shapes, not abstraction, but people, women, in the flesh—not intellectualized, personalized, romanticized, anything-ized."

"De Kooning also—"

"When I look at my father's paintings, I get that same sort of kick you get on the street when you apprehend a stranger, whole."

"Are you an artist, too?"

"No," said Ruby. "I teach English at a public high school on the Lower East Side."

"Well, it's admirable how passionate you are about your father's work."

"Well," said Ruby, "you're passionate about it, too."

"Of course."

"But you're wrong about abstraction."

"No doubt," he said without conviction.

Teddy came back in, carrying the cake on top of dessert plates, two forks in one fist. She set it all onto the table; then she bore away the soup pot. Ruby didn't get up to help her mother.

When Teddy was out of earshot, Ruby said, "I think it's hard for my mother to talk about my father like this. She was crazy about him. I've never seen anyone so crazy about anyone else as she was about him. He loved her back, but in a totally different way."

"Must be wonderful," said Ralph, "to be the daughter of two people so in love."

"Not especially."

"That's not what I expected you to say."

"My grand theory about my parents is this. My mother was the lover and my father was the beloved. From watching them, I drew the conclusion that it's best to be the lover, the one who adores and pursues. Love is tangentially about power, and the beloved has less power than the lover, all appearances to the contrary. In other words, my mother had more power over my father than he did over her. That's always how it works, no matter how it may appear on the surface."

"Always?" said Ralph, mostly to keep her talking. "What about balanced relationships, where two people love and are loved in equal measure?"

"Oh, please, that's impossible. From what I've seen anyway. One person is the adorer and cherisher and the other is the adored and cherished. Whenever Mom distanced herself from Dad, which was rarely, believe me, he sort of fell apart. I could see it, even as a little girl. He needed her; she made it a point not to need him. But she loved him."

"That's interesting," he said.

"Sometimes it works the other way; sometimes a man is the lover, the uxorious husband. . . . That's a word that means pathologically proud of his wife. Isn't that a great word? No one uses it anymore. My brother-in-law, Ivan, for example. My sister is much younger than he is. She's not intellectual really, although she's smart and has a B.A. in art, and she's a painter, but she never paints because she's got two kids under four. Meanwhile, Ivan has a doctorate in biochemistry and is a senior research fellow at the

Starr-McGee Institute. She's thirty-nine; he's fifty. He possesses and controls her. He needs to know where she is every minute. I think he's the real reason she's not here today; he doesn't want her doing anything without him. I'm sure he took the car to keep her a prisoner in their house. And she loves this kind of treatment! She plays right into it. She always wanted to be close to Dad but never could, so obviously Ivan makes up for that in many ways."

Ruby splashed more wine into her glass, drank some, set it down again, all while Ralph waited.

"Of course, my mother is proud that she was never controlling of my father, but that depends on what you mean by *controlling*. . . . For example, she loved to bait him and goad him and get him to go off about this and that in front of other people, show him off. She'd be right there, contradicting him so he'd reveal more and more of himself. She was so proud of him, of course; she adored him. . . . But it was a kind of power mongering, in a way. In a way, she controlled him with her love."

"But what about her lack of possessiveness?" Ralph asked.

"Her lack of possessiveness was an illusion," Ruby said.

"You mean," he said cautiously, darting a glance toward the kitchen, "she gave him free rein as a paradoxical way of keeping him?"

"Yes . . ." said Ruby. "Exactly. But there's more to it than that."

Teddy stuck her head through the door and said, "Ruby, coffee?"

Ralph started a little; Ruby turned calmly and said, "Sure, Mom."

After Teddy had gone back to the kitchen, Ruby looked at Ralph, shaking her head. "Aren't I a terrible child, telling you my mother's secrets while she waits on us hand and foot. By the way, I don't get up to help her because she won't allow it; she's a total control freak in the kitchen. As well as in every other way. Anyway, her lack of possessiveness was an illusion. She was extremely posses-sive. Sexually, Dad was totally in Mom's thrall—it was obvious to anyone with half an eye—so if he went off and had other women, it didn't bug her. It was like the queen not minding if the king had consorts: She was still the queen. And meanwhile, kings always have their consorts; it's part of the deal. Emotionally, she was very jealous. Like, for instance, she wouldn't let us be close to him, his own daughters. She kept us all apart. She allowed him to go home to his poor fat wife only because she didn't want him underfoot all the time and didn't want him to get tired of her. . . . Did I mention that she's a control freak?"

"But I don't think you can boil marriages down into such codi-fied structures. It seems more of a give-and-take to me, more of a flow. I think there must be much more to any relationship than people outside it can see."

"Are you married?"

"No, are you?"

"No . . ."

"Not yet?" he asked.

"Maybe not ever."

"Oh, I doubt that," he said. "A woman as beautiful as you are."

"Thank you," said Ruby warily.

She'd meant to imply that she didn't want to get married, and he'd meant "beautiful" as an abstract compliment; he hadn't at all meant to come on to her, but all the same, an invisible bubble suddenly enveloped Ralph and Ruby and sealed them off, the filmy bubble of sexual possibility, which was awkward for them because they weren't attracted to each other, but the continuation of this conversation, spooling itself out unspoken between them, nonetheless suggested something along those lines. Neither knew how to delicately convey this absolute lack of attraction to the other, so they just sat, not looking at each other, in a silence made more uneasy by the fact that it rode in the wake of their torrent of wine-fueled words, until Teddy strode in with the coffeepot and two cups and started pouring matter-of-factly, as if she hadn't heard every word they'd said.

PART TWO

Four

Maxine Feldman woke up early in a state of panicky despair and decided to clean her studio, one of her preferred solutions to any emotional upset. (The others, none of them mutually exclusive, were chain-smoking, brushing her dog, Frago, with a Love Glove, taking baths, and/or listening to turbulent music at full volume—Beethoven or Sonic Youth, it didn't much matter which.) As she cleaned, she chain-smoked and listened to Dave Holland's *Conference of the Birds,* which wasn't turbulent; it was flat-out joyful, but that suited the morning sunlight. She was wearing men's black trousers, size twenty-six long, thirty-two waist (Maxine liked to think of herself as squarely built rather than squat) and a baggy gray short-sleeved sweater that had once been all cashmere but now was at least half dog hair. Frago lay under her worktable, well out of the way of all the activity, but keeping a close eye on it nonetheless.

Maxine's assistant, Katerina, had confessed the day before that she had fallen in love with someone. Whether this someone was a woman or a man, she didn't say, and Maxine was too proud to ask. Katerina was thirty-eight, or so she claimed; Maxine suspected that either she was almost ten years older than that or the Soviet diet had caused her to sag a little at the jawline prematurely, not that it mattered or diminished her appeal. She was a *jolie laide* Hungarian with a sweet, gamine, slightly gap-toothed face and the kind of gymnast's body that had always driven Maxine mad: petite, leggy, broad-shouldered, slim-hipped. More than that, she was intelligent, courageous, stalwart, loyal, and warm, all the qualities Maxine felt she herself lacked but had nonetheless always yearned for in a mate.

Anyway, that wasn't going to happen. It had been a ridiculous idea. She was almost fifty years older than Katerina, for God's sake.

As she worked at setting everything in order, she ignored the twinges, some more painful than others, in her back and shoulders and the joints of her elbows and knees. She hated being old. She caught sight of herself in the mirror by accident: Her face was sagging and consternated, her mouth awry, the eyes behind thick glasses squinting in concentration. She looked to herself like an ugly dwarflike toad.

All around her, hanging on walls and leaning against tables and lined up on shelves like books, were her paintings, finished or in progress or temporarily abandoned. She didn't dare look at any of them in this mood. It was so hard to wake up every morning and manufacture the energy to continue this whole endeavor when she had all but lost faith in it. Who cared? None of it mattered. Wisps of black on canvas after canvas. Why black? More important, why wisps? When she was younger, she'd stayed up all night working. Each fresh black mark on the white canvas was an electric impulse generated by the energy in her head. Black because it was the negative image of the hot light she saw. Negative because she rebelled at positivity, the finiteness of a figure, the decadent arbitrariness of a full palette of color. The shapes were the only thing that varied from painting to painting—feathered or blunt edges, large or small wisps and blobs, curves or angles. What moved her brush was whatever impulse issued from her core, the spark created by the intersection of whatever was in the room and outside it, in her head and outside it, her mood and the weather, the political climate and the condition of her stomach. She had used her body as a source of light and heat, a high-speed muscle car that needed periodic pit stops to refuel and regenerate.

The ashes of that self-immolating fire were stored in the urn of her skull now, her memorial of that young artist who had believed so fervently in art, her own art especially. Now, mired in cynicism and defeat, she wondered whether it had really been so wonderful, the heyday of her artistic career. She had drunk too much booze, slept with a lot of women who'd hurt her badly, and never found lasting love. She'd made some money, it was true, and established some degree of a name; her paintings hung in the Modern and other museums around the world, but she'd never achieved the kind of fame that her ambition required of her. In her own mind, therefore, she was a failure. As the years wore on and she felt herself and her name fading, disappearing, being replaced by fresher talents, names, egos, canvases, and careers, she found it increasingly difficult to prop herself up every day, to resurrect her flagging drive through willpower alone, since hope was gone. And so it went for anyone who'd lost his or her faith. "I can't go on I'll go on." Because what else was there to do? It wasn't as if she were being tortured or oppressed or forced to endure in a Third World stew of horror. No one needed her except Frago, a midsize mutt who had been listed as a Lab-boxer mix when she'd rescued him eight years before from the ASPCA, although he resembled a mournful miniature hippo more than anything else. But Frago's needs were minimal and had a built-in end point. If she didn't paint, she might as well die, and that was all there was to it.

As she was cleaning a jar's worth of sable brushes soaking in turpentine, her cell phone trilled the little melody it had come programmed with, a cascading tumble of tinkly notes. At first, she heard it as part of *Conference of the Birds* and ignored it; then suddenly the phone's chirps separated themselves aurally from the music and she realized someone was calling her.

Katerina!

She put the brush down, took the lit cigarette from between her lips and stubbed it out in a nearby ashtray, fished the phone from her back pocket, and checked the little screen on the cover. It wasn't Katerina; it was a number she didn't recognize. She said, "Fuck," flipped it open, and said, "Yeah."

"Maxine Feldman?" said a hesitant male voice.

"That's me."

"This is Henry Burke, your brother's biographer?"

A lot of professional white men under the age of about forty-five, Maxine had noticed lately, were doing something that a few decades before had been the clichéd provenance of Valley girls, ending declarative sentences with a question mark. But unlike those prepubescent mall rats, they weren't verbally sequestering themselves in a trendy colloquial clique; they were trying to declaw and deball themselves by appearing as unthreatening and sensitive as possible. Blatant masculinity was, unfortunately, out of favor.

"Henry," said Maxine. She'd liked him well enough when she'd met him, despite his blandness. She might have felt differently about him if he hadn't been lucky enough to contrast favorably with that other one, Rupert or Rufus, that pompous *shwartze* with his chummy condescension. He'd seemed to think that by subtly allying himself with Maxine and flattering her, he could win her over and get her to reveal things about Oscar that weren't already a matter of public record. She could smell a mile off that he was only trying to bamboozle her by capitalizing on his knowledge of the rift between her and her brother. Ralph, his name was, she remembered then. Ralph's little game of being "on her side" had conveyed the implication that it was generally understood that Oscar's side had been diametrically and personally opposed to hers. This irked her no end. She preferred Henry's strategy, which was to be openly worshipful of Oscar and wary of her: Maxine tended to feel more at ease with people who didn't seem to like her than with those who tried to collude with her.

Not that these boys were going to get anything interesting out of her. She had decided to appear cooperative and sweet as pie, but to tell no one a damn thing he couldn't learn by spending some quality time on Google. "Oscar was a confident and boisterous kid, whereas I was more shy and studious," and "Oscar was never happy in art school—he was too rebellious—and that's why he dropped out after one semester," and "From a very early age, maybe even birth, Oscar loved his power to charm women," that sort of claptrap. She had announced these things first to Henry, then to Ralph, with a confidential air meant to suggest that she was sharing secrets. Maxine hated the whole idea of someone writing Oscar's biography. Part of it was her general distrust of the biographical venture and part of it was sibling rivalry—profiles in art periodicals aside, no one had written a full-length biography of Maxine yet, and here were two being written about Oscar! But he'd had to die first, so she supposed it was a fair trade-off.

"I was wondering," Henry was saying, "whether I could come by today. If you're not too busy?"

"Well, I'm busy now and there's a dinner party I have to go to later on," Maxine said then. "Come at five. That should give us plenty of time."

Henry started to tell her that was the worst-possible time for him to come, because his wife had asked him to stay home with Chester from 4:00 to 5:30 P.M. so she could go to a yoga class.

"Better make it four-thirty, so I have time to bathe and dress," Maxine said, interrupting him. "See you then. Good-bye." She shoved the phone back into her pocket and stalked over to the window, harrumphing a little as she lit a fresh cigarette. She was not in any mood to entertain today. When Frago lurched to his feet and ambled to her side, she bent down and took one of his silky ears in her hands. "Frago Fragonardo Fragonard," she crooned. "My sweetest pea, my sweet good boy. Who's my sweet pea?" Frago looked into her face, his eyes seemingly devoted but, Maxine knew, totally unfathomable. Even so, she felt an answering well of love for him as pure as any feeling she'd ever had. On their walk this morning, she'd lost her temper with him. She liked to feed him his breakfast kibble as they walked, instead of giving it to him in a bowl; even after all these years, he'd never learned to heel very well without a steady stream of bribes, and she no longer had the strength to restrain him if he pulled too hard. Sometimes her fingers and his mouth suffered a misunderstanding, and today had been one such time: She'd held the kibble too deeply in her bunched fingertips, so his teeth had had to sink into her fingers so he could tongue it from her grasp. It had hurt her, but usually this passed without remark from Maxine, since they were both too old to learn otherwise. Today, however, the indignity of being bitten by her own dog as she was feeding him had been too much to stand. "Fuck you," she'd muttered, giving his muzzle a quick squeeze, so hard that he'd squealed. Just then, she'd met the eye of the Korean woman in front of the deli on the corner. For some reason, every time this woman saw Maxine, she happened to be in the grip of her worst self: haggling over the price of coffee, falsely accusing the cashier of shortchanging her. . . . This terrible, low morning, caught in the woman's gaze, Maxine had felt herself at once reduced to the evolutionary status of a slug.

"Frago," Maxine crooned now. He nuzzled her hand with the same nose she'd squeezed to the point of pain; she wished the Korean woman could see him now. Outside, the street below was still fairly empty, but before too long it would be thronged with the usual slow-moving herds of tourists and outer-borough nimrods buying three-hundred-dollar pairs of shoes and low-level TV stars and other horrible people. Maxine's loft, which she'd bought for "nothing" (actually, $27,000) in the seventies, was on the fourth floor of an old factory on Greene Street. Most of the old SoHo artists had long ago fled to Brooklyn or Chelsea and been replaced by male models, Eurotrash, and bond traders, but Maxine had stayed, stubbornly. Where was she supposed to go, anyway? For about the past ten years, sales of her work had pretty much been in the crapper, but she had saved enough from the flush eighties to keep her going, she hoped, till she croaked.

Maybe, it occurred to her now, these biographies of Oscar would shed a little secondary light on her. . . .

Oh God, she was going to die alone.

Maxine mashed her smoked-down filter into an ashtray and

went back to the brushes. By the time Henry was due to arrive, her worktable was austerely clean, the floor mopped, paints and brushes, tools and inks perfectly organized. She'd sorted through a lot of new sketches and drawings and put them away in flat files, emptied months' worth of jars full of gray turpentine, and even scrubbed the little toilet in the tiny hallway. Katerina always offered to clean the studio, but letting someone else clean in here felt intrusive and stressful to Maxine, even Katerina, who kept the rest of the loft beautifully tidy and mopped.

Maxine waited in her kitchen for the water to boil for Earl Grey, put some gingersnaps out on a plate, then noticed she was out of milk. Well, Henry would just have to drink it without. She had never been much for entertaining; she always invited people to show up between mealtimes so she wouldn't be called upon to provide food.

She was bone-weary, she realized suddenly. She'd awakened at 7:30, which was very early for a night owl like her, and had walked Frago over a mile; then she'd cleaned steadily all day in a state of manic despair, without stopping to eat, and she'd smoked too much. She wanted nothing in the world so much as to crawl into bed and pass out. Her heart was fluttering arrhythmically, the way it did sometimes. She'd be damned if she'd go to a doctor, though. All they ever had was bad news and cures that just made things worse. She'd made it this far; she was as tough as a weed.

The buzzer rang. She got up and went to her front door and pushed the button to open the door downstairs without bothering to ask who it was over the intercom, then went back to the table and slumped in her chair and fell into a momentary waking nap. She heard the elevator doors clang open and shut, but she didn't move until she heard Henry's irritatingly soft knock on her door.

To her consternation, he was carrying a backpack that contained a baby. Even worse, it had a pinched-looking face, whose expression suggested that he either had a foul-smelling diaper or was about to launch into a two-hour squall. How rude, to bring a baby!

"Come in," she said through clenched teeth.

"Sorry about the kid," said Henry, who was red-faced and a little sweaty. "It couldn't be helped; it was either this or wreck my marriage."

"I've made hot tea," said Maxine crabbily.

Henry took the backpack off and scooped the baby from it and cradled him in one arm. With his free hand, he extricated a notebook and pen from his shoulder bag. It was almost feminine, his way with the baby. And why did so many younger men wear shoulder bags now? Men were turning themselves into women now, the way women had turned themselves into men during the feminist heyday. Maxine, despite the fact that she was a rather mannish-looking lesbian who'd always lived her life on her own terms, nurtured a great fondness for the 1950s, the era of cartoonish sexual display, glossy painted lips and pointed breasts and full skirts on women, men in squared-off suits and hats shaped like circumcised penis heads. . . . "People knew who you were then; girls were girls and men were men. . . ." She was with Archie Bunker all the way, in that at least.

"Have a seat," said Maxine, setting out two cups and sugar. "I'm out of milk."

"I don't need it," said Henry in a reassuring tone, which made Maxine suspect he did indeed take milk but was assuaging what he incorrectly took to be hostessy anxiety.

Henry unwrapped the baby from his gummy-looking swaddling blanket and spread it on the industrial-linoleum floor of Maxine's kitchen, then set the baby down on his back. The baby, to his credit, appeared to take this indignity in stride. Frago, under the table, growled in the back of his throat but didn't pounce.

"Chester likes to be on the floor, for some reason," said Henry.

"Bodes well for his future," said Maxine.

"Does your dog do all right with babies?" Henry asked.

"He doesn't know any," said Maxine. "But he's harmless in general. All right, let's cut to the chase. What did you come to ask me?"

Henry opened his notebook and consulted what Maxine took, upside down, to be a nearly illegible list of jotted questions. "I've been wondering about what you were saying about Abigail and Claire—or rather, Teddy, if you don't mind my calling her that."

"You can call her a two-headed hyena for all I care," said Maxine, pouring tea.

"About Abigail, too, and the dynamics of their triangle," he added, pressing on. "Do you think Oscar stayed with Abigail all those years out of guilt?"

"I see you've met Teddy and succumbed to her 'charms,' " said Maxine, hoping the quotation marks were audible.

"What I'm trying to understand is why he kept two households going. I have one, and frankly, that's more than enough. Why would a man want two? Why not divorce Abigail and move in with Teddy?"

Damn it, Maxine thought. She didn't have it in her to be cooperative and cheerful and opaque today. She shouldn't have let him come. "This biography mongering is just an excuse to stick your nose into Oscar's private business, isn't it?" she said. "A man you profess to admire and revere."

"Why wouldn't I be curious about his life?" he asked mildly.

In lieu of an answer, she took a loud slurp of tea. Then she lit a cigarette without asking whether it would bother the baby. Her own mother had smoked like a sailor through both her pregnancies and her children's childhoods, and both she and Oscar had wound up chain-smokers themselves, but so what? Not the end of the world.

"Why don't you like Teddy?" Henry asked.

"That's what you're really wondering, isn't it," Maxine said, "now that you've met her and been sucked in. . . . Isn't there anyone you just don't like?"

"Of course."

"Call it biochemical, call it taste, call it bitchiness. I really don't care what you call it. Unlike everyone else, apparently, I see right through Claire, and what I see I can't stand."

Henry leaned forward on his elbows, so the steam from his untouched teacup curled up to bathe his sweating face in yet more moisture. "What do you see?"

"Oh, think whatever you want," Maxine said. "I have no interest in dredging up all that old shit with Oscar's little mistress. That's the last thing I feel like talking about. I've had a bad day."

The baby opened his mouth and began to scream.

"So have I, actually," said Henry. He picked up the baby and held him against his shoulder, gently patting his back. This looked to Maxine like a plausible solution, but it didn't help. The baby wailed. Henry reached into his bag and pulled out a bottle. He stuck the nipple in the kid's mouth. The kid fussed initially, then shut up and started to suck. "Breast milk," Henry said. "Expressed from my wife's breast, to be deployed in case of emergency."

"I never had kids myself," said Maxine. "And I don't envy those who do."

"I'm in no mood to argue," said Henry. "Believe it or not,

though," he added, "it's not *all* screaming and shitty diapers and sleep deprivation."

"Really," said Maxine.

"Every now and then . . ." Henry gave himself over to watching Chester's mouth suck at the bottle. "It's like they say. All the old clichés are true."

"Probably why they're old clichés," said Maxine. "Listen, I'm sorry to cut this short, but I've got to take a nap before I go out tonight. Was there anything else—"

"Why don't you like Teddy?"

She blinked at him. "You are persistent," she said. "I suppose that's an admirable quality."

Henry waited; she didn't say anything more. He switched to another tack. "Why did Oscar stay with Abigail?"

"I find it flattering that you credit me with the assumption that I would know the answer to that."

Again, he waited; again, she clammed up.

"Why didn't Oscar leave Teddy any of his paintings, or any money?" he asked.

Maxine finished her tea. "I guess because she had no claim to any of it."

"I'm sorry to keep you," said Henry. "I'm just trying to—"

"Was there anything else?"

"Why do you ignore Oscar's daughters?"

"You mean Teddy's daughters," she said before she could stop herself.

"Why do I mean Teddy's daughters?"

"You'll have to ask them that."

"But how do you know what they'd say if you never see them?"

"I pick things up through the air, like a radio."

With a victorious expression Maxine didn't care for at all,

Henry said, "I will ask Ruby and Samantha. But I'm very interested to know why you chose not to recognize them as your nieces."

"Chalk it up to a complete lack of interest," said Maxine. "In children, you could say."

"And in Teddy's children especially."

"It's no secret," said Maxine, "what I've always thought of her."

"You've only said you don't like her. You haven't said why."

Maxine declined to respond to this.

"Oscar was a complicated man," said Henry. "A very different kind of man from me. I don't judge him; in fact, I wish I were more like him. It's an honor, writing his life, talking to his family."

"I'm happy for you," she said, standing up.

"Before I go," said Henry without making a move to leave, "let me just say that I love your work. It makes me think of Franz Kline crossed with sumei painting—something about the powerful tension between control and wildness, your fluid and subtle but rigorous and tough-minded brushwork. Nothing sentimental, nothing extraneous, but what's there feels both unerringly and passionately executed." He took a hasty sip of tea. "I hope it's all right that I said that."

"Of course the Franz Kline comparison is music to my ears," said Maxine. She was suddenly feeling a little more alert. "He was a great painter, an amazing painter. He influenced me in definite ways. And sumei painting, well, yes, of course sumei painting . . . I use Japanese brushes and techniques. But you wouldn't tell a man his work was tough-minded. That's something men say to women as a compliment, and it really means 'masculine.' "

"You seem to have it in for men," said Henry with a smile. "I'm used to it by now. My wife does, too."

"I have nothing against men," she replied. "I like men. Actually, I can't stand most women, except the ones I'm attracted to.

But I'll be ninety in six years. I've had plenty of time to observe a few things."

"I meant that your work is tough-minded," said Henry, "like Kline's. There is a similar achievement of absolute beauty without wishful thinking."

Maxine cleared her throat. "Thank you," she said against the upswell of words in her throat: I was always a much better painter than my brother; it was just that I was quiet. I didn't make waves. I was never comfortable with interviews, publicity, all that. I just painted. Oscar was a showman, a charmer, an attentionmongerer, a flirt, even as a little boy, and I was a good girl, and look where it got me. . . . I never learned to play the game; I just waited on the sidelines for someone to notice me and see me for what I was, like the peasant girl in the fairy tale.

"Thank you so much for your time today," said Henry. He bounced Chester a little in his arms, preparing to wrap him up and carry him back down to the car.

"The truth is, I've always felt like the peasant girl in the fairy tale," said Maxine. It came out sounding strangled.

Henry closed his notebook and put it into his shoulder bag. "What do you mean?"

"Oh," she said. "Just kvetching."

"Why would you feel like a peasant girl?"

Maxine warmed to the surprise in his voice and felt her opposition to his questions soften a little, like slightly warmed wax. "There's only so much fame that comes to those who don't make themselves notorious in some way," she said. "My greatest mistake was not allowing an aura of scandal around my name. I'm queer, as they say now—you'd think I could have turned that to my own advantage, but I've always been so naïve about those things, making the personal public, and vice versa. It's not that I don't have secrets. I have some great secrets. I just always preferred not to tell them."

She walked off to the studio area of the loft, lifted something from a bowl on a table and looked at it, then set it down again and wandered absently from one table to another, patting the surfaces, fingering other objects—a brush, a glass, a charcoal pencil. Henry had taken his notebook out again.

"I admit I'm genuinely surprised to learn that you imagine yourself to be in the shadow of your brother. Do you not see him as all but forgotten now?"

He put his pen down. As he waited for Maxine to say more, he glanced around her small living area. She had cordoned off about two hundred square feet when she'd first moved in, forty-odd years before. Flanking one corner, in the kitchen area, were a deep enamel sink, a gas stove, a Formica counter atop two side-by-side floor cupboards with two wall cupboards above, and a refrigerator. On a shelf by the stove, the spices were arranged meticulously, as if she'd bought them, lined them up like knick-knacks, and forgotten them except to dust them every so often. The pots hanging above the stove gleamed with disuse, and the countertop had not one crumb on it. In the middle of the kitchen was the large oak table where Henry sat, its surface scarred with dark cuts and small burn marks, which made Henry imagine a tableful of drunken artists sitting around with cigarettes and penknives. Dividing the kitchen from the sleeping area was a hanging Persian tapestry curtain, open now. Looking past it, Henry saw a neatly made bed, two bureaus, and a wardrobe. Against the opposite wall were a beat-up red couch and a large bookshelf that contained, among other things (he knew from his last visit, when he'd scrutinized it while she was in the bathroom), novels by the likes of Williams Gass and Gaddis, art books (along with the more obvious Kline and Kandinsky, Matisse and Fragonard appeared, inscrutably and incongruously—a master of the cutout and a rococo lightweight?), and, it appeared, every book about Sherlock Holmes ever written. Her living quarters were uniformly shipshape and orderly, but Maxine clearly had given extreme precedence to her work over her life; her studio sprawled over fifteen hundred or so square feet. Last time he'd been here, it had been a dismaying jumble, but today it bristled with cleanliness.

"Oscar's success was not really about how good a painter he was," said Maxine. "His women were so outrageously plural, so literally sexualized. . . . Looking at his paintings is like looking at the outward manifestation of his dick. Pardon my language. But it's smutty, his work. . . . He fucked them with brushes. Even his own daughters as little girls. Scandalous. Brilliantly scandalous. Now no one gives a shit, but back then, it was a big, loud, bold statement. He was a good-enough painter to make some real waves. Clement Greenberg loathed him. He once wrote in a review, 'Feldman hammers the same anachronistic note over and over, badly and off-key.' Oscar just laughed. He liked being hated by Greenberg. He found it perversely flattering."

"Greenberg also hated Oscar's dealer, Emile Grosvenor."

"He blacklisted the Grosvenor Gallery," said Maxine, "so Emile moved his paintings to Grosvenor West. Oscar's work sold in California through the sixties and early seventies. Back then, his biggest collectors were Hollywood directors and producers, the Roman emperors of their time." She held up a small white object to the light, showing Henry, who squinted at it, unable to make out what it was from that distance. "This is a shark's tooth. I use it to scrape lines in paint when I need fine definition. I like the idea of a shark's tooth, but it also makes distinctive marks I can't get any other way."

"You used it in *Night of the Radishes*?" asked Henry. This was easily the best-known of her works. It was a triptych completed in 1967, which now hung at the Modern and was generally considered her masterpiece: Over three panels were amorphous blooms of black paint and razorlike black projectiles, a juxtaposition that had served through the decades as an aesthetic Rorschach test for feminist scholars, Marxist art historians, Freudian and Jungian art theorists, postmodernists, and various other-ists, who'd invested it with whatever qualities best suited their ends. Henry thought Maxine's work was beautiful but stringently monochromatic, despite what he'd said to her earlier, but even he couldn't deny that *Night of the Radishes* was the real thing, possibly a great work of art.

She nodded at him with a glimmering of respect. "Oscar took photographs of girls as a teenager. Black-and-white snapshots, just girls being girls, some pretty, some plain, girls in their bedrooms, riding the IRT, walking on the street, shopping, eating ice cream at Schrafft's, whatever. He even took some of me, shooting from his bicycle as I rode mine up First Avenue, but as you can imagine, he had no trouble finding willing subjects."

"I haven't seen them," said Henry, almost hyperventilating. And he had been on the verge of leaving. Thank God he hadn't let her throw him out. "I didn't even know they existed. Where can I get my hands on them?"

"Easily," she said. "They're at Brooklyn College."

"He donated them to his college."

"That's right. They're still there."

"But he was an art history major! He wasn't an artist until years later."

"He fancied himself a good photographer. I admit the photos aren't bad, some of them, especially the ones he took of Abigail as a girl. He kept all those photographs in a box in his studio for years. He donated them to the college's archives only a short time before he died. I don't know whether anyone at the college fully realizes what they are. It seems that they've been kept in a drawer, undisturbed since the day Oscar took them in."

Henry shook his head. "No one knows about them."

"Well, they're awfully silly."

"Why?"

"They were of silly movie star–struck, soldier-worshiping Jewish girls on the Lower East Side in the forties, mostly daughters of immigrants. Our European cousins were beaten and raped, gassed to death, skeletal, shivering with cold, while we put on lipstick and read Emily Dickinson. . . . It was just the luck of the draw. No doubt our cousins would have done the same in our shoes."

"Why aren't they known, these photos?"

"Well, they've been right there all along," she said. "For some reason, I thought you might already have somehow magically divined they were there and dug them up. You have that eager-beaver look about you."

"Yes, and I'm going to eager-beaver my way over there as soon as I can," Henry said. "I'll give you five bucks not to tell that other biographer about them."

"You're joking," she replied, "but I won't tell him because I don't like him, so that's your good luck."

"Thanks," he said. "Would it be an intrusion if I asked to see some of the work you're doing now?"

"Not at all," she said, gesturing to her studio. Paintings hung on walls and leaned on the floor in stacks. They were, without exception, composed of spare, feathery black fillips against a white background. This new work was more austere even than the older works Henry was familiar with.

"This is my primary work surface," said Maxine. She pointed to a long steel table painted gunmetal gray, on which, lined up like ammunition in an armory, were a series of tubes and brushes. "I use fifteen different blacks and seven different whites. All oils, of course. I buy them at two different places. One is Pearl Paint, which of course you're familiar with, on Canal Street. The other is a tiny hole-in-the-wall in the East Village, a place any painter would be smart to know about. And these are my brushes. Sable, camel, and so forth. I am passionate about my brushes and don't let anyone else touch them."

Henry set his notebook on the edge of the table while his son lolled against his chest like a drunk in a deli doorway.

Maxine's cell phone rang. She answered it with mingled hope and dismay. "Yeah?"

There was a brief silence. Henry, who wasn't looking directly at Maxine, nonetheless felt a sudden chill blow off her skin like dry-ice fog. "I'll have to call you back. Henry Burke is here at the moment and we're in the middle of—"

"You wrote my best friend a threatening letter," Teddy shot back from across the East River. She was standing in her living room, looking out at an eighteen-wheeler that was trying to negotiate a turn onto her little street, making a hog-killing ruckus of squealing and hissing and grinding as the driver maneuvered its cab between parked cars and tried to ease the massive trailer after it. Why did these meathead truck drivers even try? "Why on earth should she call you before she talks to the biographers, assuming they even contact her?"

"Like I said," said Maxine with little pointy icicles emphasizing the spaces between each word, "I can't talk right now."

"Don't bother hanging up on me," said Teddy. "Leave Lila alone. She'll say whatever the hell she wants to anyone."

"Except me, apparently," said Maxine, feeling her lips stretch into the thin reptilian smile of a Dickensian villain. "Since you're calling me on her behalf."

"You're worried she's going to say something about the bet," said Teddy. "You didn't think I knew about it, but I do." The truck driver's potbellied partner had climbed down from his comfy shotgun seat high up in the cab and was now standing between two parked cars, trying to wave his arms, as if that would thread the truck through the eye of the needle. The driver went right on with his fruitless racket. What the hell did they want with India Street? Maybe they thought they were taking some sort of crafty shortcut up to McGuinness, inexplicably bypassing the wide, smooth, easy-to-negotiate Greenpoint Avenue.

Maxine was pacing around her studio, trying to seem nonchalant while she felt both of Henry's inner ears waving all their little antennae toward her conversation, even though he was pretending to be absorbed in his baby. What sort of friendship do Lila and Claire have, Maxine wondered, if Claire knows about this? Maxine had no close friends, unless you counted Oscar's widow, Abigail, and her assistant, Katerina, but these were friendships born of proximity and shared concerns, not inspired by deeply personal confidences exchanged over tea or bourbon, or whatever people exchanged them over. The habit of solitude was too deeply innate and ingrained for Maxine ever to even think of seeking out someone else's company for no other purpose than exposing her soul and seeing another's laid bare. Social commerce was nothing but a big chore. She didn't understand what hidden, silent, well-oiled mechanisms linking two people would cause Lila to tell Claire—or maybe Oscar had told her.

Here was Henry's scandalous little secret about Oscar. Of course he could never find out about it.

"I will call you back later," Maxine said. "I have your number stored in my cell phone now."

"Isn't that a neat invention," said Teddy; she hated the very thought of cell phones and had kept Homer Meehan's monstrous old telephone, which appeared to date from the dawn of the Touch-Tone era. It still worked fine except for a loose wire; you had to jiggle the receiver every so often, but it always paid off.

Maxine grunted a good-bye, then closed her phone, shoved it back into her hip pocket, and strode in horror about her studio, which suddenly looked as unfamiliar and naked in its new anal-retentive cleanliness as her own shorn head in the mirror appeared to her after a particularly blistering haircut.

"That was Claire," she informed Henry. "As the old Italians say, she gives me *agida.*"

"Is that unusual for her to call you?"

"Unusual," said Maxine, "like a sighting of the Loch Ness monster, or even more so, because she's never called me before. I think she wants to make nice, now that you boys are poking around. Extend the olive branch."

"And you weren't biting."

"I'll call her back. We'll kiss and make up."

"My first biography was of Greta Church," said Henry, "which was published three years ago and which I bet you haven't read."

"Who is Greta Church?"

"A great twentieth-century poet. Anyway, while I was almost

finished researching the biography, the woman I had thought was her great-niece suddenly revealed that she was really Greta's granddaughter, and her mother Greta's daughter, whom Greta had given up to her younger sister to adopt at birth. I was the first person outside the family to know. She wanted the record to be straight, that was all."

"Why are you telling me this?" Maxine asked with some uneasiness she tried to mask.

"I don't know," said Henry, whose inner-ear antennae, as Maxine had correctly sensed, had picked up more from her side of the conversation with Teddy than his conscious mind was yet aware of. "Maybe because Teddy—I mean Claire—suddenly wants to reconcile after so many years of this—is *cold war* the right term?"

"Not bad," said Maxine, uneasy.

"What I mean is that I find it interesting how the unexpected suddenly comes to light among the living in the course of writing about a dead subject's life."

"What's your book called?"

"*Sing Me a Cloud of Tears.* It's from her poem 'The Cloud.' It begins, 'Sing me a wall/ Of bread so I may eat./ Sing me a cloud/ Of tears that I may feel./ Oh you choral tongues,/ You cannot know the need,/ You cannot know the terror and the need.' " He paused.

Maxine cocked her head and squinted at him. "A little melodramatic," she said.

"No," he said, "it isn't when you hear the whole thing, and especially when you know about her life, it's all in context. She was a morphine addict at the end of her life. She could hardly write."

"Well," she said, "that sounds very sad for her, but not so terrible in the scheme of things. Go on, recite the rest of it."

But Chester chose that moment to empurple his face with his own cloud of tears, his own terror and need, so Maxine had to content herself with trying to imagine where on earth the poem might have gone to redeem itself from there, and what, given Henry's evident predilection for aggrandizing mediocrity, Oscar would have made of the biographical company he was in.

Five

That evening, Maxine stood in one corner of Michael and Natalie Rubinstein's dauntingly enormous and radiantly lit living room, holding a sweating glass of whiskey and ice. She couldn't see a single person she wanted to talk to. One thing about getting old was that your openness to new people shrank through the years from a naïve embrace to a narrow squint. By the time you hit old age, you barely had the ability to be civil for one minute to any stranger, let alone get through a whole evening of "interesting" conversation.

The real problem was that the human race was so disappointing. Why had she expected it to be otherwise? As a young woman, Maxine had tended to leap with open arms, like a wet-eyed, splayed-out nincompoop, toward everyone she met, but she had quickly encountered enough snideness, selfishness, neediness, cruelty, rejection, and indifference to enable her to gradually develop the social crankiness that had by now become thick and insuperable as an old toenail.

The Rubinsteins had said she should "feel free to bring a friend" tonight. Well, she had come alone in a taxi, and so what? She had left Katerina a message this morning asking her to come, but Katerina had never called her back. Of course she hadn't, Maxine told herself with characteristic self-cruelty; she was making violent Slavic love with a Ukrainian man with ice blue eyes, a man who was good with his hands. Anyway, being here with Katerina, standing shoulder-to-shoulder with her, aware of the warmth of her skin, would only have made her feel even more abject and lovelorn.

She swallowed some whiskey and enjoyed the hot-cold burn in her gullet. It was that awkward hour when people were still arriving and no one was drunk yet and the hors d'oeuvres were off to a slow start. Even more so than usual, Maxine didn't feel like talking to anyone tonight, but luckily for her, an ugly and unfashionable old woman standing alone generally attracted no attention. As long as she could keep herself out of Natalie's sight line, she might be left in peace to eat her dinner unnoticed while everyone around her talked among themselves, then thank the hosts before dessert, make a hasty getaway, and be home in bed by 10:30. Everyone was secretly glad when old people had to leave early.

"Oh, you can't ever believe what he says," she heard a male homosexual voice announcing just behind her.

"I always believe him," said a slightly deeper but just as obviously homosexual voice. "That's my problem."

"Your problem," said the first voice, "is that you believe everyone. You're such a child."

They were speaking softly, not theatrically, so Maxine assumed they were a couple and this conversation was private, which only made her want to eavesdrop more. She half-turned so she could see who they were, and with a flash of a glance, she beheld two slenderly muscular young men with identical haircuts, short and sleek as ocelot pelts over their scalps, which accentuated their features. One of them was exotically olive-skinned and black-haired, with almond-shaped eyes. The other, a redhead with bright blue eyes, had a tricky complexion, the pale, mercurial kind that flushed easily and sunburned badly and broke out in pimples and rashes and boils.

"I'm not a fucking child," said the redhead.

"About him you are," said the olive-skinned one. He caught Maxine's eye, realized she was listening, and looked blandly away.

Natalie Rubinstein appeared in front of Maxine with a glass of red wine in one hand and kissed her on both cheeks. She wore a very expensive-looking, subtly matronly sleeveless burgundy silk dress that showed off her full breasts and her round, dusky arms without eroticizing her in any way. Her dark hair tumbled around her shoulders; her brown eyes glowed with the ease and goodwill born of the confluence of financial security and a lucky disposition apparently free of fatal introspection.

"Maxine," she said, "I'm so sorry. I got waylaid. I'm so glad you're here! How are you?"

"I've been better, truthfully," said Maxine, but she smiled back at her hostess. Natalie was the devoted, unflappable mother of three small children, a self-professed "huge, huge fan" of Maxine's work, and also, it happened, the wife of Maxine's longtime dealer, Michael Rubinstein. In spite of herself, Maxine genuinely liked her—it was impossible not to—although she didn't understand a thing about Natalie, and vice versa.

"Oh, why?" said Natalie.

Maxine waved a hand. "Old age is nothing but a big drag. Do everything you can to stave it off."

"Seth and Charles," said Natalie, "come here and meet Maxine Feldman. She's a great, great, great, very famous painter Michael has the incredible honor to represent."

The two homosexuals dropped their conversation and obediently extended their hands to Maxine. Their hands were smooth and warm as suede.

"Seth's my little brother," said Natalie, slipping her arm through the olive-skinned boy's and drawing him closer so he had to enter Maxine's radius. Charles automatically followed Seth as if by magnetic pull; now they formed a little social clump, which had, of course, been Natalie's aim all along. "He's visiting us from Chicago."

Seth glanced at his sister, a complicated look filled with roughly equal parts affection and bemusement; Maxine imagined that the latter was caused in a larger sense by something to do with his visit, but more immediately by being forced to make conversation with the old bag who'd been spying on his private conversation a second before.

"That's right," he said briefly.

"And I hope you stay here forever," said Natalie.

"Well, if I do, I promise I'll get my own place."

"We have plenty of room," said Natalie.

Seth gave his sister another complicated look.

Natalie smiled joyfully at the cozy little trio she'd created, then sidestepped away to greet a newly arrived couple, kisses on all cheeks.

"Are you enjoying your visit to New York?" Maxine asked Seth, throwing the question into the sudden cold pool of silence like a depth-sounding pebble. As senior member of this enforced huddle, it was the least she could do.

"He's actually moving here," the redheaded Charles said, looking at Seth, "but he can't admit it yet."

"So you're a painter," said Seth to Maxine, ignoring what Charles had said.

"I am a painter," she replied, as if she were saying, "I'm nothing but a pawn in this lovers' spat and I wish I were home right now."

"So is Charles," said Seth cruelly.

"Who are some of the artists you admire?" Maxine asked; the old trick of sussing out the competition.

"I love your work," said Charles with endearing alacrity. "De Kooning, Kandinsky, Kline, and Rothko are great influences also."

"Anyone more contemporary?"

Charles looked at Maxine with sidelong hesitation, as if he were trying to gauge her own opinions before he answered in order to avoid offending her. "A lot of what I see these days, I can't relate to," he said. "I guess that makes me an anachronism. That seems to be the general opinion anyway; I'm still trying to get a gallery to show my work." His face was mottled now.

"Getting a gallery solves very little," said Maxine. "It only creates more headaches and terrors than you had before."

"I'll take them," said Charles. She saw the force of ambition undergirding his quip like a massive glacier slow-moving in the sunlight.

"I invited him here to meet my brother-in-law," said Seth, "but he's too shy to let me introduce him."

"Not yet," said Charles. "I just got here."

"You mean," said Seth, "you're not drunk enough yet."

"I'll introduce you," Maxine told Charles. "I'll say you're my protégé. That carries more weight with him than a family connection."

"You've never seen my work," said Charles.

"Don't shoot yourself in the foot," Maxine snapped. "Come with me. Play along."

She turned and stumped toward the kitchen without looking to see whether he was following. If he wasn't, that was his mistake.

"He's not my boyfriend," she heard Charles mutter behind her. "Just a friend."

"Glad to hear it," she shot back. "What's your last name?"

"Emerson," he said. "Thank you so much for doing this."

"Oh, painters are like a big Irish family in the potato famine: There's never enough of anything to go around—collectors, galleries, grants, prizes. . . . But I'm so old now, I've got nothing to lose."

Michael Rubinstein was standing by his own refrigerator, deep in conversation with a very young woman with cocoa-colored skin who was wearing a slinky vintage cocktail dress and a lot of berry-colored lipstick. In the time it took to cross over to them, Maxine deduced that the girl worked at Michael's gallery, he wasn't sleeping with her, and they were flirting around the fact that he could if he wanted to.

"Michael," said Maxine, interrupting them without apology, "I'd like you to meet Charles Emerson. He's a painter. You should take a look at his work."

"Hello, hello," said Michael to both Maxine and Charles, kissing Maxine on the cheek, shaking Charles's hand. He was a short, broad-chested man in early middle age, with a lionlike head. "Sorry, your name is?"

"Charles Emerson," said Charles. He cleared his throat. "It's a pleasure to meet you."

"You'll remember his name, Liza," said Michael to the girl. "Maxine, of course, you know."

Maxine the person, of course, Liza didn't know, but the name at least she recognized. "Nice to see you," she said, and shook Maxine's proffered hand. She had an English accent. "Hi, Charles," she added brusquely, not bothering to meet his eye.

Liza was, Maxine was certain, a painter herself, for whom every day as a minion at the Rubinstein Gallery was like working as a scullery maid in a house she hoped to own someday. To her, Charles was nothing but competition. Maxine was certain Liza would have decided to forget his name and everything else about him by the time his slides arrived, or his CD, or whatever they sent around now.

Maxine took a swig of whiskey, swallowed, and said to Charles, as a veiled threat to Liza, "Listen, Charles, I'll call you in a week to make sure you've sent your work to Michael."

"Thank you," said Charles with a tentative disbelief that touched her. It was so easy to help someone, so nice when they showed proper gratitude. Good, now she was free to die: she'd passed the torch, however tenuously, however disingenuously. Out of nowhere, she had a vision of her body being slid into a crematorium oven, her soul finally having decamped from squatness and thwarted ambition alike.

Michael leaned in toward Maxine, his eyes narrowed in that deliberately charming way she had always found laughably obvious but was always suckered in by all the same. He asked in his intimate, gravelly voice, "How are you, Maxie? Are you working?" He liked to call his artists by pet name—like diminutives, as if he thought of his gallery as a species of animal charity, a caretaking project for barely domesticated beasts. His breath smelled sweet and rich, like roast chestnuts. He was the human equivalent of advertising, in your face but impossible to resist.

Just as it had been with her brother, she saw through his charming warmth to the amoral selfishness beneath and loved him anyway. "I'm a fucking genius, Mikey," she told him.

"Of course," he replied.

"Really," she said, "I'm doing some of my best work."

"When can I come and see it?"

"Very soon."

Slender young men and women in black pants and white shirts began rushing about, setting out baskets of bread on tables, uncorking wine.

"Almost dinnertime! Better find Natalie," said Michael. "Excuse me."

Charles and Liza had struck up a conversation. Charles looked terror-stricken, Liza focused and impatient. "Well," he was saying, "for now, I'm most interested in the possibilities of pure color and shape."

"I'll let you two chat," said Liza, and disappeared.

"You're Oscar Feldman's sister, aren't you?" said Charles.

"My one claim to fame."

"What was it like to have a brother who was a painter, too?"

"We argued. We were hard on each other. We both wanted to be right; we both had something to prove. Now he's been dead for five years, and two young men are writing separate biographies of him."

"That's great," said Charles uncertainly.

"After a glass of whiskey, I'm glad he's getting his due. It was good to meet you, Charles," she added, shaking his hand, "and you must send those slides to Michael."

"I promise," he said. "Thank you."

"And now I'd better find my table."

Natalie and Michael subscribed to the inevitably awkward convention of place cards. After some simple sleuthing, Maxine found, at the table nearest the apartment's front door, which would facilitate her retreat in an hour or so, a card with her own name on it, flanked by those of two men she hadn't met but both of whose names she recognized in the usual art-world way. This table had only six instead of the usual seven chairs; Natalie had evidently thoughtfully left an opening for Katerina, or whoever Maxine might have rustled up as a date. She went around the table and beheld cards for Jane Fleming, who she'd heard was now a tenured art history professor at Columbia, and with whom she had had a brief but passionate affair more than thirty years before. Next to her was Michael Rubinstein himself, and on his other side, of all people, was Paula Jabar.

Maxine looked up and down the long, crowded room. Jane Fleming was a small, pale moth of a woman, or at least she appeared so initially, until you got to know her; she could easily go unnoticed among these forty-plus guests, but Paula Jabar's ostentatious coppery dreadlocks would have attracted the notice of everyone in the place within twenty seconds. So either Paula hadn't arrived yet or she wasn't planning to show. Maxine felt simultaneous twinges of anticipation and disappointment; she disapproved of Paula and her work and everything she said and stood for, but at least she could hardly be called boring, and boredom was Maxine's bugbear.

"There you are!" came Jane's familiar voice over her left shoulder.

"We're both midgets," said Maxine, turning to smile at her. "If just one of us were taller, I'm sure we'd have seen each other an hour ago."

Jane kissed Maxine's cheek and looked into her face with an open, steady, unblinking expression.

"I look like crap, I know," said Maxine. "But don't forget I'm eighty-four."

"I've missed you, Maxine," said Jane.

"You have?"

"Well, yes." There was a very brief pause, with many unsaid things hanging in it. "I know I could have called you," Jane went on, "but it wasn't that kind of missing; it was the kind where I wanted to run into you at a party."

"And here we are."

Their affair had begun and ended remarkably civilly at the end of the summer of 1978. After several months of extremely good sex (great sex, really; Jane was hotly sensual, uninhibited as a dolphin; not only did she laugh a lot in bed but she had a way of taking Maxine's nubbin, as they called it as a private joke, between her lips with a vacuum suck and mashing it with exactly the right amount of pressure with her tongue and then backing off at precisely the right instant, thereby giving Maxine orgasms the transcendent, intense likes of which she'd never known before or since) and interesting conversations and mutual respect and all that, they had agreed that they liked each other, but they weren't in love, and they were much too busy with their careers, both of them, to see each other so often if it wasn't going to be a grand lifelong passion. But something had always rankled a little about this for Maxine: She'd half-suspected, whenever she'd thought about it later, that they'd let each other off too easily. They were a lot alike, which was part of their mutual attraction—equally driven, reserved, proud, independent, determined not to need anything from anyone. The trouble was, any lengthy love affair required at least one participant who was willing to be the fool, and ideally two; maybe the real problem had been that neither was willing to fall, to lose control. So they had let each other go.

Maxine, twenty-three years older than Jane, had been in the throes of what she'd half-mockingly called her "midlife crisis" that summer, so she was acutely aware that her pursuit of a much younger woman might mean she was a desperate, aging dyke. It was anyone's guess why Jane had put *her* cards down and left the table, but in hindsight, Maxine sometimes wondered whether it was a similarly misguided pride. Back then, Jane was thirty-three and still working on her Ph.D. thesis, whereas Maxine was enjoying the beginnings of her professional heyday, a sudden, inexplicable ten-year-long interest in her work that translated into articles and interviews and a rash of sales that, thanks to shrewd and timely investments and frugal habits, might last the rest of her life.

"How have you been?" Jane asked.

"I have a new assistant," said Maxine. "She's a young painter, Hungarian, very talented, and she came to me out of nowhere and offered to work for me for almost nothing. Now I don't know what the hell I ever did without her."

"I see," said Jane.

"How have you been?"

"Oh," said Jane. "Well. I'm dating someone new these days, a colleague for a change. Also for a change, a man," she added. "I wanted to bring him tonight, but he couldn't make it."

Maxine tried not to show how shocked she was by this. And something else besides shock, something more personal. "I hope he's nice."

"Oh, very nice," Jane replied with a sly sidelong look no doubt meant to convey something erotic.

"Well, I'm happy for you," said Maxine. "Listen, there are two different guys writing books about Oscar right now."

"Good for him," said Jane with some skepticism; she had barely known him, but even so, she had never thought much of Oscar, either as an artist or as a person.

"Just in case they contact you," said Maxine. "Don't say a word about that bet."

"They would never in five million years contact me, because I hardly knew the guy," said Jane. "But, Maxine, nothing would give me greater pleasure than to see the truth get out about all that."

Maxine smiled. "Between you and me and the place cards, I feel the same way, but I have a good reason to want to keep it a secret."

"Well, it must be a very good reason, that's all I can say," said Jane.

Before Maxine could reply, Michael bore down on them with two men in tow.

"Maxine Feldman, I'd like you to meet two of your collectors!" he said. "This is Saul Unger, and this is his partner, John Sipperley."

"We *love* our new one," said Saul Unger, the shorter, older, uglier, and no doubt richer of the pair.

"And we've given it a prime spot over our fireplace," said John Sipperley, who was probably in his early fifties but was still willowy and elfish—he looked like a ballet dancer turned choreographer.

They all took their places at the table. Maxine's previously unknown collectors flanked her. She felt very grateful to Michael and Natalic for putting her between them, essentially giving her their ears, the opportunity to sell them new work over the course of a friendly dinner.

"Where do you live?" she asked John.

"In New Canaan," he replied. "We bought an old barn and moved into it."

"I bet it's beautiful," said Maxine.

"It's all right," said John.

"Of course it's beautiful." Saul leaned across Maxine to say this sternly to John. "John designed the whole place."

"You're an architect?"

"No," said John with puckish apology, "just an amateur decorator. He talks me up too much."

Waiters set down bowls of vegetal consommé with tiny bits of green, algae probably, floating on top. Maxine took a spoonful, thinking as she did so that this was the kind of food invalids were given when they were almost dead, either to bring them back from the brink or to sustain them on their journey to the underworld.

Across the table, Jane and Michael were discussing Paula: Where could she be? Why hadn't she come?

"Michael tells us you have a new series under way," John said to Maxine with what looked to her to be genuine interest. "What's it like?"

"I'm obsessively preoccupied with mortality lately," Maxine said after a slight pause. "I'd be silly if I weren't, at my age. It's a few lines here, some brush strokes there, a lot of bare white canvas. Philip Larkin has a great poem about getting old and dying called 'The Old Fools,' but I promise I won't bore you by quoting from it. It's about how old people are protected from the constant, crazy-making terror of death by an emotional trompe l'oeil; otherwise, we'd all be bonkers. I'm trying to remove that illusory perspective, show what it looks like when you force yourself to see where it's all going to end up."

"I love it," said John.

"I'd like to see them," said Saul.

She took another spoonful of soup and settled more comfortably in her chair, which had padding on the seat, the sort of luxury Michael and Natalie would naturally have, even on chairs they'd rented.

"There she is!" Michael said, looking at someone coming through the front door.

"It's Paula Jabar," John crooned under his breath to Maxine, turning to see. "I've never met her."

Maxine hunched over her cooling soup.

"I am so *sorry*," came Paula's voice, which managed to be both loud and velvety at the same time. "I got held *up*. Where's Natalie? Hey there, girl! You're looking *good*."

She passed by Maxine in a cloud of flowery smells, something ghetto and feminine, undulating dreadlocks, a dress made of a shimmery tropical bird—colored material, cut to reveal just enough luscious thirty-five-year-old café au lait skin, heavy on the lait.

The soup bowls were whisked away and plates of summery salad replaced them: a Japanese woodcut sea of curly pale green frisee lettuce on which floated almond slice rafts, each holding a tiny, near-translucent poached baby shrimp as pink and naked as a newborn. Crisp blanched haricots verts darted through the sea like needle-nosed fish. Cerise-rimmed radish slices bobbed here and there like sea foam. The dressing was a briny green lime juice and olive oil emulsion. Maxine stared at the thing, trying to imagine the person who had so painstakingly made it. It would be demolished in three bites. She would have been perfectly happy with a wedge of iceberg with a glop of bottled Russian dressing, like you got in the olden days. Food had become so fussy and contrived.

Paula took her place between Jane and Michael with a quick sidelong comment to Jane that made Jane laugh and lean over and give her a kiss on the cheek. How did they know each other well enough for that? As Maxine munched a big forkful of the fussy, preposterous salad, Michael performed the requisite hostly introductions so that everyone at the table could know beyond any doubt that Paula Jabar had just landed in their midst. The waiters came around and refilled wineglasses with a feathery-light, crisp white wine—Maxine had no idea what, but on top of her glass of whiskey, it was making this whole thing infinitely more tolerable, especially now that the easy warmth she'd felt at the table was now revealed to be as fugitive as all unexpected intimacies.

"Hey, how have you been, Maxine?" Paula asked suddenly.

Maxine set her salad fork down and gave her the fish eye. "Very well, Paula, and you?"

"Working, working. Sometimes I think that's *all* I do." Paula tossed a handful of dreadlocks over one bare shoulder. Maxine looked somewhat curiously into her eyes, which were impenetrable, as if they'd been spray-coated with something shiny and tough.

"How is your work going?" John asked tentatively, as if it might be construed as rude to inquire.

Paula's face gave away nothing. "Today not at all, 'cause I had these people, asking questions."

"What are you working on now?" Jane asked.

Paula had made a career out of making small dioramas, the shoe-box worlds children made in grade school—or rather, used to make, back when children did such things. Her best-known one was *Beautiful Day in the Hood*, which showed a woman in a project apartment cowering with her daughters on a couch as gangwarfare gunfire raged outside; the gunfire was represented by "Pow!" and "Ak-ak-ak-ak-ak!" coming out of the windows in a dialogue bubble rimmed with fiery orange and red. And so forth. Paula Jabar was about as famous as you could get in the art world these days. Four of her "ghetto boxes" had been shown in the previous year's Whitney Biennial; she had even made an appearance on *Oprah*.

Maxine happened to know, because she'd read an interview with Paula a number of years ago, back when Paula was less savvy about marketing herself and more unguarded about the truth of her past—that after the age of five, Paula's childhood had taken place miles from anything resembling a ghetto. Moreover, her white maternal grandparents had moved to the States from France, and her father was a lawyer from Algeria. Paula had, it was true, been born in a scruffy neighborhood; her parents hadn't had much money then, because her father was still in law school, while her mother supported them as a high school French teacher, but once he had passed the bar and joined a law firm, the Jabars had bought a house in a tony suburb and Paula's mother had quit her job; the three kids were sent to private schools, and Paula later studied art at Bennington. She had been more naïvely candid in that long-ago interview, but these days, being much smarter about her career and image, Paula allowed her interviewers to gather that she'd grown up on the South Side of Chicago and had gone through some hard times.

Fortunately for her, even if the truth had come out, it was considered poor manners to question anyone's racial authenticity. She could have countered any untoward skepticism with the line she'd used in that interview: "There's a saying among Jewish people when their racial purity is called into question by their fellow Jews: 'I'm Jewish enough for the ovens.' Well, I'm black enough for slavery."

Maxine looked over at Jane, who was avidly awaiting Paula's answer about those damned dioramas. When had Jane become so enamored of Paula, and, more important, why? Paula was exactly the sort of person Jane and Maxine might have made fun of privately together back in the old days. Either Jane had lost her sense or Maxine was completely out of touch; Maxine was unwilling to investigate the likelihood of the former.

"I'm doing a new series. Michael knows," Paula added, nudging him.

"It's brilliant," said Michael briefly, not looking at Paula, with his manner suggesting a fleeting but marked self-consciousness Maxine had never observed in him before.

Were they sleeping together? *Were* they? Maxine thought of herself as impossible to shock, but for some reason, this truly surprised her. It seemed unlike Paula somehow to sleep with her dealer, no matter how appealing and successful he was, and Maxine would have bet that although Michael's appetites would eventually lead him to adultery and excess, he was still on the right side of things; his conscience and ego seemed approachably cloudless. No, of course they weren't sleeping together. But their relationship seemed sticky and intertwined nonetheless.

"What's the new series?" Maxine asked Paula, wishing she could shoot a privately amused, colluding look over at Jane and have Jane return it, as she would have a long time ago. Instead, Jane turned her gaze toward Paula to await her answer.

"I'm building replicas of certain, quote/unquote, clichés of African American family life," said Paula. Michael didn't look at her as she spoke; he looked thoughtfully into his wineglass. "Life-size. The miniaturizations of the boxes were greatly effective but have run their course. I'm fabricating a couch in an apartment in the projects, family watching TV, no father; a Kentucky Fried Chicken booth with a family eating dinner, no father; a car of the A train heading up to Harlem, whole family coming home from shopping, no father. Like that. My visitors today were from

MOMA, of all places. It would be a real statement to get a replica of a KFC booth into the Museum of Modern Art."

"Was that what they were interested in?" Michael asked.

"Well, they liked the A train, too. . . ." She held up her fingers, which were theatrically crossed.

"How would you characterize what you're doing?" Maxine asked. Her voice resounded with a certain hollowness, but no one seemed to notice.

"What do you mean?"

"I mean, I suppose, aesthetically."

"Aesthetically," Paula repeated in a teasing voice. "I don't know about aesthetically, but essentially it's just one statement, part of an ongoing dialogue. Conceptually, it's about shifting the paradigms while engaging in the act of replicating something real and making it as lifelike as possible, to scale, in an artistic context. And thematically, it's about the African American matriarchy. I'm dialoguing in mainstream, accessible terms about an underrepresented sector, giving a voice to the voiceless and, in the process, playing with the traditional power structures of representation. To put it colloquially, in black culture, women are the ones who step up. Sure, black teenage girls are having babies, but the family raises them together, grandmothers, aunts, cousins. Black men are off in prison or on the streets and the women are holding everything together with faith and discipline and courage."

"Yes, I see that," said Maxine. "What I don't see is how life-size subway benches or fast-food booths can be considered art in the same way as a Kandinsky painting or a Rodin sculpture."

"That's partly the point," said Paula. She sounded as if she were congratulating Maxine. "The African American family structure is, of necessity, self-invented and free-form in the same way African American art has to be. We have to make it up. We have to invent.

We have to use what we've got, which is nothing. Our own lineage was broken by slavery. Our heritage was lost. Our families were divided and separated again and again—out of existence. African American art is pure American energy, tapped into something positive instead of the negativity of gangland killings and crime and unwed motherhood and drugs. It's the flip side, the bright side of ghetto darkness. You could say that we have to write our own song, and we are singing it any way we can."

"Beautifully put," said John softly.

"And, all due respect," Paula added with a glint of fight in her eye, "but you haven't seen these replicas. Radically different subject matter aside, they are solidly part of tradition, if you want to get into that. I'm dialoguing with Ed Keinholz, of course, and Red Grooms . . . Duane Hanson and H. C. Westerman. . . . And just because they were white men and I'm a black woman doesn't mean it's any less valid as art, Maxine. You, as a woman artist, ought to know that as well as anyone."

"Bravo," Jane said, tapping her fingers together in miniature applause.

Maxine opened her mouth to ask Paula how she could possibly consider herself an African American descended from slavery when her mother was of French descent and her father was from Algeria and she'd grown up in the suburbs and gone to Bennington.

Instead, she said, "I have done my best to avoid becoming familiar with conceptual art. It seems like a lot of clever, cold hoo-ha to me. As for so-called dialoguing—if that is really a verb—I have no idea what that means. I paint out of direct experience, and I'm not talking to anyone when I work, least of all to myself. I have to get everyone out of my head, including my own voice, in order to be able to paint. Please excuse me if the answer is obvious and the question is retarded, but what the hell ever happened to truth and beauty?"

The whole table erupted into conversation all at once.

"So is it really *art*?" said Saul Unger softly in Maxine's ear. "That's the question. It should be called something else, because it *is* something else."

Maxine looked over at him, surprised to have an ally at the table after all.

"Really," Saul said stubbornly. "The same way Scientology is not a religion, this is not art. Yom Kippur is not easy. Kandinsky is not easy."

Suddenly, another plate appeared in front of Maxine, this one containing two grilled lamb chops, boiled new red potatoes, chickpea-mint salad, and steamed baby squash. The chickpeas looked like round infant heads with cowlicks. So whoever was masterminding this dinner was attempting nothing less than the re-creation of the history of evolution, from primordial soup to water babies to land babies. She supposed there would be meringue chicks in baklava nests for dessert. She could imagine the cook back there, his breast simultaneously puffed with pride and racked with despair: No one would understand his brilliant work, no one would apprehend its true meaning, and then it would be gone.

"Speaking of aesthetics," she said jovially across the table to Michael, indicating her plate. "This is like the upscale version of *The Discreet Charm of the Bourgeoisie.*"

Michael responded with an impatient, tight look Maxine felt was meant to function as a slap. She surmised in a flash that she had committed a double faux pas. Apparently, you weren't supposed to question Paula's artistic merit; rather, you were supposed to say, "This dinner is amazing. Who is your chef?" instead of comparing it to a Buñuel film. But why the fuck not? It made no sense, any of it. In the old days, the painters at such a party could well have been pissing in corners, drunk as bums, arguing so hard that they spat at one another. She missed her brother with a sharp pain in her chest; she thought for a moment that she was having a heart attack until she realized that it was just nostalgia.

Six

The brush was moving on the canvas as if it had volition, liveliness, as if it were made of nerve endings and electrical impulses instead of dead wood and hair, or as if it were a dog or a badger, something instinctive, intent on prey. It leapt over the surface and left tracks, deposited a trail of feathery flakes, then a smudge, as if the wind had smeared it. The tracks ended before the entire bare right side of the canvas. It looked as if the creature had become airborne and lifted off.

Ashes and Dust, Maxine had named this series. She stood back to look at what she'd done. From this angle, at this remove, it pleased her, but Maxine knew all too well that the eye of the beholder was a fickle thing when the beholder was also the maker. Five minutes from now, from another angle, it would look like shit.

"Ralph Washington will be a little late," Katerina called from the office area in the back of the loft, which was little more than a desk made of a door on two filing cabinets, with phone and computer on it, stacks of papers, bills to be paid.

"What?" Maxine called. Whenever Katerina was here, she took charge of Maxine's cell phone, which was a relief, but even so, Maxine hated to be interrupted when she was working, even by Katerina. Being dragged from the world of painting back into the world of life was as difficult as forcing herself from the world of life back into the world of painting. A thick but permeable membrane separated them. Going from one to another required a shape-shifting in the brain. She was never entirely safely ensconced in either world; the demands of the other one could be heard, muffled from whichever one you were in, so no matter where you were, you felt a tug of anxiety that something might go wrong in the other one in your absence, something you'd failed to account for before you left. It would have been much easier if the transition could have been accomplished through a series of soundproof air locks, decompression chambers. It felt as if there were only room in one lifetime to inhabit one of these parallel worlds, but here she was, trying to cram them both in. Each parallel life sucked the air out of the other one. When she was deep in her painting, she felt how short her time there was and panicked because she would never get to do it all before she died. It only got harder as she got older, harder because, as with sleep, she could never be as fully in either world as she'd been when she was younger. The membrane had become worn and weakened with age, like everything else.

Katerina didn't bother repeating what she'd said, but that was to be expected; Maxine knew that Katerina knew she'd heard every word.

Maxine dipped her brush in the paint and sent it on another

series of animal skitterings up to the shoreline of what she now imagined was a frozen lake. She wanted the shock of so much unfilled whiteness to evoke a sort of internal gasp, both a dying breath and a living astonishment that so much space was left unexplored. She could feel her own lungs suspended as she worked, and she forced herself to inhale, suddenly frustrated by the insurmountable inability to make the paint correspond exactly and precisely to what was in her head. It was always doomed from the outset, but here she was, making another goddamned painting.

It was 10:00 A.M. Katerina had come at nine o'clock, as she did every Wednesday. She had settled right in to work, as always. No small talk had passed between them; they had met once, at the coffeemaker in the kitchen, to pour themselves fresh cups, but Maxine hadn't asked why Katerina had never returned the weekend's phone call, and Katerina hadn't offered any apology or explanation. Now an hour had gone by and it hadn't come up, so Maxine was fairly sure it never would: The window of opportunity had passed. Katerina wasn't the type to apologize or overexplain things, which Maxine, in her current frame of mind about Katerina, suddenly found irksome and impolite. Before today, she had always loved Katerina's stoic reserve, but during these past few days she had worked herself into a state of not caring about Katerina, which had involved a lot of tricky mental gymnastics. She had twisted and warped Katerina's stellar character traits into a craven bunch of faults, had pinned all her good qualities to a corkboard and viewed them, squinting, through a cynical lens until they morphed into manipulations and illusions. It had taken some doing, but Maxine was skilled at doing this to people who had disappointed her; she had had a lot of practice. That damned Slavic stone face, the nerve of it.

Five years before, Katerina had come here to see Maxine, a

stranger whose phone number she'd looked up in the White Pages, an artist she considered one of the greatest living painters. She had asked for the minimum hourly wage to perform the most menial of tasks in return for the privilege of watching the master at her work. Grudgingly, Maxine had agreed to let Katerina come once a week, on the condition that she stayed out of her hair when she was working. This, she had done.

When Ralph had called a few moments before, Katerina had been sorting Maxine's receipts into two piles: those that were tax-deductible and those that weren't. Her understanding of the American tax system had improved vastly since she'd gotten her green card and become a taxpaying citizen. She worked as a waitress at a cheap Polish restaurant in the East Village, the primary advantage of which, besides the great kindness of the elderly owners, was that it was only four blocks away from the one-bedroom apartment she shared with two fellow Hungarian émigré artists, a young married couple in their late twenties who fought passionately in the kitchen over cigarettes and straight vodka, then disappeared into the bedroom. Katerina, who was almost never there except to sleep, had only the pullout living room couch and a small bureau in the entryway. Because of this economy, she had a tidy savings account and could just barely afford the small studio, a cubbyhole in an industrial loft she shared with seven other painters, in a patchy neighborhood in Brooklyn, four stops in on the L train. Out of both economic necessity and a perverse pleasure in being smart about what little money she had, she was stringent and disciplined with her own deductions and receipts, and she brought the same zealousness to Maxine's finances. She considered anything other than groceries, toiletries, or clothing tax-deductible. Paints were, of course, and so were MetroCards, restaurant receipts, and books. Since Maxine was haphazard, disorganized, and stubbornly lax about remembering to put all her receipts into the box Katerina had marked "For Taxes," she always went through Maxine's coat pockets, her grocery-carrying backpack, and the bits and pieces on her bureau. Still, she could never make it add up to enough to make a real difference. Katerina was often tempted to augment Maxine's patchy receipts with some of her own, but she had thus far resisted the temptation to bestow this sort of ridiculous and unasked-for charity on someone who would grumpily wave it away if she ever caught wind of it.

"So what time is what's his name coming?" Maxine shouted suddenly.

"He said he'll be about fifteen minutes late," Katerina said, smiling. "He will be here soon."

Maxine heard the smile in Katerina's voice and felt murderous. She could smell Katerina's new love affair on her like a cheap perfume.

"Didn't he ask everything last time?"

"Should I tell him not to come?"

"What is the fucking point of all these goddamned paintings?"

Katerina didn't answer. They both went back to work.

A moment later, Maxine called, "Come look at this painting, would you?"

"Okay," said Katerina, approaching the canvas with a cautiously eager expression. Maxine despaired at the sight of her; Katerina was dressed in a black tank top that revealed her muscular arms, and a pair of olive green canvas pants with many pockets that rode her narrow hips, low-slung and fetching, showing an inch or so of flat belly. Her face looked wide open, soft, like a small child's, as if she had just awakened from a deep sleep and was anticipating ice cream. Maxine felt strongly that her advanced age should have granted her some kind of immunity from the humiliation of unrequited lust. That it didn't was yet another of the many indignities of old age.

After a moment, Katerina said slowly, "Mostly negative space. A quiet painting, a little bleak."

"Bleak," repeated Maxine.

Katerina paused again. She had learned by answering wrongly that these requests of Maxine's to tell her what she saw in a particular painting always had one right answer only. Last time, Katerina had looked at cross-hatchings of black, a claustrophobic schemata of webbing and fencelike filigree, and said the painting created a feeling of suspense and anticipation. Maxine, not bothering to hide her disappointment, had told her that actually the painting was supposed to make her feel buried alive. The one before that had been intended to make her feel punched in the gut. Apparently, Maxine's paintings were intended to punish the viewer for failing to see what they were about.

"There is just bare white on the right side," Katerina went on, "and very small black marks on the left side. . . . It feels unfinished."

"Yes," said Maxine. "Anything else?"

"Well . . ." Katerina took a deep breath. It made her feel as if she were being drowned? dragged by horses? dismembered and eaten alive by a polar bear?

The cell phone in her hand chirped. She pressed the green button, put it to her ear, and said, "Maxine Feldman's studio, Katerina speaking." It was her own choice to answer the phone in this way; Maxine had never told her what to say.

"Katerina," came a robust but unmistakably elderly female voice. "This is Claire St. Cloud. May I speak to Maxine, please?"

"Just a moment." Katerina pressed hold and said to Maxine, "It's Claire St. Cloud."

"God fucking damn it," said Maxine, reaching for the phone. "Claire," she said with guttural displeasure. "Hello? Hello? Oh good, she hung up."

"You have to press the hold button again," said Katerina.

Maxine mashed the button, then repeated—this time with less venom because she'd been distracted—"Claire?"

"Hello, Maxine," said Teddy. "I'd like to come and see you today."

"Why would you want to do that?"

"You know why."

"Oh for God's sake," said Maxine. "Come later, then. That biographer is coming here this morning."

"Henry?" said Teddy possessively.

"The other one."

"How's three o'clock?"

"Oh, all right," said Maxine, and hung up without asking whether Teddy knew where she lived. She had put her return address on her letter to Lila.

The doorbell rang then. While Katerina went to let Ralph in, Maxine turned the easel with the new painting to face the wall; then she went into the little bathroom in the back of the loft to wash her hands and face. When she came out, she could hear Katerina talking to Ralph, a bottle being opened, carbonated liquid being poured into a glass, chair legs scraping against the linoleum. She heard Ralph say, "I was unavoidably held up."

Maxine strode into the kitchen. Ralph looked up as she entered, pushed his chair back, and stood up.

"Thank you so much for your time today," he said. His face looked even blacker with its sheen of sweat. A glass of golden bubbly liquid sat on the table in front of him.

"Hello," Maxine said, trying to sound far more friendly and

welcoming than she felt. In front of Katerina, she felt compelled to dredge deep inside herself for whatever kindness and warmth she possessed, to live up to Katerina's obvious respect for her. Without her here, she could have been as crabby as she'd wanted.

"Some ginger beer?" Katerina asked Maxine with her gap-toothed grin. "I brought it. It's very cooling on hot days."

"No, thank you," said Maxine, hiding, she hoped, her extreme dislike of the stuff. She sat down.

"I'll be in the office if you need me," said Katerina, and went back to her chores.

Ralph turned on his tape recorder and set it on the table between him and Maxine, then glanced down at his notes. He took an expressionless sip of ginger beer. "I've been thinking," he began. "Maybe *wondering* is a better word."

Maxine sighed.

"You and your brother both being painters," Ralph added.

"What's your point?"

Ralph looked at the tiny bubbles clinging to the inside of his glass. "Could he have been rebelling against you in his refusal to allow his work to evolve into abstraction?"

Maxine laughed. "Do you have brothers or sisters, Ralph?"

"A younger brother."

"So you're the firstborn, too."

"That's right."

"I see." Maxine's dog, Frago, lurched up from his bed in the corner and ambled under the table to put his chin on her knee. She toyed with his ear; he snorted and burrowed his head into her thigh. "I was a girl; I was expected to produce little Jewish children. Our parents were businesspeople, and I was their worst investment. I didn't want children; I wanted to sleep with girls. Oscar at least gave them a grandson. Never mind that he wasn't much of a grandson; at least Oscar got married, and he wasn't queer."

"And two granddaughters."

"I have nothing to say about them." Maxine became aware that she was palpating Frago's ear as if she were trying to extract a pea from it. "What made you choose my brother as your subject?"

Ralph pursed his lips, which immediately irritated Maxine and made her wish she hadn't asked. "I love his work," he said with a fervent lack of irony. "He was a man who saw women clearly and deeply, and as his daughter Ruby pointed out to me recently, he wasn't painting any version of himself. When he looked at a woman, he saw her, not some projected version of his own desire." Ralph sat back in his chair and lifted his glass and turned it in midair, studying the pale gold liquid.

"You don't like ginger beer," Maxine observed.

"Frankly," said Ralph, putting it abruptly back down onto the table, "I have often thought that Oscar's work wanted to leave the runway and take off into abstraction. There are certain indications in some of the paintings that hint at an impulse toward blurring the lines between the women themselves and their backgrounds, transcending their features and bodies to show the essential fragmented nature of their personalities. . . . He stopped short of allowing his paintings to evolve in that direction, and in so doing, I believe, he hamstrung himself as an artist. It was out of some perverse rebellion. Which, I believe, was against you."

"Oscar was incapable of abstraction. He was too lazy."

Ralph blinked.

"He wasn't self-reflective or adventurous," Maxine went on. Something had risen in her gorge, and she was talking as if she could expel it with words. "His paintings have no suffering in them, because Oscar never suffered. He had all the women he wanted, and still his wife and mistress doted on him. He neglected his children, but apparently they all loved him anyway. He was not nearly as smart as he thought he was; he had an inflated opinion of his own intellect, and he had no idea how limited he really was. You couldn't argue with him—or rather, you couldn't win an argument with him in the usual sense of exchanging views and having it out on equal footing—because whenever it reached the point beyond which his mind couldn't go, he took that to mean that he had won."

"What would Oscar say if he heard you saying all that?"

Maxine smiled acidly. "It would not surprise him at all. Anyway, I recall, not that I saw it once he was past a certain age, that he had a very small penis."

Ralph was clearly shocked and had nothing to say to this.

"Well, he must have," Maxine went on. "For all his charm and all his good looks, he always refused to put himself in any situation in which he wasn't in control. He allowed nothing and no one to challenge him. He chose women who were devoted to him in spite of their superficial appearance of independence and strength. He never approached a woman he wasn't totally sure he could have. And he never did anything in his work that risked revealing any aspect of his own inner self. He refused to risk anything—rejection, failure, self-exposure. And he didn't allow himself to truly suffer, because he was too weak."

"So you think he didn't deserve acclaim and success?"

"Of course not," she said. "He painted good portraits, interesting and sometimes even beautiful portraits."

"Did your parents prefer his work to yours?"

"Our parents didn't like art. They didn't see the use of it. By 'they,' of course, I really mean our father, but our mother felt the same way—in the background, like a good wife. She was smarter than my father, by the way. We were both a disappointment to them. They were happy when we sold paintings, and happy they didn't have to support us, but to them, we might as well have been retards. That should have made us more allied, but it didn't. In the end, Oscar and I each hoped the other one would take up the slack. I felt much guiltier, being older, being the girl, and not being married. Oscar was very distant from them. He treated them with outward respect but didn't take to heart a single word they said. I, on the other hand, was embroiled in all sorts of ugly tensions and battles with them, both spoken and tacit. I got the brunt of it; he got away. I suffered because it's in my nature, and it wasn't in his. He was lucky."

"But you believe you're the greater artist."

Maxine waved the whole topic away. "Will it bother you if I smoke? I'm only asking to be polite. The only answer is no."

"No," he said.

She tapped a cigarette out of the pack she always kept in the breast pocket of her shirt. She flicked the lighter and inhaled a lungful of smoke, then put pack and lighter back into her pocket and returned her free hand to Frago's ear. He licked her palm.

"What do you make of your rival, Henry Burke?" she asked Ralph abruptly with a leering glint of hostility.

"I have never met the man."

"You two should go out for drinks, compare notes, divvy up the chores."

Ralph said, poker-faced, "Maybe so." He turned off the tape recorder, gathered his things together, and stood up. "I have taken up far too much of your time already," he said. He raised his hand to Katerina, who was waving good-bye to him from the far corner, then went to the door and, without another word or look in Maxine's direction, let himself out into the hallway.

After Ralph left, Maxine wandered around with an unsettled

feeling, smoking. She felt trembly and nauseated, maybe from the heat and cigarettes, or maybe because she had been so angry while she'd been talking to Ralph, angry without really knowing it. Damn it, it was out of her control. It was getting worse with age, not better. She had meant to be gracious and generous, knowing Katerina was listening, but the interview had run away with her—or rather, from her. Something was very wrong with having so much unrealized ambition. It acted like some kind of poison, insidious and slow-acting. So much fuss and furor, so much bitterness, envy, sorrow, and regret, all over splotches of paint on canvases.

"Katerina," she said harshly.

"What is it?" Katerina called. Of course she'd heard the entire conversation between Ralph and Maxine. She was worried about Maxine now, and expected to be lashed out at for something minor. She wouldn't take it personally; she never did. She loved Maxine, and she understood her nature.

"I don't feel well," Maxine said. "I'm going to lie down."

"Would you like some ice water?"

Maxine, ignoring the question, went into her bedroom, kicked off her shoes, and lay on her bed.

The thing Maxine had always most feared when she imagined dying was the moment following her last breath—lying there airless, empty-lunged, finished with inhaling forever: the emptiness after that last gasp, the whiteness, the freedom from need. That particular terror and literal breathlessness was what she had been trying to get into her painting this morning. She thought about the canvas as it now stood. Katerina was right: It was raw and bleak. If she added any more paint, it might tip the balance, and the painting might lose its sense of suspension in nothingness. She suspected, humbly and without ego, that it might be a very good painting. Maybe it was finished. She envisioned it on the walls of her closed eyelids with mounting internal excitement: It might be very, very good.

Katerina arrived in the doorway with a gentle clinking sound. "Ice water," she said, and came over to set it down on Maxine's nightstand.

"You heard the conversation," said Maxine without opening her eyes.

"Yes," said Katerina.

"I shouldn't have said all that about Oscar." Maxine spoke flatly, without overt regret.

"It was harsh," said Katerina. "But everyone says things like that. It's human. What's done is done."

"What's done is absolutely fucking done," Maxine repeated, smiling wryly, freed for now from the loop-de-loop of self-loathing. "And cannot be undone."

"Claire St. Cloud called again," Katerina said. "She's going to bring her friend with her."

"That bitch."

"She sounded like a bitch."

"She is a bitch. She was so controlling of my brother. . . . That little husband thief. Never could stand her. Needed a good slap. And he just ate it all up, while his poor wife stayed home alone with her *shwartze* maid and her books and her retarded son. Of course he's *not* retarded. You know what I mean."

"She's coming at three," said Katerina, smiling.

"Get out the needles and knives," said Maxine with an answering smile in her voice. "Listen, I think that painting is done."

"The one you're working on?"

"It's done."

"Can I go and look at it?"

"You can have it."

"To keep?"

"Or leave on the subway."

Katerina sat next to Maxine and took her hand. Maxine had never given her a painting before. "I can't thank you enough."

"It only took me about an hour to paint the damn thing," said Maxine. She willed her hand to lie inert in Katerina's without clutching or squeezing or betraying any feeling.

"I'll treasure it!" Katerina said.

Maxine turned her head on the pillow to find a cooler spot, happy to have Katerina hold her hand like that and react with such feeling to being given the painting.

"Now go away and let me sleep," said Maxine. "I want to rest up for that horrible little mistress."

Katerina went away, leaving the cold, dewy glass of water behind. Maxine opened her eyes and looked at it and realized that she was thirsty. It seemed to her that she'd never been so thirsty in her life. After she'd rested a little more, she would sit up and guzzle the whole thing.

PART THREE

Seven

The apartment Abigail and Oscar Feldman had shared until he died had been a wedding present from Abigail's father, a furrier who'd died a multimillionaire and left everything equally divided among his three daughters, like a rational, nondemented Lear. He'd bought this place on Eighty-fourth and Riverside in 1958 as an investment, and then, when Abigail, his youngest and favorite daughter, had gotten married, he'd given it to her and her new husband. Oscar Feldman had been a choice Abigail's father had approved grudgingly and only because of Isaac Feldman's business acumen. Back then, everyone, meaning Oscar's parents and Abigail's and even Abigail herself, had assumed Oscar would give up his notions of being a painter and go into the meat business with his father. The fact that Abigail could have known her husband so little amazed her now. The idea of Oscar getting up before dawn to trundle down to the Meatpacking District was ridiculous. He had never shown any interest in business. He'd wisely married a rich Jewish girl, and had lived off her father's money until his work started to sell, but even then, it was her father's money that had sustained their daily lives. Oscar's father hadn't been rich, although he'd been successful, but he left his wholesale meat business to an enterprising nephew and not much to either of his children.

The apartment was big, hushed, and dim, so well-insulated that no noise filtered in, either from the city or from any of the neighboring apartments. It took up the rear half of the second floor of a nineteenth-century building; there was no view, but Riverside Park was just across the street, and Abigail's synagogue was only a few blocks away. The apartment smelled clean but dense and shut-in, as if the windows were never opened. It was either an oasis or an entombment, depending on Abigail's mood. Since Oscar and her maid, Maribelle, had died, she had been feeling a little restless. Whole days went by now of almost unbroken silence, Ethan rocking, his right hand holding his left ear, while Abigail read. She had reread most of Henry James recently, and was taking a break now from Great Literature with a few light, earnest, simple contemporary novels by women. Whenever she ran out of books, she went on-line and ordered more from Amazon.com. Because of the Internet, which she used to order not only books but also groceries and clothes and just about whatever else she and Ethan needed, she almost never had any real reason these days to leave the apartment; she took Ethan to Shabbat services most Friday nights but no longer bothered on Saturday mornings, and once or twice during the week she took him down to the park for some fresh air. Except for these excursions and an occasional visit with

Maxine or her one surviving older sister, Rachel, who lived on Long Island, Abigail spent her days in the apartment with Ethan, completely alone except for the girl who came to clean the apartment and run small errands on Mondays and Ethan's nurse, a soft-spoken young man named Marcus, who came every other day to bathe him and give him physical therapy.

She was therefore nervous and excited about Henry's visit today. The first time he had come, about two weeks before, she hadn't realized how oddly satisfying it would be to talk to him.

This morning, she'd made up her face and despaired at how fleshy and drooping it had become. She had never been much of a beauty, but she'd always had what Oscar had called "a beguiling softness" about her. He had always made her feel attractive—it was one of the many things she had dearly loved about him—but it had been a long time since she'd thought much about how she looked. The last time Henry had come, she had worn her usual comfortable elastic-waist pants and a white button-down shirt that had been Oscar's. Today, she had put on a pale turquoise silk pantsuit, which by some miracle was a little loose on her now, her pearl necklace, and low-heeled pumps; yesterday, she had had her short faded red hair colored its original auburn and styled in a new way, springier, curlier.

She'd ordered in Oscar's favorite delicatessen food from Zabar's so Henry could experience firsthand the sort of lunch that Oscar had liked: smoked whitefish salad, potato salad, sliced chicken breast, and smoked Gouda, along with grainy mustard, sour dill pickles, and rye bread that was crusty outside and soft inside. It was easier than trying to make something from scratch. Abigail had never been much of a cook, but she knew good food when she ate it. Early in her and Oscar's marriage, she had hired a West Indian woman, Maribelle, who had lived in the little maid's room off the kitchen for more than forty years. She had been a great cook, which, naturally, had caused Abigail to get increasingly fatter as the years went on. Five years ago, Maribelle had died, very shortly after Oscar. Abigail had to admit, but only privately, to herself, that she missed her housekeeper more than she missed her husband. Maribelle had been her faithful and constant companion, and he had not.

One day, Oscar had asked Maribelle out of the blue to take all her clothes off and pose for him right then, in the living room, and she'd done it. He had never before painted at home; he worked in his studio on the Bowery and often stayed there several nights in a row, or so he said—of course, he was probably at Teddy's. He'd covered all the furniture in drop cloths for a couple of days. Standing there unselfconsciously, Maribelle had started to sing while he painted, old torch songs, so he'd painted her as a nightclub singer, with her head thrown back, eyes half closed, mouth open in song. It had been festive, but Abigail couldn't remember now why she had found it so exciting and entertaining to have her maid standing there singing naked in her living room while her husband wielded his paintbrush with his usual predatory jabs. What an odd life it had turned out to be, living in a cloister with a son who was totally imprisoned in his own mind and body, a husband who went wherever and fucked whomever he wanted, and a black maid as her best friend. Abigail had planned as a girl to get a graduate degree in literature, become a professor, never get married or have children. Anyway . . .

Should she have bought some wine? She would have bet anything Teddy had served him wine. She felt a flare-up of jealousy like a tongue of flame in a defunct oil field. Henry and Teddy had probably gotten tipsy together while they talked about Abigail's husband. They had probably liked each other. Teddy had always been beautiful. Was she warm? Abigail had never had an impression of warmth from Teddy, but why would she have?

It was so odd, looking back at it all. This woman knew Abigail's husband as well as Abigail did, but very differently; had given birth to Oscar's twin daughters. Abigail and Oscar had never once talked directly about any of this, but of course Abigail knew everything. She wasn't stupid. And of course she minded, but she and Oscar had always been more friends than lovers; she couldn't meet his needs that way. She had always preferred to sleep alone. She was taken up with Ethan's needs, because she refused to send him away to an institution, although everyone assured her it would be the best thing for everyone. He was her only child. Yes, she had always been horribly jealous of her husband's mistress, but it was unfair of her to mind. Abigail's main feeling about Teddy, besides this natural and uncontrollable jealousy, had been curiosity. She remembered seeing Teddy at Oscar's openings, knowing who she was and knowing Teddy knew who she was, but both of them, naturally, pretending ignorance. At least they hadn't had to stare at each other on gallery walls, because Oscar hadn't painted any portraits of either of them, but they'd had to look together at other women he'd painted and, more often than not, slept with.

Whatever and whoever she was besides, Teddy had been the antithesis of Abigail for Oscar. That had been the whole point of her role in his life, as far as Abigail was concerned: an overflow valve to catch all of Oscar's excess appetite and energy their marriage failed to absorb and feed. She could see no other reason for his dual life than the fundamental but entirely natural incompatibility with his wife that underlay their otherwise-good union; and so egotistically, and admitted only to Maribelle, Abigail had always viewed her husband's need for his mistress as the waste product of their marriage. She hoped that nothing she might learn, either inadvertently or directly, in the course of this biography Henry was writing would contradict this necessary belief.

Abigail opened her apartment door as Henry came down the hallway. She let him in right away. "Let's sit in the kitchen," she said before he could apologize for being late. "I've got Oscar's favorite lunch, and he always wanted to eat lunch in the kitchen. He said it was *haimish.*"

Henry followed her into the narrow, somewhat cramped kitchen, at the very end of which was a breakfast nook, whose table was set and laden with food.

"He spoke Yiddish, then," he said.

"Well, but you have to understand, he spoke it ironically. He always made fun of American Jews of our generation who tried to sound *echt,* as he called it, again ironically."

Abigail fluttered over to the fridge, aware of the three bottles of beer in there left over from a visit from Maxine months before. Maxine had brought a six-pack of Mexican beer and drunk two herself, while Abigail had sipped carefully at about one-eighth of one and poured the rest down the sink later.

"Would you like a beer?" Abigail asked Henry, trying to sound as if she said this every day.

"Sure," he said with enthusiasm as he slid into the kitchen nook and sat next to Ethan, who was humming to himself in a tone so low, it was almost like Mongolian throat singing, and who seemed not to notice Henry's presence at all. Henry got out his notebook and, there being not one inch on the table that wasn't covered with food or dishes, tucked it under his thigh and put his pen behind his ear. He took a swig of the bottle of Tecate Abigail handed him.

Ethan stopped humming and rocking. Without looking directly

at Henry, he sent a gentle, fluttering hand over to touch Henry's shoulder.

"He's saying hello," said Abigail. "Help yourself to lunch; it's from Zabar's."

"Do you keep kosher?" asked Henry.

"Well, I'm Conservative," said Abigail, "so no, not strictly, but I try."

"Do you take care of this place all by yourself?" he asked her.

"Oh God no," she said. "A girl cleans it once a week. I use the word *clean* very loosely. Since Maribelle died, it's been a big problem. No one seems to know how to dust moldings or get behind couches. Maxine told me to hire a Filipina, but they all seem to be taken, or else I just don't know how to find one."

Henry took a daub of whitefish salad, a piece of cheese, a few lumps of potato salad, a piece of rye bread. "This looks great," he said.

"He hated lox and cream cheese. And bagels. He said it was all too slippery. The texture of the bagels, slippery. Lox, slippery. Cream cheese, ditto. He called them 'the Jewish Unholy Trinity.' "

Henry laughed. Abigail sat down, afraid she was babbling. She spooned whitefish salad onto some bread and took a big bite to shut herself up, then did the same with another piece of bread and put it onto Ethan's plate. Ethan, without looking at it, immediately lifted it to his mouth, touched it to his lips, then set it down again.

Henry took another swig of beer. "I wonder," he said through a gentle burp, "whether you remember those photo portraits of schoolgirls Oscar took in high school. I went out to Brooklyn College yesterday and found them, and at least half of them were of you, or someone who looked a lot like you."

"That was me," she said, startled. "That's right, I'd forgotten about those things."

"I didn't realize you were high school sweethearts. I thought you met in college."

"We weren't," said Abigail. "I barely knew him in high school. Frankly, I hardly remember him shooting me, but now that you mention it, he did come around me a lot with a camera. I thought he was very funny; I knew he was out of my league romantically, so I didn't even bother playing coy with him. When he asked me on our first real date in college, when I was a freshman and he was a senior, I was very surprised, but of course I went, but even then I felt there weren't many sparks between us, so I didn't bother getting too worked up about it."

"But he really liked you," said Henry.

"He kissed me good night, sure, but to me it felt friendly and polite. We didn't become, as they say, romantically involved until I was a junior and he was living in the Village. . . . In my mind, it happened by default, since we were hanging out together so much, so I tried not to expect anything from it. The girls were all crazy about him, and none of them took his thing with me seriously. They kept buzzing around even when I was there."

"What did you and Oscar do on your dates?"

"We went and heard a lot of jazz, which I hated, and he thought it was the funniest thing, to hate jazz. One day, he asked if I would marry him. We were out at Coney Island, on the roller coaster, of all places. What a way to propose! I said I'd think about it, I was so surprised. Inside, I was just singing. I always thought we were mostly pals, and sleeping together was just something our crowd did back then—to be different from our parents, I guess. Well, we really were just pals, but we were great pals, and it turned out that's the kind of wife he wanted."

"I had the strong impression," Henry said, "seeing those photographs, that he was in love with you even in high school. I could see it in how he kept the camera on you. And you were so—"

"If you say pretty, I'll laugh," she said.

"I was going to say 'comfortable with yourself.' "

She shot him a shrewd look. "Oscar liked to say he married me because he knew he would always feel he could be fully himself with me. Not the most romantic reason, is it?"

"How long did it take?" Henry asked, writing doggedly in his notebook. "Before you accepted?"

"My sister Rachel said to me when I told her about it, 'He's a good man.' Rachel is one year older than I am, a psychiatrist in Great Neck, or was—she's retired now. Even back then she knew I didn't have it in me to be a professor, which was what I always said I wanted to be. I always loved to read, but I didn't do so great in college. I didn't like to think that way about books; I just liked reading them. All that analysis gave me a headache. So Rachel told me to marry Oscar because she said I'd be much happier that way. I knew she was right; plus, I loved him like crazy. The next day, I told him the answer was yes. He seemed relieved, which shocked me. . . . He acted like he'd been really worried I'd say no. Ethan," she said suddenly to her son, "let me do it for you." She picked up his piece of bread and held it to his mouth. Ethan took a snapping bite and began to chew savagely, staring sideways at the ceiling.

"I imagine he broke a lot of hearts when he married you," said Henry. He checked his watch by tilting his wrist slightly and stealing a quick glance.

"Of course not," said Abigail quietly. His glance at the time, along with the question, had hurt her feelings. She tamped down her disappointment. It wasn't Henry's fault, it was her own. In the old days, she wouldn't have minded. Maybe she had spent too much time alone with Ethan. She never should have gone to so much trouble to get her hair done and all that; now she felt foolish.

"Actually," she said, her voice steady, "it broke some sort of tension, a question hanging in the air between Oscar and all the girls he flirted with. He was off the market, but that just made him somehow more interesting to them, so they wanted him even more. And they got him, or part of him anyway. I'm just conjecturing. I don't know this for a fact."

He stopped writing, looked up. "Why didn't Oscar paint portraits of you? He obviously loved having you as a subject in those photographs."

"I wouldn't let him," she said, wiping Ethan's mouth with a napkin.

"Why not?"

"I didn't like how it made me feel. I had to be quiet and try not to move while he looked at me. Some painters talk while they paint, and maybe he talked to his other models, but I could feel myself disappearing. I told him to stop and walked away, and that was the end of it. Later he asked why, and I tried to explain, but it was the one thing I think he never could understand. The real reason was, when he painted me, it was one of the rare times with Oscar when I felt—" She stopped talking abruptly. How could she be revealing these things? She was a private and dignified person, or at least she always had been, until now. She had been about to say that it was the only time Oscar made her feel like a purely sexual object, and she hadn't liked that feeling at all.

The telephone rang then, and with relief Abigail got up and went out to the hall and picked up the cordless phone from its bay. "Hello?"

"Abigail," came Maxine's harsh voice. "Can you come down

here this afternoon? That horrible Claire is coming to talk about something, and I think you should be here."

"Claire!" said Abigail.

"Yes, I know," said Maxine. "I need you to be whatever it's called in duels, the person who hands the pistol over, then carts off the body or escorts the victor from the scene, whichever."

"A second?" said Abigail. The last person she wanted to see was Claire, but she was not in the habit of standing up to Maxine. "What is this all about, Maxie?"

"Eccch, it's these biographers," said Maxine.

"One of them is here right now," said Abigail.

"The black one or the white one?"

"The white one," said Abigail. "Why is Claire coming?"

"Because I sent a note to her best friend. They're both coming at three. Can you get here at a quarter of?"

"Why did you send a note to her best friend?"

"I want to explain all this in person. I don't know whether Oscar ever told you about this, but if he didn't, I can imagine that you're going to need a little time to adjust to the news before she arrives."

Abigail pinched the bridge of her nose between forefinger and thumb. She wanted to say, So there's some big secret that I don't know about but that you, my dead husband's former mistress, and her best friend are all in on that you're going to drop on me fifteen minutes before I have to protect you from her? Hell no!

"Gosh," Abigail said instead. "Like I said, Henry Burke is here right now. I'm not sure I can get away."

"Well, if you can't, you can't," said Maxine in a tone that suggested that if Abigail couldn't, she was a terrible person. "Anyway, I have to go."

Abigail hung up the phone and went back into the kitchen. She was shaking.

"I'm so sorry, Henry," she said with a thundercloud in her chest. "Where were we?"

He was peering through reading glasses at the old leather-bound diary of Oscar's she had loaned him the week before. "Let's see," he said. "I had a couple of questions about June 1984. His childhood friend Morris Treitler totally falls off the radar screen after June seventeenth. There is no other reference to him anywhere in Oscar's diaries or calendars. Did something happen?"

"Yes, but you'll have to ask Moe about that yourself, because Oscar wouldn't tell me, but look out, he's an unreliable windbag. He lives down in SoHo, not too far from Maxine. Speaking of which." She blew out air through her nose. "That was Maxine on the phone just now. She asked me to come down this afternoon. I'll need to leave in about an hour."

He looked up at her. "Okay," he said after a moment. "That's no problem."

"Are you sure?" she said. "I know you blocked out this afternoon to work on the 1980s."

"We can get as far as we can and then finish another time," he said. "I can give you a lift if you'd like. I drove here."

"Oh, no, I'm sure it's out of your way."

"I honestly don't mind."

"Well," said Abigail, "gosh."

About an hour later, after Abigail had put the remnants of the lunch away and cleaned up and discussed nearly a year of Oscar's life day by day while Henry filled many notebook pages with jotted notes, Abigail and Henry led Ethan into the elevator and rode it down to the street, where Henry's car was parked not too far from Abigail's front door. Ethan moved sideways, scuttling crablike, staring up at the sky, his knees slightly bent, arms flapping gently from the elbows; Abigail was always afraid, now that she was old and not strong, that she wouldn't be able to support him if he tripped, but somehow, he rarely did.

After they'd managed to fold Ethan into the backseat of the car like an enormous, gawky bird, they were off. Ethan shrieked for the first few blocks, disoriented by being in an unfamiliar car. Abigail made a constant shushing sound but didn't look at him or touch him. Finally, he stopped and seemed to accept his new whereabouts. Henry took the West Side Highway down the island; Abigail leaned back in her seat and looked out the window at the rotting, monstrous, gorgeous old cruise-ship docks. She caught a glimpse of herself in the little mirror on the side of the car and remembered that her hair was freshly dyed and styled; she felt suddenly glad that she had gone to all the trouble of fixing herself up. Seeing Claire, even now, was going to be tricky enough without having to worry that she looked like a wreck of an old woman. She felt Ethan's fingertips on top of her head, touching very lightly; then they were gone, quick as a spider. She looked back at him. He was looking out his window with an expression of aching blankness. His face looked exactly the same to her as it had at five, eleven, twenty-four. He hadn't aged; he was still as perfectly beautiful as he had always been.

She had always believed, like most of the other mothers of the most deeply autistic children she had met, that he understood much more than he could show, but he was so completely locked in that his IQ was untestable. She was always careful to talk to him in a low, steady voice, because whenever he heard a sudden, loud, or piercing noise, he flapped his hands by his ears as if it caused him physical pain. It was almost exactly the same gesture Oscar had used when he thought someone was being stupid or nuts. When

Ethan did it, she found it poignant, even now that he was forty-seven years old. When Oscar had done it, she had often laughed. Even though she had never fully understood his manifest, arrogant, and (in her opinion) unjustified impatience with his fellow man, she could see the humor in his impatient hands flapping by his ears, unless he was reacting to something she herself had said or done, in which case it hurt her feelings. She thought she should have been granted immunity from Oscar's judgmental superiority, she who so devotedly forgave his transgressions against her and their marriage.

"For some reason, Ethan reminds me of a certain poem by a poet named Greta Church," said Henry. "It starts like this: 'There is a thing within a thing./ The thing itself is all it is./ The thing is just the thing it is,/ No more no less than what is it,/ It is the thing within the thing.' "

"Is that the whole poem?"

"No, it goes on, but that's the part Ethan has been making me think of. It's called 'On looking at El Señor de la Misericordia in the Cathedral at San Cristóbal de las Casas, April 1949.' "

Abigail laughed. "What a mouthful of marbles! What exactly about Ethan reminds you of that?"

"Well," said Henry. "Something about the way he stares so blankly, without seeing, his presence so mysterious but embodied. I think the poem is about some of the ways in which art has become different from religion."

"Which is how?"

"People pray to a statue of El Señor in a glass box in the cathedral. He's crawling on his hands and knees, bleeding, supplicating. Women especially. They stand in front of it and weep, and pray. I went all the way to Chiapas just to see it in the course of writing her biography. It's completely different from how people look at a work of art. The second stanza goes, 'Sometimes a thing is not a thing./ It's something other than a thing,/ A thing that's greater than a thing,/ Beyond, above, beside a thing/ It is the pure, the only Thing.' "

"That reminds me of a children's nonsense rhyme."

"It's not nonsense," said Henry. "The significance of the statue of El Señor is far greater than the thing itself. It is literally Jesus. Instead of being created aesthetically, it was made to provide an outlet for prayers. An artist's rendering of Jesus is a work of art, in and of itself. She says it so much better in the poem. Modern people don't pray and weep to artistic representations of Jesus as if they were Jesus himself. That's one of the differences between religion and art."

"In Judaism," said Abigail, "iconography is frowned on. Oscar was very daring to paint figures, raised Orthodox the way he was. I think that was a big part of why he did it."

Henry turned to look at her, blinking with the force of this revelation.

"I hope this isn't some sort of an emergency, you having to go down to Maxine's so suddenly," he said. "I don't mean to overstep, but is she all right?"

"Maxine?" said Abigail with a short laugh. "She's never all right."

Henry looked as if he weren't sure how to respond to this.

"Actually," she added with a touch of asperity, "she called me to come down because Claire and her friend will be there."

Henry looked abstracted, as if he were remembering something. "Does this happen often?"

"This happens never."

He pulled up in front of Maxine's building. As Henry helped Abigail and Ethan out of his car, Abigail had the sense that he was dying to be invited up to witness this historical moment. She thanked him with enough finality to forestall any such request, then guided Ethan across the sunstruck pavement to ring Maxine's buzzer. After Katerina's garbled squawk issued from the box, Abigail pushed the door open and waited for the elevator to make its lumbering way down.

Maxine stood at the door of the loft, waiting for her. "Well, hello," she said with her usual brusqueness. "Let's sit at the kitchen table." She stumped over to the table. Abigail followed her and parked Ethan on a chair. He was gently shrieking from the unpleasantness of being moved around from place to place.

"I'm having a bit of whiskey," Maxine announced. She took down two glasses and poured a shot into each. She set one glass in front of Abigail. Abigail looked at it. This was unusual. Normally, Maxine failed to offer anything to eat or drink, knowing that if her sister-in-law wanted something, she would just get it herself.

Abigail took a tentative draught, as the nineteenth-century novelists called it, a word Abigail had always loved. She put her other hand over Ethan's, which was trembling on the edge of the table. He had gone abruptly quiet. Her baby, her little bird. His eyes were as blank and his face as pure as those classical Greek sculptures of young men. She wondered for the gazillionth time what went on in there. The whiskey tasted like medicine she needed. "So," she said, "what is all of this about?"

"It's about the painting called *Helena*," said Maxine.

"*Helena*," said Abigail. "One of Oscar's best paintings."

"Yes, except for the fact that Oscar didn't paint it."

"Of course he painted it," said Abigail. "What are you talking about?"

"I made a bet with him. I won and he lost. It was during a big argument we were having in a booth in the Washington Square Diner in 1978. Oscar took a catsup packet and a thing of saltines and squooshed them out onto the tabletop and said he thought that mess was as good as the average abstract painting. I told him he was full of shit. The upshot is that I ended up betting him a thousand dollars that I could paint a painting in his style, a portrait of a lady, and he couldn't paint one in mine. To prove that it was worthy, it had to be accepted into the other one's next show."

Abigail laughed. "So what happened?"

"Oscar painted a train wreck that my dealer at the time rejected in no uncertain terms, and I painted *Helena*. It went in his next show, paired with *Mercy*, since his dealer thought they were a matched set. Claire's friend Lila Scofield bought both paintings and had them reframed, and the framer noticed my mark on the back of *Helena*. He asked Lila about it. Lila recognized it and called me to ask me what my signature was doing on Oscar's painting, and foolishly I told her the whole story, although I could have lied. She was upset, understandably, but she decided not to tell, to keep the painting and keep her mouth shut. We agreed that to do otherwise would just be silly, but I did offer to reimburse her for the damned thing. She refused, and that's the last either one of us has said about it in all these years, at least I thought so, but now it turns out she told Claire."

Abigail rubbed both hands over her face. "Why are they coming here?"

"When these biographers started poking around, I wrote a note to Lila and asked her to give me a call. I don't want her spilling any beans. But Claire called me instead, which was unpleasant in the extreme. Goddamn it, I cannot stand that woman." Maxine fished her cigarettes from her pocket and lit one.

"Well, I can't say I'm too shocked or upset by this," said Abigail. "I don't much care one way or the other, actually. Oscar painted enough other paintings, seems like he can spare one."

"Well, don't tell anybody."

"Why exactly?" Abigail said, puzzled. "I would think you would want it to get out!"

"I would," said Maxine, "but Oscar was my little brother, and when it comes right down to it, I can't."

The two women looked at each other without blinking for a moment, Maxine with her eyes bulging a little, Abigail quizzical.

"Those biographers can't find out about it, either," Maxine went on. "Can you imagine the field day? I don't want to give either of them the satisfaction."

Abigail said with her eyebrows knit, "But what about the truth? For the sake of art history?"

"Does it really matter?" Maxine asked. "Who did what, who painted what. That painting is pretty damn good. Me, Oscar, it's the same genes, same last name. It says Feldman on it."

"It says Oscar on it."

"I can't damage Oscar's reputation like that."

Abigail scratched her cheek, squinting, picturing *Helena,* the portrait of a naked, pale thoroughbred of a girl in front of a bare white wall, floating in an incongruously ornate frame in the long gilt-edged museum salon where the holy hush of Art permeated the air like incense. And next to it, its sister painting, *Mercy,* depicting a black woman with a wide red mouth, head thrown back, singing, also naked. Both women's skin tones were unusual colors for Oscar, azure shadows, touches of electric mauves and greens and hot pinks, even though one woman was clearly black, the other just as clearly white. The two were a matched set, a diptych. Or so she had always thought. . . .

"This is *Helena* we're talking about here," she said. "A famous painting, hanging in the Met, and you painted it! What could be the harm to Oscar's reputation? *Mercy* hangs right next to *Helena*, and Oscar did paint that, am I right?"

"As far as I know," said Maxine, "but I wouldn't rule anything out."

"Well then, I would think everyone would love finding out about that. It would create a lot of attention for you both."

"Maybe," said Maxine, "but the point is—" She stopped and took a drag of her cigarette and looked away from Abigail. "I made a promise to Oscar before he died. Not on his deathbed literally, but pretty near it. His death couch, maybe."

"What exactly did he make you promise?"

"To keep this a secret."

"Oh," said Abigail. "Then that explains it."

"You backed me into a corner," said Maxine. "I was going to try to come off as noble and altruistic, but your argument just makes too much damn sense for me to keep this up."

"You know, he wouldn't know a thing," said Abigail.

"Abigail! He begged me. Said it was all he wanted from me. He couldn't stand to think that it might get out, and in fact he was furious when he found out I'd signed it, secretly. Of course, when Lila discovered the mark, I painted over it before she donated it to the Met, so there was no danger of its being discovered by anyone who didn't already know."

"He won't know a thing," repeated Abigail. "They can remove the paint and see your signature for themselves. Oscar is gone."

"Good Lord, you're a terrible person," said Maxine approvingly. "I had no idea."

Abigail took another slug of whiskey. "There might be a lot of things about me you don't know," she said then, a courageous side-long glint in her eye.

"Like what?"

"Like, oh, well," said Abigail. "Give me some more whiskey, Maxine. I'm not sure I can tell you this, but I think it might be good to tell someone before I go, and you're all I've got."

"Besides Ethan," said Maxine, pouring a good shot into Abigail's glass.

They both turned and looked at Ethan, who was fiddling with the tabletop, staring at the ceiling.

"Hello, Ethan," said Maxine in a loud, overly enunciated voice. She shared Abigail's private conviction that he understood every word they said, but, unlike Abigail, she treated him as if he were a little retarded.

Ethan fluttered his hands by his ears.

"All right, Abigail," said Maxine. "You might as well spit it out; we're not getting any younger sitting here."

"I am getting younger, actually," said Abigail. "This whiskey is making me feel about fifteen years old; it's going right to my head. Whoo!" She giggled.

"All right, no more for you. I need you to be compos mentis when the crones get here." Maxine took her glass away. "Which they will in about five minutes. That Claire strikes me as someone who shows up five minutes early to catch her opponent off guard."

"I had an affair, too," Abigail blurted out. "Not just Oscar."

Maxine set her whiskey glass down with a snap.

"In the mid-seventies. With Ethan's doctor. It lasted three years."

Maxine's eyes bulged behind her thick glasses. "How exactly did this come about?"

"He stayed the night once when there was a blizzard. We were snowed in and he couldn't get back to Larchmont because none of the trains were running. Maribelle was in Queens at her boyfriend's and Oscar was with Teddy, I imagine. We stayed up talking. I don't know, the snow, the cognac. He was so gentle and literary. He loved poetry. We read Yeats out loud to each other and somehow we ended up in my bed. I was forty-eight; he wasn't even thirty. I was a middle-aged wife and he was so beautiful. His name was Edward."

"Edward," repeated Maxine tonelessly.

"That's right," said Abigail, feeling oddly defensive, as if Maxine had mocked the name. "Dr. Edward Young. Everyone else called him Eddie, but I called him Edward. He treated me like gold, brought me flowers. Oscar never brought me a flower in his life. Oscar brought me his laundry."

"You must have been a mother figure for him," Maxine said with ruminative obliviousness. "He must have been that son that Ethan wasn't."

"No," said Abigail. "We were really in love, man and woman."

"Well," said Maxine.

"Quite passionately, too."

Maxine blinked. She drank some whiskey.

"Hard to imagine, isn't it?" Abigail laughed. There was an edge of anger in her laughter.

The buzzer rang. Katerina appeared from the office area and went to the wall and said into the box, "Yes?"

A squawk came from the intercom, and Katerina pressed the button to let Teddy and Lila in.

Abigail suddenly felt sweat well under her arms and her jaw muscles tense and her heart thud. She cast a wild eye toward the door.

"Steady," said Maxine. "You're here for backup."

"I'm here because you asked me to come," said Abigail. "But just so you know, this is not the easiest thing for me."

"It'll do you good," said Maxine. "Face down the enemy."

"Maxine," said Abigail through a thickness in her throat, "I'm doing this as a favor to you. In no way for myself. On the contrary."

Maxine flapped an impatient hand at her. They waited in silence until they heard Teddy's knock on the door.

Eight

Katerina opened the door with a motion of her arm like a knife through water. "Hello," she said. "Come in." She stepped back and let Teddy and Lila enter. Teddy came in first, of course, striding past Katerina with her head held high like a ballerina's, her spine, Abigail thought, almost unnaturally straight. Then came Lila, a plump, pretty woman with curly white hair, smiling furtively, timidly at the back of Teddy's head.

"Have a seat," said Maxine by way of greeting, not bothering to stand.

Teddy and Abigail looked at each other for an instant of shocked silence. Then Abigail said, "Hello, Claire."

"Call me Teddy, please," said Teddy. She took the chair across from Maxine; Lila sat facing Abigail.

Abigail could not stop staring at Teddy. She forced herself to look away, make a joke. "The seconds," she said, "are in place."

"Quiet," said Maxine.

"Seconds," said Teddy. "Ah! You mean for the duel. This is my friend Lila Scofield. The original owner of *Helena.*"

Teddy seemed collected, unfazed, even though she couldn't have known Abigail was going to be here. Shouldn't she, and not Abigail, have been the one who felt uncomfortable here? Abigail felt foolish for allowing herself to be the one who felt at a disadvantage.

"Hello, Lila," said Abigail, trying to sound as poised as Teddy seemed. "I am pleased to meet you."

"Hello, Abigail," said Lila. She looked as if she might faint. So she, anyway, was appropriately nervous about seeing the mistress meet the wife. Abigail felt somehow reassured by this.

"This must be Ethan," said Teddy, examining him with curiosity.

"We were just having some whiskey," Abigail told her. Maxine made a noise in the back of her throat, which Abigail interpreted as an injunction to shut the hell up. "Maybe you'd like some," Abigail went on. "We were drinking it neat, but you'd probably prefer it over ice."

"Oh," said Lila, startled and excited. "That would be delicious."

Abigail got up and set about making a drink for Lila. "Teddy," she said, finally turning to look directly at her again, "do you want one, too?"

"Well, yes," said Teddy. "Thank you."

Abigail and Teddy looked at each other for an instant. There was nothing in Teddy's expression but uncomplicated amicability. Abigail felt herself relax. What was there to be upset about now? Oscar was dead. It was all over.

"Goddamn it," said Maxine, "give me another one, then."

When everyone had her glass of whiskey in front of her, there was a general sense of this meeting's being called to order, along with an implicit acknowledgment that Maxine, on her home turf, was the chairman of this meeting, and Teddy was a visiting enemy, equal in stature to Maxine. Ethan sat quietly, as expressionless as a judge.

Maxine cleared her throat. "Well, so this is why we're all here," she said. "We need to discuss these biographers, what we're going to tell them. We need a united front. And this united front must be that we won't tell the truth about the painting *Helena.*"

"I don't care about *Helena,*" said Teddy. She shifted in her chair, curled one long elegant leg around the other like a cat around a pole. "I have no need to tell anyone anything. Doing so would be to your benefit and no one else's. I can't for the life of me imagine why you've refrained from trumpeting it to the world."

"She made a deathbed promise to Oscar," said Abigail.

"Abigail!" said Maxine sharply.

"Ah," said Teddy.

"Sorry," said Abigail, surprised at herself.

"Oscar asked me to keep his secret before he died," said Maxine. "That's why I want it kept. If it were up to me, of course I would let the truth be known. I'm not an idiot."

There was a brief silence and then Lila, her eyes slightly averted from Maxine's, said, "I have been wanting to say this for many years, Maxine. When I learned that you had painted *Helena,* I was angry. We didn't speak after that, so I had no chance to tell you that I'd changed my mind. I think the truth ought to come out. I think everyone should know. If it were me, I would really just burn to have it known." She flushed.

"Lila," said Teddy, "you need to write your novel."

"Are you a novelist?" Abigail asked.

"No," said Lila, "but I always meant to be one."

"She is one," said Teddy. "She just hasn't written anything yet."

"Gosh, that's great," said Abigail. She looked down at her hands on the table. They looked garish and gauche to her, covered in diamonds and veins. "I'm a big reader. I'd be first in line to buy it."

Maxine looked around at all three of their faces, as if, Abigail thought, she were wondering how Abigail had become allied so easily with the enemy. Where was her allegiance to her sister-in-law? Abigail realized, to her own astonishment, that now their rivalry was out of the way, she was developing something of a little crush on Teddy. Teddy and Lila reminded Abigail of the pretty, fun shiksas she had always yearned to befriend in college. Next to them, Maxine looked like an old warthog.

"I don't want the truth to come out, Lila," Maxine said. "I take my promise very seriously. Here I am at the butt end of my life, and having that known will make little difference to me now."

Abigail sensed, or hoped she sensed, an effort in Lila and Teddy to turn their attention back to the topic at hand.

"Yes," said Lila, "I respect that."

"Well, I frankly don't care one way or another," said Teddy. "I'm here for another reason." From her bag she pulled a small package carefully wrapped in white cloth.

Maxine stared at the package, then at Teddy. "The tefillin," she said.

"You probably didn't know it," said Teddy, "but I've had them all these years."

"I thought they got lost in the shuffle when Oscar died," said Maxine. She stood up and went over to the kitchen counter and leaned on it with her head down. From the back, she looked to Abigail like a fireplug-shaped city bus driver or plumber.

"He left them at my house," Teddy said. "My old house, twelve years ago, when his studio was flooded from upstairs. He said for safekeeping, but he never bothered to take them. When I moved, I took them along. But ever since he died, I've intended to give them back to you."

"All this time, you had my tefillin?" Maxine said, turning from the counter and returning to her chair. She didn't touch the package, but she looked at it again, there on the table in front of her.

"Yes," said Teddy. "Oscar was so clear about not wanting you to have them. I was torn, but finally I decided that this was the right thing to do."

"What are tefillin?" Lila asked, but everyone ignored her.

"He didn't want me to have them because I'm a woman," said Maxine. "They belonged first to our grandfather Avram Feldman, and then to our father, who brought them to America. Our father left them to me, but Oscar never handed them over."

"He thought they should be passed down from father to son," said Teddy. "He was sure his father had made a mistake, leaving them to you. Oscar would have given them to Ethan if he had thought that Ethan could understand what they were." They all looked at Ethan, who appeared unperturbed by this news. "I brought them today to give them to you," Teddy went on. "I would have done it sooner—"

"Then why didn't you?" said Maxine. "It's a little late now."

"Well, why the hell is this my responsibility?" Teddy snapped. "It's a long trip across the river, and Lila was generous enough to drive me, but I didn't owe you a goddamned thing. I brought them today out of nothing but goodwill. These biographers have stirred up a lot of old silt, and I wanted to make things right. I should never have bothered."

"What are tefillin?" asked Lila again. "I know they have to do with the Judaic tradition, but I've never been clear on what they are exactly."

" 'And you shall bind them as a sign on your arm, and they shall be as frontlets on your head between your eyes,' " Abigail said.

"They're the things Jewish men use to cut off the circulation in their arms so they don't think about sex all the time," Teddy said. She looked nettled by Maxine's accusations, both implied and actual.

"Tefillin are holy," said Abigail. "Jews wear them on their weaker hands and on their heads to remember their liberation from Egypt, to think of God, to stop lustful and sinful thoughts, to control and redirect those thoughts to spiritual matters. The making of tefillin is a complicated and mysterious process; the writing on them has to be perfect or the tefillin are invalidated, even if just one letter is too rounded or pointy. You can't go to the bathroom or pass gas if you're wearing tefillin. You have to be absolutely clean. These old family tefillin are sacred. If only Ethan could wear them."

Everyone looked at Ethan. He studied the air in front of his face, calm and mute as a Nepalese mountaintop guru.

"Why couldn't Ethan have them?" asked Lila.

"Because they're mine," said Maxine. "God fucking damn it."

"That," said Abigail. "And also he can never wear them because he can't perfectly control his bodily functions and he can't think of God, as far as we know."

"There's also my grandson, Buster," said Teddy. "I mean Peter.

He's three. He happens to be another male descendant of Avram Feldman."

"They're mine for now," said Maxine. "When I die, you can squabble over them."

Teddy and Abigail looked at each other.

"You can meet Peter, if you want," said Teddy. "He has a little sister, too."

"Anyway," said Abigail simultaneously, "it's good you brought them and good Maxine has them now." As she spoke, she heard what Teddy was saying, but pretended she hadn't.

"I can't accept this," said Maxine. "Do you know my father left me nothing but those tefillin? And he left Oscar his prayer shawl. But Oscar took both. And my father left all his money to my cousin Fischel. Those bastards, it's unbelievable."

"And here you are, keeping Oscar's secret for him," said Teddy. "Makes you think twice, doesn't it?"

Not looking at anyone, Maxine leaned back in her chair and shoved a hand into her breast pocket and brought out her pack of cigarettes. She shook one out, fired it up with a match, then shot a severe look at Teddy.

"How much do you know about Judaism?" she asked coolly, exhaling a diffuse cloud of smoke, inadvertently or not, in Teddy's direction.

Teddy waved her hand to clear the smoke from her face. "Not much," she said.

"Well," said Maxine. "The signature I use on my paintings is the Hebrew for *apikoros*, a Greek word meaning 'nonpracticing believer.' We're considered the worst of all the Jews. I don't know about all those other *apikoroses* out there, but for my part, I don't do the *baruchas* and obey the laws because they're a big pain in the ass and I don't have time for it. I do think Judaism is a good thing for the most part, except when it tips over into fundamentalism. And I am very disturbed that Oscar kept those tefillin from me."

"Disturbed enough to tell the truth?" asked Abigail.

"Stop right now with the talk about *Helena*," said Maxine. "One thing has nothing to do with the other." She tipped some nonexistent ash from her cigarette into the beige glass ashtray that sat in front of her, which was bristling with butts. "I don't need to punish him for this. There are things about Oscar the three of you don't know that I do and which I will take with me to wherever my ashes end up. I'll just say: I knew my brother was a schmuck before the trouble over the tefillin and I'm choosing to keep my promise to him anyway."

"What things?" asked Teddy, smoothing the front of her white blouse with one hand, slowly, as if she were caressing or comforting herself.

"Ask his old best friend, Moe Treitler, for one thing; maybe he'll tell you, but I won't," said Maxine. "Katerina," she called. "Come here."

"One minute," came Katerina's voice from the other end of the loft.

Suddenly restless, wondering what exactly she was doing here, Abigail stood and made her way over to one of the old factory windows and looked out through the enormous, grimy panes of glass, inlaid with what looked like chicken wire. The sky outside was white with heat. She heard Katerina come into the kitchen area and say, "Maxine, that was Michael Rubinstein on the phone, asking when he can come and see what you're doing."

"Take these," said Maxine, handing Katerina the unopened package of tefillin, "and put them in my safe. Tell Michael to come anytime. I have nothing to hide."

Katerina said something else, but Abigail didn't hear what because someone spoke right behind her.

"I'm so sorry," came a soft girlish voice. "I think maybe you're more upset by all this than you're letting on. I know I would be."

Abigail turned. Lila stood there, eyes squinting a little, skin aglow with heat and empathic anxiousness. "No," said Abigail. "I'm really not."

"It's my fault, in a way," Lila went on as if she hadn't heard. "I could have just ignored Maxine's mark. But no, I had to ask Teddy. I never wanted this known; I loved Oscar."

Abigail said, "I'm not at all upset. And everyone loved Oscar, Lila; he banked on being loved. Nothing wrong with that. But he did come to take it for granted. He had to prove no woman could resist him. I always wondered why he needed that so badly. I knew him from when we were kids, and he was always like that."

"How hard, to be married to someone like that," said Lila wistfully.

"Not so hard as you might think," said Abigail. She glanced over at Ethan. He seemed calm enough. "We were strangely well suited to each other. I wouldn't have married anyone else."

She and Lila exchanged a complex look.

"What do you think of these biographers?" asked Lila.

"Henry's all right. I'm having lunch with the other one tomorrow."

"Ralph?"

"Have you talked to him yet?"

"Oh, me, no. Why would he want to talk to me? I was just Teddy's friend, nothing more."

"Oh, sweetheart, you loved Oscar, too, but trust me, you were better off with your own husband; I can tell just by looking at you."

"What are you saying?" Lila asked with a faint air of sorrow.

"I have a suspicion that you're a romantic. That's a compliment. But no woman could be romantic and have the stomach for Oscar. To survive him, you had to be practical and a little bit detached from him. I wonder whether your friend Teddy was those things. To look at her, I would guess she was, and good for her."

Lila sighed, obviously wishing she were more practical, more coldhearted, more whatever it would have taken to have been with Oscar. "I have a confession," she whispered with a quick glance over at the table. "I'm in love."

"You are?" Abigail said, surprised. "Who with?"

"A younger man I met on the street! At my age! We're like teenagers."

"Well," said Abigail yearningly, imagining the thrill. She suspected that Lila had told her this to even the playing field, and she didn't blame her. "Gosh."

"I can't tell Teddy."

"Why not?"

"I don't want her to be upset. She seems so lonely these days. . . ." Lila's voice trailed off.

"You should tell her," said Abigail. "I'm sure she'll be happy for you." Her antennae had begun to sense a restlessness at the table. She looked over at them all to make sure Ethan was all right.

"Hey," called Maxine, "you two, get back here. There's another item we have to discuss."

As Abigail and Lila herded themselves back to the war table, Abigail felt renewed resentment toward Maxine but quashed it. Ethan was rocking silently, twiddling an ear with the opposite hand. Katerina was nowhere in sight. Abigail guessed she had gone back to her office, leaving Teddy and Maxine uncomfortably together in prickly silence, and this was the real reason the seconds had been summoned back to the table.

"What were you two getting up to over there?" Teddy asked.

"All sorts of mischief," said Abigail.

When Lila smiled at her, Abigail was surprised to find herself near tears. Had she really become so lonely that a scrap of proffered friendship could make her weep? Things were dire indeed. She took her place again across from Lila and tried not to look dementedly needy.

"Now," said Maxine. She poured herself another shot of whiskey and then, by way of hospitality, waved the bottle at the rest of them a little menacingly, Abigail thought, like a pirate offering his captives a last drink before they walked the plank.

"Please," said Teddy, pushing her glass forward. "Pour some all around."

Maxine gave Teddy a good-size shot, then poured markedly less into Abigail's and Lila's glasses. Ethan touched his nose a few times, fending off the sharp, caustic smell.

"These biographers," said Maxine. "Oscar would have greatly cared about the things we all say about him to these men. I want him remembered properly, the way he would have wanted to be."

"You're a good sister," Teddy burst out, half in anger and half something else—Abigail wasn't sure what, maybe admiration.

Maxine looked directly at Teddy, her face blank, and said nothing.

"Well, anyway," said Teddy in that same half-angry tone. "I've already said things about Oscar that I deeply regret."

"So have I," said Maxine, sounding oddly relieved.

The two hostile parties stared at each other. Abigail felt the air between them smooth out just a little, become marginally warmer.

"It's kept me awake at night," said Teddy. "I betrayed him."

"Nowhere near as badly as I have," said Maxine.

"Well," said Teddy. "It's true: We should all be very careful what we say about him from now on."

"The upset apple cart comes to mind," said Maxine. "As does the open barn door with the horse gone."

"I haven't said anything I regret," said Abigail, "but it does make me a little uneasy to talk about Oscar in such a way. It feels very exciting and flattering to me to have Henry there listening to every word, and I find myself telling more than maybe I should, because I do love to talk about Oscar. I do miss him so much; it brings him back to me a little."

"Yes," said Teddy.

"Yes," agreed Maxine.

Teddy looked over at Abigail and clasped her hands together on the tabletop in front of her. "Abigail," she said.

Abigail looked back at her.

"I can't apologize to you," said Teddy. "I always thought I ought to if this moment ever came, but I find now that I can't do it."

"You haven't got anything to apologize for," said Abigail. She sounded unconvinced and unconvincing even to herself.

Maxine made a sound in the back of her throat.

"I'm sure I have," said Teddy, "but I find that I can't."

Maxine made another sound in the back of her throat.

"Sounds like something's stuck in your craw," Teddy said to Maxine. "Maybe you should spit it out."

"I will," said Maxine. "Right in your face. You screwed her husband for decades."

Teddy looked at Abigail. "If it hadn't been me, it would have been someone else. Many times, it *was* someone else."

"Oh," said Abigail, wanting to agree, wanting this conversation not to be happening. She went on: "Well, yes. But it was mostly you."

"Sure," said Teddy. "He needed me, Abigail."

"I can see that," said Abigail.

"Stop being such a yellowbelly!" Maxine said.

Abigail stared at Maxine with her mouth slightly ajar. "Maxie, there's nothing to say now! What would be the point? Why are you pushing me?"

"Because you won't push yourself," said Maxine. "Damn it. You should have put a stop to it right at the beginning."

"I couldn't," said Abigail. "What would I have said?"

"Told him to dump her and stick to his little sluts," said Maxine.

"As if anyone could have," said Teddy. "It's not Abigail's fault Oscar and I carried on an affair. It was nothing to do with her."

Ethan made a sharp, high sound, as if he were reacting to this in some way.

"Nothing to do with his *wife*?" Maxine squawked.

"I can see that objectively," said Abigail with a sudden whiskey-fueled clap of rage, "but I have to say that emotionally, that strikes me as purely disingenuous."

Teddy was silent for a moment. Something worked in her face. Everyone waited for her to answer except Ethan, who rapped his knuckles softly on the table. Teddy said finally, looking fixedly at the air between them all, "When he died, I thought I was going to go insane. I did, maybe. Looking back, now I think I went a little crazy. I sold my beautiful house and moved to an old dump in a sordid neighborhood farther away from everything, and if it hadn't been for Lila, I might have literally died of a broken heart. Lila sat up with me at night because I couldn't sleep. My brain was sick with grief. I didn't talk much, did I?"

"No," said Lila, "not much at all. You asked about my grandchildren. You wanted me to talk. I always thought you never really grieved properly for Oscar."

"I didn't even know he was dead," said Teddy directly to Abigail. "He died at home, with you. Who would think to tell me? I read his obituary like most of the world. Read about it in the paper . . . that's how I learned he was gone."

"And it didn't mention you or Ruby or Samantha," said Lila.

"Well, of course not," said Teddy. "Abigail and Maxine weren't going to allow anything about us in Oscar's obituary. I'm sure if you had any control over the biographies, we'd all be erased from those, too. The reason I can't apologize is that this was between you and Oscar, Abigail. Not me. Maxine is right, but only half right. If you had tried to put a stop to his affair with me, it would have created an intolerable situation for him. He couldn't give either one of us up. He needed us both equally. If you had been the histrionic kind of woman to telephone me with your voice trembling dramatically, begging me to give him up for the sake of your marriage, your son, I would have told you it had nothing to do with me, that it was entirely up to Oscar and between the two of you."

"You have not one fucking idea," Maxine snarled. "You controlling bitch. You sucked him in and kept him there."

Ethan made another high keening sound in the back of his throat.

"I had him under some kind of spell?"

"I think you controlled him. You can call it any fancy name you want."

Teddy laughed harshly. "You think Oscar was that easily led around by the nose?"

"Not the nose," said Maxine.

Abigail had been looking intently at Teddy throughout this conversation, watching her confident way of speaking, her gracefully precise gestures, imagining that if Teddy had been Oscar's wife, he very well might not have needed a mistress. This thought both galvanized her and gave her a mournful sense of her own failings. "I was never that kind of woman," she said. "The kind to call anyone up like that. I had too much pride and what I mistakenly thought was dignity. Now I see I was laughed at and mocked."

Ethan keened again. He sounded like a wild animal.

"Never," said Lila.

"All those nights I couldn't contact him," Teddy said to Abigail. "The night I went into labor with our daughters, I couldn't call him. He was at home with you. I knew, I understood, exactly what the deal was. All along I accepted it. But when he died, I saw how much I had given up. And I don't mean because he left me nothing. I mean because, in the end, a woman needs legitimacy."

"I know those nights," said Abigail. "I had them, too. I didn't have your telephone number, Teddy, did I? And I *was* laughed at; I *was* mocked. Maxine, you mocked me."

"To your face," said Maxine. "Right to your face. It wasn't mockery. I just thought you were being a dumb bunny. He lived off your money and gave you nothing in return. Where was *your* legitimacy, Abigail? A piece of paper that pronounced you Mrs. Feldman? So fucking what. A marriage is in the details."

"All due respect, but how would you know?" Abigail said in a sudden white-hot explosion of rage at Maxine, the rage that had been rankling her all afternoon—for decades, in fact. "How would you know what marriage is, Maxine?"

Ethan's hands flapped by his ears. He rocked.

"I know," said Maxine with blunt indifference to Abigail's fury, "what Oscar was getting from you for free."

"You couldn't stand to see him get exactly what he wanted," said Abigail. She was out of breath with anger at Maxine, dizzy with it. "And he got it all and no one took it away from him. He had me and Teddy and his little chippies, as Maribelle and I called them. He had his two cakes, ate them whenever he wanted, and all the cupcakes he wanted on the side. Not to mention everything else he had. Because he was bold. He had the courage of his convictions. Shhh. Ethan, it's all right."

"That's for sure," said Teddy with a little laugh. "Absolute clarity in all things, Oscar. Never wavered, never hesitated."

"He had balls," said Abigail.

"He was not a good boy," added Lila.

Maxine looked around at their three faces. "Please," she said. "I never got silly about him. I saw him for what he was. Without the haze of sex."

"Shhh. Ethan," said Abigail again. "I promise, it's all right."

Ethan abruptly went quiet, but his hands moved by his ears and he kept rocking.

"Staking your claim," said Teddy. "You're welcome to it."

"We all saw him, in our own ways," said Lila.

A silence fell around the table. The four women avoided eye contact, as if suddenly ashamed or shy. Into the breach came the sound of Katerina singing to herself in the far corner of the loft, something in Hungarian in a raspy, slightly off-key voice that somehow managed to be beautiful anyway by virtue of the language she sang in. Her voice sounded to Abigail like a peasant girl's during wartime as she dug, squatting in a potato patch behind a hut.

Abigail said to no one in particular, "I've read too many novels. I haven't lived enough of life."

"Oh, me, too," said Lila, as if she had been thinking along similar lines.

"I wanted to," said Abigail, "but I could never quite get up my nerve. And then Ethan always needed me."

"You could have put him in a home," said Maxine. She looked over at Ethan. His mouth was twisted; he was looking at the tabletop.

"I could do no such thing!"

"Of course you couldn't," said Lila.

"Why not?" Teddy asked. "Would he have known the difference?"

Abigail said with horror, "He would have been miserable among strangers!"

"Among his own kind," said Maxine. "Cared for by trained professionals. And then Oscar might have felt he had your undivided attention, Abigail."

"Maxine," said Teddy, "that was not why Oscar—"

"Oh really," said Maxine.

Teddy and Maxine stared at each other with hatred.

"It wasn't," said Abigail. "You're right, Teddy. He didn't want my undivided attention. He wanted me distracted."

"Oscar, Oscar, Oscar," said Maxine. "Look at us, four smart old bags with plenty to think about, fixated on my putz of a brother, who's been dead for five years and wasn't especially nice to any of us."

"Time for Lila and me to be going," said Teddy. "You have your tefillin, we'll all keep our traps shut about *Helena,* we had a nice little volley of long-overdue spats and tantrums, and now I'm tired and ready for a nap." She stood up and said to Lila, "Ready?"

"Yes," said Lila. "But I just want to add one thing. Oscar and Teddy were soul mates. That was true love if I ever saw it. It didn't diminish or tarnish over all those years. I can't go home without saying that."

"Stop romanticizing Oscar and me, Lila," said Teddy. "I appreciate what you're trying to say, but really, it was as complicated and messy as any relationship between two people always is."

"Like I said," Maxine said, "I have heard enough about Oscar for one lifetime. I don't care if he and Teddy floated in fairy dust and little red cinnamon hearts together, I've had it with my fucking brother and all of you lovelorn girls who fell for his bullshit."

"Good-bye," said Teddy, pushing her chair back, standing up, smiling enigmatically. "Thanks very much for all the whiskey." She walked toward the door with her head held high and disappeared through it.

Lila fluttered around, gathering her pocketbook, hooking it through her arm. At the door, she turned and said, "Abigail, I would love to have lunch with you someday, but of course I understand if that's impossible. Good-bye, Maxine."

After the door had closed behind Lila, Maxine made a harrumphing noise that might have been just her clearing the phlegm from her throat.

"That was very tense," said Abigail.

"You were on their side," Maxine said.

"I said exactly what I thought," said Abigail. "I was being honest."

"I find it very interesting," said Maxine, "that this seemed to involve agreeing with them most of the time."

"What about the things you said to me? Calling me a yellow-belly in front of Teddy! What sort of loyalty is that, Maxine?"

Maxine bunched up her mouth, looking away from Abigail and at Ethan. "What do you make of all these crazy old bats, Ethan?" she said loudly.

Ethan clucked his tongue against the roof of his mouth. Abigail said nothing.

"I bet you think we're all out of our trees," Maxine told Ethan.

"I'm not out of my tree," said Abigail.

Maxine looked at her sister-in-law. "Well, sometimes I think I must be completely out of mine," she said. It was as close to an apology as she had ever come.

"What did Moe Treitler say about Oscar that was so terrible?" Abigail asked, forgiving her grudgingly but completely, as always.

"Oh," said Maxine. "I can't tell you that."

"Why not?"

"Because I can't. I don't know whether it's true, for one thing. I only know what Moe told me."

"Well, so tell me and I'll take it with a grain of salt."

Maxine called out, "Katerina!"

"Yes," came a faint voice from the other end of the loft.

"Did you put those tefillin in the safe?"

"Yes," came the stoic answer.

Maxine grimaced at Abigail. "I'm wrung out. That little meeting was goddamned debilitating."

"Ethan," said Abigail, wrung out herself, quailing at the thought of getting Ethan downstairs, hailing a taxi, getting him into it, then getting him out of it onto the sidewalk on Riverside

Drive and into their building's front door and elevator and finally their apartment, "it's time to go home."

Ethan said, "Unghhh." His eyes were fixed on the ceiling now. His hands had come to rest on his thighs, still fluttering, like birds landing after a storm.

Nine

The next morning before breakfast, after a night of odd and upsetting dreams (one of which was about playing Scrabble with Ethan and having to pretend "eeokiys" was a word), Abigail got out the Manhattan White Pages, found a "Treitler, M" on Greene Street, and, without stopping to consider whether or not she might be opening a can of worms, dialed the number.

An hour later, her doorbell rang.

"Abigail Feldman," said an ancient man in a slightly tattered black suit, a tattoo of a spider on his cheek. Shoulder-length greasy gray hair sprouted from his skull-like head. "You look just the same."

She stared at him while he grinned at her. He was missing a front tooth.

"It's Morris!" he said puckishly. "Moe Treitler."

"Moe Treitler," she said. Moe Treitler had always been on the stout side, stout and pink and somehow juicy.

"Esophageal cancer," he said. "That's why I look like this; I'm being eaten up from the inside. All those cigarettes finally bit me in the ass."

"Moe!" Abigail said, recognizing him now by his breathy voice and hepcat manner, his glinting no-goodnik eyes. "Come in, come in."

He followed her back to the kitchen, where Ethan sat at the breakfast nook. Morris chucked him under the chin and slid in next to him. "Ethan," he said. "It's been a fuckin' lifetime, but you look just the same, too."

Moe Treitler had been Oscar's friend from childhood. They'd grown up together, had their bar mitzvahs the same year, chased girls together. Back before Oscar and Abigail were married, when they'd gone to jazz clubs in the Village, they had double-dated with Moe and a succession of his girls, most of whom Abigail had found intimidating, humorless, sophisticated, and slovenly. Then Oscar had married Abigail, and Moe had disappeared into Alphabet City to live in a tenement flat near Tompkins Square Park, where he'd cultivated through the years first a hipster heroin habit, then a full-blown addiction, and finally a rehabilitated, clean-living persona of righteous zeal. He painted street murals and enormous abstractions on stitched-together bedsheets and cheap fabric, played free jazz on his saxophone, mostly alone in the street for loose change but also gigs with other musicians when he could get them.

In the early years in the Riverside apartment, Moe had occasionally turned up for dinner with Oscar, both of them punchy and sweaty and hungry, often having walked the whole way uptown, shouting and arguing and gassing each other about what geniuses they both were. Moe always had some crazy outfit on, tie-dyed jeans and animal-fur vests in the sixties, top hats and glitzy ties and platform shoes in the seventies, velour jumpsuits and long silk scarves in the eighties, and then he'd disappeared from Oscar's life after a blowup over something—Oscar wouldn't say what.

Abigail hadn't liked Moe Treitler much when he was sixteen and hadn't cared much for him when he was twenty and thirty and forty, but she felt almost glad to see him now.

"You want a cup of coffee or something?"

"Coffee, great. Can I smoke in here?"

"I'd rather you didn't," said Abigail, pouring some coffee for him, "but all right."

Moe settled in, stretched his legs out under the table, lit a cigarette, and fondled his coffee cup. He had always been excessively tactile, needing to claim whatever came into his orbit by touching it, whether it was a woman, an object, or food and drink. Abigail dredged up the ashtray Maxine always used when she visited, a souvenir from Maui that had come from she knew not where, and set it on the table in front of him.

"I can't believe Ockie's gone," he said to Abigail, his eyes welling up. She remembered then his habit of tearing up easily, then pinching his nose as if staunching a potential cascade of tears. "Somehow sitting here makes it real in a way it wasn't before. Makes me feel so fuckin' old."

"We are so fuckin' old," said Abigail. "I'm eighty; how old are you?"

"Yeah," said Morris. "I'm the same as Ockie, so he would have been eighty-three now if he was still around. Time flies, life."

"Time flies, life," Abigail repeated. "It sure does."

"Last time I saw Ockie, we almost killed each other. That was

over twenty years ago, 1984. I remember that day like it was yesterday. Broke my heart, but I wanted to kill that guy. I wanted his neck
between my two hands. We walked away like, pffft, it's over, a lifelong friendship. And it really was. I kept thinking, you know,
we'd . . ."

"I know," said Abigail. "He told me you two fell out, but he
wouldn't say what it was about. He also always sort of thought . . .
you know, you'd patch it up."

"Well, we never did. Maxie I see from time to time. You know I
live near her now. I see her out walking her dog, late at night. Both
of us are night owls. I call her 'Crankypants'; she calls me 'the old
nutjob.' 'Well, if it isn't Crankypants!' 'Oh no, not the old nutjob.'
She sure has a stick up her ass. She sure can pass judgment. We
start arguing drop of a hat. I say, 'Maxie, calm down. It's all one big
pot of gold we're dipping our brushes in, whatever we do with the
paint.' I was spray-painting awhile back, heavily influenced by my
very good friend Jean-Michel Basquiat. I told Maxie all about it and
she said, 'Oh, that's just a bunch of bull.' On the whole, she doesn't
care for anything too street, you know, too unconventional, too
black. Personally, I think black art and culture is all this country
has going for it. It's the only original shit we've got." Morris
clapped his hands together once and shook his head. "That's the
shit, man. That's where it's at. Black kids."

"I'm sure Maxie would have a lot to say about that," said Abigail.
"I myself have no opinion."

"Ockie was just as nuts as his sister," Morris said. He looked
over at Ethan with a paranoid grin, as if he might be a gossip
columnist in disguise. "Ockie was a bad boy, worse than anyone
but me you ever saw. We were the red devils on each other's shoulders, me and him, till we weren't anymore. There's a lot of stuff you
would wet yourself if you knew, and most of that goes to the grave

with me, or the stoppered jar, wherever I end up. I'll tell you one thing, though. He and I came up together, sort of like brothers. Brothers who fell out with each other, who ended up in hatred, but for a while there we were very close."

Abigail watched him with an expression of careful, mild interest on her face, afraid if she revealed how rabidly she wanted to hear this, he would clam up and scuttle away.

"Listen to me," Morris went on, leaning in. "No one knows this. I forgave Ockie a long time ago, or maybe I never will, but this is my hour of sweet revenge."

"No one," repeated Abigail with frank disbelief.

"That's right," said Morris. "And I know he never told anyone. It's not the kind of thing he would brag about, as you'll see."

"Not even Maxine?"

"Naw," said Morris. "Well, all right, Maxie probably knows most of this story. So, my best friend." Morris's thin shoulders hunched in a shrug. "As you well know, Ockie didn't get along with a lot of guys. He was competitive, liked women better, whatever. I put up with a lot of bullshit from him. One thing with Ockie, he had to be the alpha male. He had to be top guy, big man on campus. Otherwise, he was out of his depth. He had to leave if another guy topped him. He didn't fight; he scrammed. With me, I let him be the famous guy who married a rich girl and lived in a nice house and had a tamale of a girlfriend on the side and all that."

Abgiail flinched.

"Sorry, sorry," said Morris, leaning in closer, as if he were sucking in her pain, altruistically siphoning it off like snake venom, but drinking it vampirelike at the same time. "Anyway. Meanwhile, I was the crazy poor one in the weird situations, doing drugs and living in cockroach shit. On top, that was him; on the edge, that was me. I never fought Ockie on this. I let it ride. I wasn't competitive like that; I'm a live-and-let-win kind of guy. Whatever, if that was his thing, let him have it—that's how I saw it. And that kept the friendship together through a lot of shit. A *lot* of shit. So then I got married."

"Oh," said Abigail.

"You ever meet Carole?"

"I never met her," said Abigail. "I don't think Oscar ever even mentioned her."

"No surprise," said Moe. "This girl wasn't like the other girls I always had. This one was my own true love. Carole, her name was, and she was so good to me. I would always go for these smarty-pants Ivy League girls, younger classy babes slumming it with an old schmo like me from the Lower East Side who didn't know his ass from Thoreau. Then I meet Carole. She was younger, too, but from the same neighborhood, not Jewish, but might as well've been. She spoke the same language as me; she knew who I was. And what was new for me was, I was a step up for her; I looked pretty good after a bunch of low-life scumbags. I looked like a prince compared to those jerks, a real knight in white armor. But the thing is, she was beautiful, Carole. I mean really a knockout. Long black hair, good-tempered, easy to be around. I thought I'd hit the jackpot. I couldn't believe she loved me, too. Both of us had suffered from past heartbreaks; we'd been treated pretty rough, so we knew each other's weak spots, and we always took care to avoid causing more pain. We just plain loved each other, no drama, no bullshit."

"That sounds wonderful," said Abigail.

"It was, but Ockie had a problem with her, he said. He was concerned when I told him we were tying the knot. He thought she was a bad influence on me. He thought she and I did too many drugs together. Drugs, schmugs, what did Ockie know about that? What's wrong with it? What's wrong is, you cease to be a good taxpaying member of society, but other than that, if you do it right, there's nothing bad about it; it doesn't hurt you or anyone else. There is no better feeling than that high. So me and Carole had a nice little using-now-and-then, shacked-up lifestyle going, and Ockie didn't like it one bit. I had already been through rehab, and Ockie had seen me through the whole fuckin' thing, and paid for it, too, as you know, so to be fair, I can see why it might've bugged him. But this time around, I was smart about it. I didn't let it get out of control because I loved this girl too much, and I was looking out for her, as well."

Abigail made a skeptical noise that had been intended to sound noncommittally encouraging.

"So we get married, get on with it. She's a writer; I'm a painter and musician. We do our things—she does poetry readings; I play the odd gig. We sell stuff on First Avenue and St. Marks to make ends meet. Stuff we find rooting through other people's garbage, but perfectly good shit, you know? On a good night, we could clear plenty to score and get a little taco and go out the next day, do it again. There I was, living the sub-American dream, perfect wife, little tenement flat with the bathtub in the kitchen, the free and easy life. So, back to Ockie. The wrench in the works."

"Oh dear," said Abigail.

"I don't know if it was seeing me happy finally, or if it was because Carole didn't give Ockie the time of day. In her eyes, *I* was the great artist. She always told me, 'You have more originality in your little finger,' yadda yadda, built me up like that. She'd go, 'Don't let him act like that, treat you that way. His stuff is cornball; it's over.' She thought he was a big phony. He thought she was bad news. So there was no love lost."

"Yes," said Abigail, "I'm gathering that."

"Well, it's important that you do, because what happens next is so shocking. Afterwards, Carole and I went our separate ways. At first, though, I knew, I just knew, I felt it in my bone marrow, that we'd be together till the end. And then it all exploded in my face."

Abigail looked right at Morris. "Well, I can see it coming like a regular commuter train," she said.

He looked at her and shook his head without surprise. "I bet you can," he said. "But I didn't. And I never got over it. To this day, I am still not over it." He paused dramatically.

"So?" said Abigail, twitching a little with impatience to hear the worst.

"Maybe it was seeing me happy," said Morris. "Maybe it was that he could tell she didn't think much of him. I don't know, but for whatever reason, Ockie had to break us up, and he knew the only way to do it. And I mean the *only* way. Carole could have killed my mother, fucked everyone in Rikers, eaten a pound of human feces every morning for breakfast. I would have kept her with me through nuclear fallout. But Ockie . . . I truly don't know how he did it. I can't imagine how he got around her."

"I can," said Abigail.

They exchanged a look.

"I bet you can," said Morris with far more pity than anger.

"Oscar slept with your *wife*," Abigail said, as if this affirmatively answered a question she'd asked herself for many years.

"Not only that," said Morris, "but he had the evil balls to pretend he did it for my own good, so I would see what a user she was, how she was bad news for me. He pretended he did it out of friendship!" He gave a hollow, sorrowful cackle. "He did it to save me from myself! He looked me right in the eye and said, 'Moe, now you see what she is.' Is that pure evil?"

"No," said Abigail. "I don't think it's evil."

"Did you know about this?" Morris asked her.

"No. But it doesn't surprise me. Oscar was competitive, just like you said. Like a two-year-old. You found something, and he couldn't leave it alone."

"I wanted to kill him. I would have bashed his head in with a baseball bat without a second's thought if I had ever seen him again, but he had the sense to stay the fuck away from me. Wanting to kill her came later. Then she cried her guts out till she almost puked, swore she hated him, that he hypnotized her or something. Hypnotized, my ass. I physically threw her out of the house with all her crap. It was something like two o'clock in the morning, but I didn't give a fuck, and I never spoke to her again. I would cross the street to avoid her for years. Leave parties where she was. Sent her the divorce papers in the mail. But at first, I blamed Ockie one hundred percent. It turned out that he was just as furious at me for being so stupid, as he called me. Well, maybe it was time for us to end that friendship and she was just the catalyst. I've never murdered anyone, but I came close then with Ockie in that last conversation between us. He said to me, 'Of course I used a rubber with her.' He told me some other shit I didn't fucking want to know. Did you ever feel like the world made no sense whatsoever? It's like the laws of gravity were canceled and I woke up to find everything floating off into space. For years after that, I was a walking shell."

"Yes," said Abigail, "I can well imagine you must have been."

"I have never trusted anyone since, although I've had my share of companionship. But trust and love like I had with those two, that is rare; that only comes around once or twice in a lifetime." Morris looked at Abigail. "So now you know."

"You can't tell me anything new about him," said Abigail, smiling as if her mouth hurt.

Morris stared at her. "This is *funny* to you?"

"You couldn't get mad at him. You couldn't hold him to any-thing."

Morris examined Abigail's face for any sign of disingenuous-ness or self-deception.

"Well, then what kind of love did he have to offer, Abigail?" he burst out.

"An honest kind of love. No illusions for either of us. How of-ten can you say that?"

Before she was finished with her last sentence, he said, "I never understood why you put up with him."

"Maybe Oscar really was trying to help you," Abigail was saying, "however misguided he may have been. Did that never occur to you?"

"In recent years, it did," Morris said. He rolled his eyes. "But come *on*. He fucked my wife."

"To answer your question," said Abigail, "I always gave Oscar the benefit of the doubt. That's how I put up with him."

"Carole died," Morris said. He pinched the bridge of his nose between two fingers and blinked a few times. "She OD'd."

"I am so sorry," said Abigail.

She was loath to say this aloud, but she found it extremely hard to believe that Oscar would have seduced his best friend's wife solely to teach that friend a lesson, a woman he claimed he didn't even like. Oscar wasn't that altruistic; he was far too concerned with his own desires and needs to sacrifice himself sexually for another person, even a close old friend. Maybe Morris was delu-sional and heartbroken, but maybe he was telling some kind of truth, some version of what really happened. She wondered what Oscar's side of the story would have been. She would have bet any-thing he'd had the hots for Carole, so he'd seduced her, being un-able to resist anyone he was attracted to. Where the story about doing it for Morris's sake had come from was anyone's guess. What a schmuck Oscar had been; Maxine was right, but she was wrong in thinking Abigail didn't know that.

Shortly after Morris had gone, Ethan's male nurse arrived, and Abigail was free to go downtown to meet Ralph for lunch. She stood on West End Avenue with her arm up while the occasional cab went by with its lights off, people in the backseat. She was damp with sweat under the cream-colored linen suit; she'd worn it because it reminded her of what Teddy had been wearing the day before, but she knew she looked nothing whatsoever like Teddy in it. She felt rumpled and flustered.

Finally, a taxi stopped. She had a little trouble hoisting herself into it. She was old and creaky—that was the main problem—but the door was very heavy, and the handle stuck, and the man didn't offer to help her open it. The instant she'd managed to get in and get the door closed, he sped away into the downtown traffic, lurching her against the back of the seat so suddenly, she lost her breath.

"I'm going to Chelsea," she said, and gave the address. He said nothing, didn't indicate in any way that he had heard or understood, but he did manage to get her there with alarming speed, so she wasn't late. She paid him, tipped him, and got out as fast as she could; she sensed his impatience to be off in search of younger, nimbler fares, although all he did was sit staring straight ahead.

The place was tiny. She felt out of place and shy. It was dim inside. She caught a glimpse of two young men in waiter's outfits laughing by the cash register. There was a lot of red cloth, an aquarium; she heard soft classical music playing and after a split second identified it as a late Beethoven quartet.

Seated at a table against the far wall was a young black man. After the brightness outside, she couldn't make out his features, but he wore a short-sleeved white shirt and had some sort of complicated hairdo. He gave a quick wave to get her attention, as if he recognized her, although they had never met before. Of course, he must have recognized her from the photographs Oscar had taken of her when she was younger.

"You must be Ralph," she said as she approached his table.

He stood and held her chair out for her and said, "Thank you so much for coming, Mrs. Feldman."

They shook hands. His hand was dry and hot. She hoped hers wasn't too sweaty.

"Oh!" she said. "Please call me Abigail. My gosh, no one calls me Mrs. Feldman." She sat in the chair and was happy to find that the seat was cushioned. She took a sip of ice water and blinked as her eyes adjusted to the soft lighting. "What a lovely place," she said. "It's air-conditioned!"

"Well, it better be," said Ralph. "It's so hot today, you can hardly breathe out there. I came from Brooklyn on the subway."

"Well, I came in a taxi, and the guy drove like a bat out of hell. I was lucky to get here alive."

Ralph laughed. One of the willowy waiters stepped over and proffered one-page menus, elegant mottled cream-colored cardboard on which a very few dishes were listed in careful calligraphy and described in painstaking detail. The prices almost gave Abigail a coronary, although of course she could afford this; she could afford anything. Ralph ordered a bottle of sauvignon blanc. Abigail asked for sparkling water. The waiter wordlessly inclined his head, eyes lowered. He was a sloe-eyed, pale Pre-Raphaelite beauty with a mole by his lush lower lip and a lock of curly dark hair on his forehead. Abigail took him in, then looked back down at her menu; his beauty had been created to appeal to a sex different from hers.

"Will you have some of the wine?" Ralph asked her.

"Oh," said Abigail, about to say no. "I'd love some."

"Two glasses, please," said Ralph.

The waiter went away; there were only a few other diners, and the room was so small, Abigail could have heard everyone's conversation if she'd tried. The whole restaurant was about the size of her bedroom. A moment later, the waiter was back with a bottle of wine in a bucket of ice. He set about uncorking, pouring a smidge into one glass, waiting for Ralph to taste, then pouring for real; then he held up his pad and waited interrogatively; Ralph asked for the fresh pea soup and the cockle salad. Abigail deliberated aloud a moment. Trout meunière was such a classic, dependable dish, and you hardly ever saw it anymore, not that she went out to many restaurants anyway, but that cockle salad sounded so intriguing—it came with asparagus, her favorite, and a mango salsa, which she wasn't familiar with, but she loved mango.

"Do the cockles come in their shells?" she asked the waiter. "Cockles are those little clamlike things, aren't they?"

"They're taken from their shells, rolled in buttermilk, dredged in cornmeal, then lightly fried," said the waiter. "It's one of our most popular dishes."

"Oh," said Abigail with lust; there was something about the word *dredged.*

"Have both," said Ralph.

"All right," she said, surprised but not at all put off at his familiarity. Very rarely, this happened when she met people; she felt as if they somehow already knew each other, and finding out the details and filling in the blanks was just a formality.

"Excellent choice," said the waiter, collecting the menus. Ralph smiled up at him and the two men exchanged a quick look.

"I have been thinking a lot as I research this book," said Ralph to Abigail when the waiter was gone again, "about magnificence." His tone was earnest and ruminating, as if she had asked him a question and he had been mulling over his answer. "Oscar's work immediately appealed to me as an adolescent, when I first saw it, because, whatever flaws it may have, whatever limitations, his work has real magnificence—meaning grandeur, beauty, and passion all together."

"Well," said Abigail, "he would have liked to hear that." She drank some wine. It was fizzy and metallic-tasting, with a strange, fishy aftertaste; she didn't care for it at all. Disappointed, she took another sip to make sure.

"I watched him paint our housekeeper," she said. "She stripped naked right there in our living room one day after lunch and he got out his paints. *Mercy*, he called it."

"*Mercy* and *Helena* were the paintings I first saw of his," said Ralph with hushed excitement. "What was the real-life Mercy like?"

"Her name was Maribelle. She was one of my best and dearest friends. She lived with us for many years and died shortly after Oscar. Well, I thought he didn't do her justice at all in that painting! He missed the point of her, I thought. She was so much smarter than I ever was. We would talk about everything, she and I. He painted her as a singer. Is that not a cliché, a black woman singing?"

"What isn't a cliché about black people when you get down to it?" Ralph said.

"She and I discussed religion, politics, art. We went through the radical age together, she and I, a housewife and a housekeeper. We sat in that apartment like two gerbils in a cage and we read the newspaper and listened to the radio and we discussed everything. We read *Ms.* magazine from the very first issue. We wanted to go to the big demonstrations, but we felt too self-conscious; we worried we'd get laughed at by the real protestors. But that didn't mean we weren't aware! We heard about other women having consciousness-raising groups. We weren't that formal about it, but we had our own sort of ongoing discussion group, Maribelle and I. And Maxine would come over, of course. She really spiced up the conversation. Her life was so different from ours."

"Oscar must have been there a lot of the time, too. What did he make of all this?"

"We waited on him and didn't rock any boats. It never occurred to me to try to change anything in my *own* life. But oh, I admired those women who just *left* their husbands and went off on their own! A lot of them with children, to graduate school and into the work world! Maribelle was one of them, but she never saw herself that way."

"Did she sing a lot?"

"Only around the house. Ethan liked her voice."

"So it wasn't out of the blue for him to paint her singing."

"Oh no! She was singing while she was posing for him."

"Then how did he miss the point of her?"

She picked up her wineglass and said abruptly, "Is this wine supposed to be so fizzy?"

Ralph swirled the wine around in his glass very fast, keeping the glass on the table, then lifted it to his mouth and inhaled before he tasted it. "It tastes excellent," he said, puzzled. "Spot-on, in fact."

"Oh," she said. She took another sip, determined to choke it down and not look like a schnook. "He missed the point of her," she said, "because he didn't really know her. He didn't take the trouble to know her. Not out of racism, but because to him, it must have been like when he painted me, and why I didn't let him paint me after a couple of times. The way he looked at you while he was painting you . . ."

Ralph compressed his lips uncomfortably, glanced down at the napkin in his lap, then looked up at Abigail again. "How was that?" he asked patiently.

"As if he were using you for his own ends," Abigail replied shortly, having strongly sensed Ralph's distaste for this topic. She sighed and tried another sip of wine. It tasted exactly as horrible as it had on her first sip. Well, the food would arrive soon, and then she could busy herself with a good lunch.

"But he was famous for not doing that," said Ralph.

"Well, of course," said Abigail, immediately regretting having said anything negative about Oscar, the way they'd all agreed they wouldn't. It was funny, the way she felt so loyal and loving toward him in her heart but came out with critical-sounding things when the biographers started asking about him. "That's right. I don't know why I felt that way. Maybe it was all in my head. And also, he was my husband. It was probably very different to model for him if you didn't know him that well. Are you a painter?"

"No," said Ralph, "not at all. Just a writer and an appreciator."

"You have a degree in art history, I think you said?"

"A master's," he said modestly, "from Columbia, and I'm thinking of going back for my Ph.D. I'd like to be a college professor, ultimately."

"So did I, once."

"In what?"

"English literature. I'm a big reader. But I'm not an academic type; I don't like thinking about books that way. You have to have a very analytical mind for that kind of thing."

"That is true."

"I would get into a classroom and just go mute. I would have thought so much about a book like *Jude the Obscure*, and then when my classmates started talking about all the themes and images and whatnot, my mind went completely blank. I only cared about Jude and Sue as people. How terribly, unbelievably sad the book was. And it spoiled it for me to have to think about how it was constructed; it felt like pulling apart your favorite toy as a kid to see what was inside." The wine must have been going to her head; she felt quite worked up about this all of a sudden. "It just killed the magic for me," she added before she could stop herself.

Ralph looked at her expressionlessly for a moment. Abigail thought she must have sounded like an ass.

"Something similar is happening for me with Oscar, but in the opposite direction," he said with measured precision, as if he were resisting the temptation to match her vehemence but privately shared it. "Maybe I should have written a purely intellectual book about him and never tried to find out about his life. But they convinced me that a biography was the way to go."

"Who is 'they'?"

"My agent," he said. "And the editor who acquired the project. They both said it would be a better book if I wrote it from a biographical standpoint, and so I started to feel like that might be interesting and worthwhile, to do the research and tell Oscar's life story." He pushed his gold glasses up the bridge of his nose.

His soup and her salad appeared. The cockles were golden puffballs. They weren't at all what she'd expected from the waiter's description. She stole an envious look at Ralph's soup. It looked cool, green, and light.

Ralph picked up his spoon and took a small, appreciative taste of his soup while Abigail speared a cockle with her fork. Finding it sizzling hot against her tongue, she set it back down and nibbled an asparagus spear.

"How is everything?" the waiter asked Ralph.

"Wonderful," said Ralph.

The waiter sighed and glided off. Ralph watched him go.

"Can I ask you something?" Abigail said.

"Well of course," he replied warily.

"This is very forward of me. I don't want to offend you. But this might be the only chance in my life to ask this question."

"Go ahead," he said even more warily.

"Oh, I've overstepped already," she said, horrified at herself. "Never mind."

"Please feel free. I can always choose not to answer it."

"Oh, well," she said. She took another sip of the fizzy fishy-tasting wine to steady herself. "I was just wondering what it's been like for you," she said in a tentative voice. "To be who you are."

"A black man?" he said. "You're wondering what it's like to be black?"

"Yes," she said. "Black, and . . . and, well, and homosexual. I wonder how that is, because I imagine it must be very hard. I'm asking out of great sympathy, believe me, thinking that you've had a hard time. I admire those who struggle with their identities and . . ." She stopped and looked down at her plate. Ralph was silent, staring at her, his expression unreadable. "I have terribly overstepped. I apologize."

Ralph still didn't say anything.

"Well," said Abigail, laughing, trying to hide the fact that she was close to tears of mortification. "I certainly have ruined a nice lunch!"

"No," he said. "Not ruined. But I never said anything about myself. I just wonder how you got that idea. About me."

"Oh, I always know," said Abigail, unbearably contrite. "I don't know how, but I do." She shrugged.

"You just *know*?" he said. There was an unmistakable note of teasing in his voice, almost relief that she had guessed his secret. "No one ever guessed before. My brother has no idea. My best friend from childhood keeps introducing me to girls. I mean women. I have a very straight personality."

"Well, maybe you could let all that go," she said.

"Why would I do that?"

"Because it's . . ." She ate a cockle. The crust was crisp and savory; the little animal inside was meaty and sweet. "Oh my! This is very good," she said.

"I'm not one of those people who needs to tell the whole world every detail of his life."

"And you don't mind, you don't feel lonely, that your brother and your best friend have no idea . . ."

"I prefer it that way."

"But what if you fall in love and want to be with someone . . . settle down with him?" She put down her fork and held up both hands. "I'm overstepping again. I know, I know, but I'm very interested."

"If and when I fall in love, I will make a decision based on that particular relationship and that particular individual. I'm in no rush."

"Well, I think that's fascinating," she said doubtfully.

"But truthfully, I imagine I will remain alone. That suits me. I enjoy having the possibility of defining who I am without labels or promises to anyone else. I have worked very hard to free myself from entanglements and obligations. It would have to be someone very unusual to make me want to give that up."

"Someone like Oscar," said Abigail before she could stop herself. She changed the subject. "Do you earn a living from your writing?"

"No," he said. "I work at the moment as an office temp. A temporary secretary. I have a long-term position at Citibank. I have a decent salary and good hours, and I can take days off when I need them. It's not ideal, but it's good for now. When I go back to school, I hope to have a teaching fellowship. If this book is at all successful, it should make it much easier for me to get into a superior program like Columbia's."

"Your future is all laid out for you," she said admiringly. "How old are you? You look about twenty-three."

"I'm thirty," he said.

Abigail couldn't tell whether he was miffed or flattered, but she suspected that although a straight man his age would be slightly insulted, Ralph, being a homosexual, would be glad to look younger. One had to appeal to women, the other to men. "When Ethan was a little boy," she said, "before he was diagnosed, when I thought he was normal, I used to think about his future. It was the best part of having a very small child. Because a small child is all potential. Nothing much else to rejoice about when they're two and three. It's a lot of mess and work and panic. But the reward is thinking about later, when all that work pays off."

"But it didn't pay off," Ralph said, perturbed.

"No, it didn't," she replied.

They ate in silence for a moment.

"No, it continued," she said.

Ralph looked up from his soup bowl.

"I work as hard for Ethan now as I did when he was a small boy," she went on. "When I die, I don't know what will happen to him; I've provided for his care at a small private place upstate. But will he like it there? Will he be all right?"

"Will he even know?" Ralph asked. He scraped his bowl, ate the final bite of soup. "Not to be unfeeling, but how aware is he of his surroundings? He is unusually deeply autistic, am I correct?"

"Oh! He's keenly aware, almost painfully so at times. I try to keep things regular, simple, calm, and quiet for him because he gets so overwhelmed by change, or noise, or upheavals. My death and his move will be a shock to him. I hope he can survive it."

"How do you know he knows if he can't tell you?"

"Because other autistics who aren't as locked in have explained what it's like, and they've described a whole world of sensation different from our own, but related. It's not verbal. It's not interpersonal. But it's no less real for that."

Ralph drank some wine, thinking about this.

"And," Abigail continued, "I think it's even more intense because there's no shield of words in your head, no comfort of knowing everyone else feels what you feel. Language and society keep a lot at bay for us. Talking to ourselves and to one another. Autistic people have no such armor."

The waiter returned, took away their empty first-course dishes, poured more wine into both their glasses, and then was gone.

"Why didn't you have more children?" Ralph asked Abigail.

"Neither Oscar nor I wanted more children," she said. "That is the short answer. I couldn't take care of anyone else but Oscar and Ethan. They both needed me so completely and in such different ways, there was never any room for anyone else. And Oscar . . . well, he had more children, just not with me."

"Right," said Ralph, as if he weren't sure how much he was supposed to ask or know about Oscar's relationship with Teddy where Abigail was concerned. "And the long answer?"

"The long answer is a little more complicated," she said. "No more children came along, although every now and then we would open ourselves to the possibility. With ambivalence on both sides, I have to add. So I think we were both relieved when it didn't happen. Our parents thought we should try for more, though, so we did. Ethan wasn't enough for them. They wanted a 'normal' grandchild. Especially Oscar's parents, since Ethan was all they got. I have two sisters, and they had three children each, so my parents had plenty of normal grandchildren to look for the afikomen at the family seders."

Ralph caught the eye of the waiter as he glided forth from the kitchen laden with plates. Abigail had a sudden image of Ralph and this beautiful young man entangling their limbs, white and black, in some imaginary realm of classical marble statues on a dappled Impressionist riverbank with the Italian Renaissance artists' idea of Jerusalem in the background, those sheer, high, topographically unlikely mountains with their dizzying gorges and plunging waterfalls, strange black carrion birds wheeling high overhead.

"Everything all right?" asked the waiter.

"I haven't had trout meunière in so long," said Abigail. "This is terrific!"

The waiter fluttered doelike lashes and was gone.

"Oh!" Abigail exclaimed in a burst of wine-warmed chumminess. "Do you know what Teddy's friend Lila said to me yesterday?"

"No," said Ralph.

"She's in love, but she can't bring herself to tell Teddy—you know, Claire. Amazing that she told me, when she had only just met me. But I suppose that was safer. She said she's afraid Teddy will resent her happiness or feel left out. And she's seventy-four. . . ."

"That's something," said Ralph with blank wonderment.

Abigail could tell that he couldn't imagine being that old and feeling much of anything at all. Back when she was his age, old age had seemed as distant as a faraway time zone or planet. She had imagined the state of agedness as being like a Rembrandt self-portrait: the subject lit from within by a golden, ancient light, inscrutably wrinkled, at one with his achievements and beliefs, about to slide through the terrible black tunnel between this world and the next. The very idea of two people falling in sexual love at that fragile, faraway stage of life used to make her mind quail and shut down. The thought of old bodies conjoined, old faces mashed together, quavery voices making guttural sounds had seemed so undignified to her, it was obscene.

"This is a terrible time to be young," she burst out.

"What do you mean?" Ralph asked.

"I love the computer; I spend as much time using it as anyone else. Maybe that's why I'm saying this. I can see how much my life has changed. The feeling I get about what's going on, which, I admit, is only from what I read, is that the young are highly sophisticated now, bright and educated and articulate, but no one is questioning the way things are in a massive, organized way. Kids' lives are abstract, cerebral. There's no cultural or political revolution, no upswell of anger. But there's never been more to protest! Gosh, do I sound like an old crackpot." She quoted in a high, self-righteous bleat, " 'When I was your age, I walked ten miles to school barefoot through the snow.' "

Ralph laughed. He held his wineglass up and looked off into the distance behind her left shoulder. "Things feel pretty hopeful to me," he said. "Don't worry about us."

"I do worry about you," she said, "and all of us."

Ralph smiled at her. "Older people always worry about younger people."

"And younger people always think they know what older people don't know," said Abigail, smiling also. "I have a business proposition for you."

He looked startled. "You do?"

"Hypothetically," said Abigail, "say I offered to stake you to graduate school. You could quit your job, study whatever you wanted. I have plenty of money, and nothing really to do with it all."

"Why would you do that?"

"Because," she said, "in return, you're going to write a book praising Oscar without reservation. That other guy, Henry Burke, is probably going to try to stir up controversy and trouble. I want one biography of Oscar at least to be flattering."

"I can't!" he said, surprised.

"I knew you'd say that," she said, "but just think about it. Oscar gave you so much, he inspired your career, and it's the least you can do to repay him."

"That may be," he said. "But I don't like feeling as if I'm being bought."

"You're not being *bought*; you're being paid extra to write the book you want to write. Just think about it; that's all I ask."

Ralph stared at Abigail for a while. The whites of his eyes were aggressively white and showed top and bottom between his eyelids and corneas, which made him look intense and intimidating.

Abigail stared right back at him, silently urging him to acquiesce to her will.

"I'll think about it," he said.

The feeling of triumph this gave her—premature though it may have been—was like a snort of cocaine, not that she had ever actually tried cocaine, but she had read enough about it to know its biochemical simulacrum when she felt it.

PART FOUR

Ten

"I can't have breakfast this morning," Lila was saying to Teddy in a tone of bashful apology.

It was Saturday morning, just half an hour before their standing breakfast date. It was Lila's turn to come to Teddy's; Teddy had just been slicing fruit. The hand that held the receiver was slightly sticky with plum juice even though she'd rinsed her hands quickly when the phone had rung.

"Are you feeling all right?" Teddy asked.

There was a brief silence on the other end of the phone. "Oh, yes."

"Then why can't you come?"

Another silence.

"Stop being coy! It's that man, isn't it?"

"His name is Rex," said Lila, laughing a little. "Yes, he's here right now."

Teddy blinked in surprise. She hadn't actually thought Rex was at Lila's; she had only been teasing. For some reason, she had assumed that Lila's not coming over today had had something to do with her grandchildren.

"At your house?"

"Right here," said Lila. "Next to me."

"You're still in bed?" Teddy asked, choking slightly on some foreign emotion.

Another silence.

"Well, you can bring him over if you want to," said Teddy. "I'd like to meet him, and there's plenty of food. I was thinking of making a kielbasa omelette; men love sausage, don't they? Oscar always did."

"Thanks," said Lila, purring in spite of herself, Teddy could tell. "I think we're all right where we are. Next Saturday, though, I promise, rain or shine."

"All right," said Teddy, "I'll eat all the food myself. Say hello to him, assuming he knows who I am." She hung up and stalked back to the kitchen, not hungry anymore. It was a hot, overcast morning, and the air felt like a wet towel. The back door was open; the smell of exhausted foliage blew in on a limp-wristed breeze. Teddy half-consciously hefted an uncut plum in one hand, squeezing it gently, the way physical therapists teach stroke victims to squeeze rubber balls to rehabilitate their hand strength. She took a small bite of it, then another bite. It wasn't perfect, but it was pretty damn close. Juice ran down her chin, and she didn't bother to wipe it off. So Lila and Rex were having a full-blown affair, and from the sound of Lila's voice, it had been going on longer than just one night. When had she planned to tell Teddy about this? Maybe it was unfair of Teddy to mind having their breakfast canceled at the last minute because of a man, but she did mind. She didn't begrudge Lila her sexual happiness, of course . . . or did she? No matter what, it just seemed impolite to call half an hour before Lila was supposed to arrive, after Teddy had shopped for their meal and was already preparing it.

Teddy threw the plum pit out into the yard, where it disappeared into the greenery. Now what? It was 7:30 on a Saturday morning, and the whole day lay yawning in front of her. Maybe because she had expected to have company, her loneliness, which she normally kept at bay, felt intolerable. Normally, she had a number of activities in reserve as bulwarks against this common sort of loneliness, among them reading *The New Yorker* carefully, from "The Talk of the Town" to the movie reviews, playing solitaire at the kitchen table while she listened to NPR, weeding the garden, or, in moments of real desperation, creating a time-consuming, nitpicky task like sorting through her thousands of recipe cards or piles of catalogs or boxes of papers. . . .

She marched back to the telephone, picked up the receiver, and dialed Lewis's number. He answered on the eighth ring, just when she had been about to give up.

"Hello?" He sounded out of breath.

"Were you running?"

"Teddy!"

The frank gladness in his voice cheered her up immediately. "Hello, Lewis. Lila just stood me up for my usual Saturday-morning date, and I just made fruit salad and walnut coffee cake and I've got a kielbasa and half a dozen eggs and some fresh chives and red peppers. Want to come over for breakfast?"

"Red peppers give me dyspepsia," said Lewis.

"Lewis!" She laughed. "No one gets dyspepsia anymore."

"Bring it all over here," he said. "I'll send Benny for you in the car. I have to stay home today because I'm supervising the decorator, who will be here in about an hour and who has to be watched every minute. She wants me to spend more on this living room than the queen of Persia."

"How much did the queen of Persia spend on her living room?"

"Will you come?" Lewis asked.

"Why don't I just call a car service?"

"Darling, you're just over the Queensboro Bridge. He'll be there before you know it."

"The Midtown Tunnel is faster."

"But the toll!" said Lewis.

She laughed again; Lewis was as rich as the queen of Persia, whoever she was. "I'll be waiting with my little basket of delicacies all packed up."

"Put on your bonnet," said Lewis. "It looks like rain."

Forty minutes later, a black Town Car pulled up in front of Teddy's house. She got into it with a plastic shopping bag filled with food. Inside the car, it was air-conditioned and quiet and smelled of leather.

"Hello, Benny," she said to Lewis's driver. Benny, as always, looked very dapper. Today, he wore a plaid driving cap and an orchid yellow sweater vest over a flesh pink Oxford shirt; his smooth pink face was so well shaved, he gave the impression of being either prepubescent or unable to grow whiskers. His full head of short black hair gleamed with some sort of unguent.

"Someone's over the moon that you're coming," he said in the Dickensian-orphan Cockney accent he never tried to modulate into anything more upper-crust.

"Is he," said Teddy, settling back against the leather seat and watching scruffy, sweaty Greenpoint slide by, the store awnings—

UNISEX SALON, FLORIST, BUTCHER—aluminum siding, spindly little trees growing out of the sidewalk. "As it happened, I was free to-day."

She and Benny had for years shared the tacit knowledge that visiting Lewis was a bit of a chore for her. Lewis never came to Teddy's house, not, she suspected, out of any snobbism about her neighborhood or the circumstances in which she lived, because Lewis was not a snob in any way. She suspected the reason was that he didn't want to be reminded of Oscar, even though Oscar had never set foot in the India Street house. Greenpoint had been Oscar's turf, and Lewis's feelings for Oscar when he was alive had been complicated and mixed at best. Lewis had been Oscar's lawyer, and, as such, had had to tolerate being taken for granted and treated by the great artist as a sort of repository for his furies and resentments toward the art world. Oscar was given the brush-off by one of his best collectors; when Emile Grosvenor died, his son Laurent had taken over the gallery and started giving Oscar fewer shows; the modern art museum in Amsterdam hung one of his subway nudes in an alcove, which he had considered insulting; always, Lewis had been there to take the brunt of Oscar's outrage, although there was very little he could do about any of it. And meanwhile, Lewis had been not so secretly in love with Oscar's mistress, who also happened to be his own secretary. Now that Oscar was dead, he had become something of an out-and-out bugbear for Lewis, his bête noire.

Benny made a left onto McGuinness Boulevard and the car went straight onto the Pulaski Bridge, crossing the Newtown Creek to Queens over a low-lying landscape with church spires and old houses that hearkened back to a nineteenth-century village just across the river from Manhattan. Teddy, who had never had a driver's license, had always loved being driven through the city, looking through car windows as it all went by. Her daughter Samantha often said she turned into a cat when she rode in a car, staring unblinkingly and indiscriminately and fixedly out the window, sitting very still and tense, as if she were about to pounce on prey.

As she rode along, she pictured Lila lolling amorously in her big bed next to a good-looking, slightly younger man, both of them naked. In her mind, Lila was an odalisque, glossy, voluptuous, and aglow.

"The view of Manhattan from this bridge is one of the wonders of this city," she said out of nowhere to Benny as they climbed high into the sky, heading east above Queens on a sinuously curving ramp, past billboards that seemed to float in thin air, and then curved around 180 degrees onto the Fifty-ninth Street Bridge.

"I never tire of it," said Benny.

Benny had lived in the States for more than thirty years, but his accent was as strong as if he were still in London. Teddy's father had been the same way; he'd lived in New York for almost twenty years, but he'd spoken like a British nobleman till the day he died, but he wasn't moneyed from birth; although his family had lived on an estate in Gloucestershire, the old family money was fairly well depleted by the time he came along. He had been educated, but just barely. As a young émigré to New York, in the 1920s, out of some maverick financial genius native only to him and evident nowhere else in his lineage, he'd made millions on Wall Street out of thin air, and that was where it had all gone back to when Teddy was nineteen. Still, riding in a chauffered car all these decades later was still as ingrained in Teddy as Benny's accent was in him. No matter where you ended up, you never lost where you came from, never shook that particular dirt from your feet.

As Benny pulled up under the awning of Lewis's building, on

East Seventy-seventh between Park and Lexington, the doorman was immediately on hand to open Teddy's door for her and help her out of the car. "Miss St. Cloud," he said with slightly bowed head. "Mr. Strathairn is expecting you." He took her bag of food from her and ushered her through the lobby, with its bronze-framed mirrors, hand-painted wallpaper, and brocade upholstery, and then into the elevator, finally relinquishing the bag of food just before the doors closed.

Lewis was standing at his open door when she stepped out of the elevator. He immediately took her bag from her while kissing her fervently on both cheeks. They were about the same height. Lewis, like Teddy, was thin, and he was almost completely bald. His face was lean, angular; he had piercing blue eyes that were now examining her with frank rapaciousness.

"You're really here," he said. "Come in, come in."

"I hope you're hungry," she said, walking past him, bracing herself for the inevitable attack of claustrophobia. Lewis was constantly redecorating the place in hopes, perhaps, of creating spaciousness, letting in a little air, but he and his longtime decorator, Ellen, had been locked for years in battle over his accumulation of things—bric-a-brac and mementos from his travels, old *Playbills*, dog-eared paperback books, enamel dishes filled with paper clips, foreign coins, defunct subway tokens, fortune-cookie slips, cuff links, heaps of "claptrap," as Ellen called it. He even stockpiled the flyers that were handed out to passersby in the street, those glorified coupons for a free eye exam or trial gym membership or cell phone with purchase of a package plan; there were always twelve or fifteen of these on his coffee table alone.

"I'm very hungry," he said, laughing. "But don't worry, if I weren't, I would pretend to be."

Teddy headed straight into his kitchen, the one room in the apartment that had a little space to move around in, if only because Lewis wasn't a cook and had little in the way of equipment. Still, the countertop was covered with stacks of old *Sports Illustrated*s. "Move your porn, please," she commanded, handing him an arm-load.

Teddy unpacked the bag, found a skillet in a cupboard and some butter in the refrigerator, and got to work chopping the red pepper and chives and sausage, beating the eggs. When the omelette was done, she cut it in half, spread it thickly with sour cream, and put the pieces on two plates with a mound of fruit salad on each. She carried the plates into the dining room and used one of them to shove aside a stack of mail on Lewis's place mat. She set the other plate on the place mat across from his chair and sat down. He had set the table with cutlery, glasses of orange juice, and cups of hot coffee, finding room to put it all amid stacks of mail, half-read books and magazines, an inexplicable bag from the hardware store, and eight or ten equally inexplicable carved masks. Teddy busied herself with cream and sugar while Lewis leaned his face over his plate and happily inhaled sausage-scented steam.

"You've outdone yourself," he said. Lewis loved to eat well, but he had never bothered to learn to cook. Teddy knew, because he had told her, that he ate his dinners at a little candlelit bistro on Lexington or stayed in and heated up ready-cooked gourmet meals from a private catering company. But nothing, he'd added pointedly, tasted as good as a meal made by someone he loved. Teddy had chosen through the years to ignore this appeal; she made a deliberate point of not cooking in his kitchen more than twice a year. She was not and had never been particularly wifely, and she'd never wanted to give Lewis any romantic encouragement of any kind, because that would lead immediately to a profound and intense entanglement she had always been a little afraid of, although she had never been exactly sure why. Anyway, it galled her that he wouldn't simply take it upon himself to learn to grill a simple filet or steak, steam some broccoli, for God's sake. Cooking was far too easy, and Lewis far too intelligent, for him to have to resort to eating either restaurant or premade meals. Also, he could easily have hired a cook.

"Where did the masks come from?" Teddy asked. "And more important, why are they on the table?"

"Bali," said Lewis. "Ellen thinks they'll go up on that wall above the sideboard."

"What's in the hardware-store bag?"

"Hardware," said Lewis with a grin.

"To hang the masks?"

"I guess so. Teddy, this omelette is superb."

"It would have been better with chorizo or Italian sausage, something spicy and piquant instead of smoky. Lila loves kielbasa; that's why I got it."

"Why did she stand you up this morning?"

"A man," said Teddy. "She met him in the street and now he's staying over, apparently."

"Lucky him," said Lewis with one of his sidelong looks at Teddy. "Lucky both of them."

She brushed him off, as she had done for decades. "Indeed," she said. "When is Ellen arriving?"

Lewis had the grace to look sheepish.

"I knew it," she said. "Why would she come on a Saturday? Someday you'll have the good manners to come and visit me in Greenpoint."

"You know why I don't want to," said Lewis. "And I always send Benny for you."

"You don't want to because you're afraid Oscar's ghost will come out and say boo."

"I would prefer not to encounter Oscar in any form."

Teddy examined Lewis's face. As usual, his expression was benign, seemingly blank, with the barest hint of a self-mocking lift at one corner of his mouth, even while he chewed. She wasn't taken in by his apparent mildness, which was merely the lawyerly habit of many years, even in retirement, of presenting an impassive facade; behind it, his thoughts were always simmering, his feelings always churning. As a boss, he had been quietly exacting and not so quietly appreciative, at first merely of Teddy's efficiency, tact, and integrity, but then after his movie-star wife had run off with one of her directors, his admiration frankly and immediately expanded to include her beauty, wit, charm, and physical being. One night, she'd stayed at the office late, asked to have a word with him, went into his office and shut the door, and told him, frankly and without fuss, that this turn in his feelings had made it difficult for her to continue as his secretary. Lewis had asked her whether she and Oscar were having an affair, she'd replied that they were, had been for many years, and he'd immediately agreed to transfer her to one of his colleagues and hire a new secretary, since it was now impossible for them to work together under such circumstances. Their friendship had continued through the years unimpeded by romantic complications, if only because Lewis, passionate as he felt about Teddy, had proved pragmatically capable of transcending his desires. "I'll take as much of you as I can get," he had told her more than once. This must have fulfilled certain needs for both of them. The fact that a man as intelligent and successful as Lewis would have chosen to languish for decades with unrequited love for Teddy, his former secretary, made no sense unless she took into consideration the real possibility that after his wife had left him, he had preferred simple un-fulfilled yearning to messy conjugal complexity.

"He died owing you a lot of money," she said with teasing sym-pathy, "and you chose not to dun his widow for it."

"His widow had other things to worry about, and it was money I could easily spare," Lewis said, taking the bait.

"He could have paid you," Teddy said.

"Oscar chose not to pay me because he didn't like the fact that I failed to urge him to sign the exclusive contract with Barbara Solomon. Of course, that was my fault. Never mind that I told him, 'My job is not to advise you about career moves; it's to advise you about a contract's soundness.' He took a pass and regretted it and then blamed me for every bad thing that happened to him there-after."

"More coffee?"

"Please." Lewis cast around under a stack of bills and pulled out his fake ceramic cigarette and clamped it between his teeth.

"Your oral-fixation device," Teddy remarked, pouring each of them a fresh cup.

"I wonder," said Lewis, "whether I have now become irre-sistible to you due to the vicarious thrill of Lila's new romance."

"You wonder that, do you," said Teddy.

"I can't help but remark on your sudden appearance at my doorstep bearing seductive foodstuffs."

"Kielbasa is seductive?"

"Very seductive," said Lewis.

Teddy found to her surprise that she had no ready comeback to this.

"I will take that as a yes," said Lewis, watching her closely.

Teddy looked steadily back at him. "I bought the kielbasa for Lila," she said after a moment.

"Teddy," said Lewis. "Do you honestly plan to go to your grave without replacing Oscar?"

"My grave," said Teddy, laughing. She stood up and began to pace around the room. "Why are you bringing up my grave, of all subjects?" She picked up one of the carved masks. It bore a resemblance to a wizened monkey and reminded her of a death mask. She put it down again quickly, as if it were red-hot.

"Well," said Lewis. "I've been thinking a lot about my own lately. How near I am to it."

"Have you really been alone all these years since Deborah left you?"

"No," said Lewis, looking her in the eye.

"You've had girlfriends?"

"I've had women."

"All these years that you and I have known each other," said Teddy, "I've never known you to have so much as a date."

"You assume I tell you everything."

"I do assume that," she said, surprised.

"Well, don't."

Teddy lifted another mask. This one looked like a tragic owl. "Well, did you have dates with one woman or a series of them?"

"What difference does it make?"

"I'm just curious."

"I've been involved, as they say, with several women over the years."

"Ellen?" Teddy asked. Ellen was wildly unsuitable for Lewis, Teddy thought; she was so shrewd and brassy.

"Well, I could be, if I wanted."

"But you're not."

"Not yet, anyway," he said. His tone was light, teasing, and tender.

Teddy set the mask down and ran her finger slowly along the sideboard, then examined her fingertip for dust. There was none.

"You're jealous!" said Lewis with delight.

"Of Ellen? Oh, come on. How could you possibly fall in love with Ellen?"

"Who said falling in love had anything to do with anything?"

She rolled her eyes. "Coffee cake?"

"Coffee cake," Lewis repeated as Teddy went into the kitchen. She came back with two plates of cake and set one in front of Lewis.

"Fresh-baked this morning," she said.

"How do you stay so slender when you eat so much, Teddy?" Lewis asked her. "Do you go into the bathroom after meals and stick your finger down your throat?"

"Of course I do," she said, sitting down.

"Waste of good food."

"Oh no, I regurgitate it whole, predigestion, then box it up and donate it to the poor."

"Lucky poor."

"They appreciate it."

Lewis took a bite of cake. "Good cake."

"Of course it is."

"*Joy of Cooking*?"

"Is that the only cookbook you've ever heard of?"

"There are other cookbooks?"

They ate in easy silence for a moment.

"Teddy," said Lewis, putting his fork down. "I think it's really time we went to bed together."

Teddy choked on a piece of brown-sugar topping. "You think it's really *what*?"

He was looking intently at her. "You heard me."

Coughing, she waved him away. "And wreck our friendship?"

"I'd happily wreck our friendship if it meant going to bed together."

She regained control of her windpipe. "Good Lord," she said. She cleared her throat. "What's gotten into you?"

"All this talk about the grave." He laughed. "What have we got to lose?"

Teddy smiled inscrutably at him. The clock behind her ticked loudly in the silence—*tick-tock, tick-tock*—hollow, skeletal clicks, too apropos for comfort.

Lewis sighed and said, "Two biographies about Oscar. Who cares about art anymore anyway? Who really gives a fig?"

"About art," said Teddy, "very few people give a fig. About Oscar, even fewer. But these two boys have wild hairs. Well, not really so wild. Tame hairs. One of them, the white one, Henry, seems to see Oscar as an emblem of lost manliness, a kind of visceral, unapologetic masculinity that's gone out of fashion. The other, the black one, Ralph, sees him, I would say, as an aesthetic maverick, but slightly disapprovingly so, or so it seems to me; he seems to think Oscar hamstrung himself by eschewing the abstract. But he reveres him nonetheless; they both do. The white one, who's rather cute actually and extremely sexually frustrated, keeps quoting some hackneyed female poet he wrote a biography about, which gives me some pause. This poet; Oscar. Clearly he has no standards. Oscar was no genius, let's face it. Henry seems to think they're both unjustly forgotten."

"I love how brutal you are," said Lewis.

"I know you do," said Teddy. "It's entirely for your entertainment."

"I think you're being a little coy. Of course you think he was a genius."

"Not coy at all," said Teddy. Throughout this conversation, she had been half-aware of the fact that she had been watching his mouth more closely than usual; now she was noticing that his upper lip had a cleft above it, as if pressed there by a small child's finger in clay. "A genius is someone who changes the fabric of his own time and stands above everyone around him. Oscar Feldman kicked around with the best of them, but he didn't transcend them or show them the way."

"Hitler was a genius?"

"An evil genius."

"I like this sophomoric little game."

"Sophomoric in the extreme!"

Lewis and Teddy both laughed.

"I'm planning a trip to Tuscany," said Lewis. "Want to come along? My treat."

"When?" Teddy asked with longing.

"November, December, whenever you want."

"Why are you planning to go?"

"To get you to come with me."

"Oh, Lewis," said Teddy. She sighed. "You know I love you. You know I think you're the best man in the world."

"Besides your grandson," said Lewis, as if he were forcing himself not to take too much pleasure in the compliment because of the implicit rejection behind it.

"He's three."

"And now that Oscar's dead."

"You're a far better man than Oscar ever was."

"That is so true," he said, his blue eyes flashing, "but what mystifies me . . . I don't need to say it. My wife left me for a real turd. And you stuck with the likes of Oscar."

Teddy looked piercingly at Lewis for a moment or two. "I wonder why," she said finally.

"Women seem to find assholes irresistible," said Lewis. "It's Darwinian, I guess. You want to be put in your place, left slightly askew, because then you know you're with an alpha male. I have no desire to put you in your place or knock you off-kilter, which apparently translates into erotic nullity. But I'm arguably an alpha-male type. I just don't care to beat my hairy breast and bellow about it the way Oscar did."

"You're pretty smart for an old guy," said Teddy, laughing.

"Maybe Ellen wants to go to Tuscany."

"I mean it. Most men of our generation don't have a clue about women."

"Well, the nice ones do, because we have plenty of time to study you without the mind-sapping distraction of actual entanglement."

"I thought you said you'd had women."

"I have," he replied vehemently. "I'm no monk."

"Why haven't you fallen in love again?"

"I've been pining for you. It's the truth."

"No one pines this long. You must have wanted to pine."

He said, "I haven't entirely enjoyed it."

They looked at each other.

"Lewis," said Teddy.

"Teddy."

She tried to say something, failed, then shook her head decisively. "I'm a bit flummoxed all of a sudden."

"That's a new one."

Teddy stood and made her way over to where Lewis sat. "Stand up," she said. "I want to try something."

He stood, nudged his chair aside with his leg, and faced her. She looked right into his eyes and put her hands on his shoulders. "Dance with me a little," she said.

"What are we, geriatrics?" he asked, laughing. Still, he put one hand on her waist and with the other lifted and took her hand from his right shoulder. He began to lead her in a medium-tempo fox-trot. They hadn't broken their mutual gaze. Their eyes were almost on the same level. "We're too young for this," said Lewis. "Let's get drunk instead."

"Dance with me, I want my arm about you," Teddy sang in an unpracticed voice that cracked a little with laughter. "The charm about you will carry me through to . . ."

Lewis laid his cheek against Teddy's and danced her purposefully into the living room. "There's liquor in here," he said.

"Indulge me," she said. "We're characters in an old movie."

"They drank whiskey in old movies," said Lewis.

"Heaven, I'm in Heaven," Teddy sang on, smiling but no longer laughing, leaning her head against his, feeling the satisfying intimate hardness of another human skull against her own, "and my heart beats so that I can hardly speak . . ."

"At least you can carry a tune," he said. "It could be worse." He turned his head and kissed her without breaking the dance.

"And I seem to find the happiness I seek," she sang against his mouth as if she didn't know it was there, "when we're out together dancing cheek to cheek." Then she stopped singing; they stopped dancing. It should have felt far more odd than it did, kissing Lewis, but instead it felt like something long overdue and inevitable. He knows what he's doing, Teddy thought, surprised. His mouth was firm and sensitive. She had not imagined it would be so; she had imagined he would be either overly enthusiastic with his tongue or that his lips would feel dry and uncommitted. Instead, his lips felt like something live and exciting against hers, dancing with her mouth; his tongue was barely there, tantalizingly. Their bodies pressed together warmly, with equal pressure, equal need. Suddenly she was so aroused, she could hardly stand up. She started to laugh again, out of giddiness and surprise rather than amusement. "Lewis!"

"I tried to tell you," he said. "Now come to bed."

In his bedroom, she clawed at his clothes. He stood, chuckling, helping her, while she undressed him. Then she stripped off her own clothes and they fell together onto his bed, naked and necking. The light coming in his bedroom window was bright and clear; she could see every gray hair on his chest, every small sag and wrinkle on his body, and she knew he could see hers, but they were both still slim and well shaped. Their bodies looked good together, like a matched set. They both looked so much better than she had expected. His thighs were well muscled, his flanks were lean, and his stomach was flat but endearingly slightly rounded, like a small boy's. She wrapped her arms and legs around him and rocked him a little, looked into his blue, ardent, eternally humorous eyes, and was struck both by how well she knew him and how exciting this was. His skin against the length of her body felt warm and velvety; the hairs on his chest and legs rasped against her smooth skin, so she felt small, intensely pleasurable electrical shocks everywhere.

"Hello, sailor," she said.

"Hello, beautiful," he whispered back. "You should have done this about twenty years ago. I had a real erection to offer back then."

She took his penis in her hand and looked down at it; it was just about firm enough for her purposes, and perfectly shaped. "Your cock is beautiful," she said with joy. "You should have warned me!"

He was silent for a moment, his head pressed between her breasts, shaking with laughter. Then he looked up at her and said with a roguish smile she had never seen on him before, "I really should have warned you about my cock."

She laughed, too, and then they had nothing more to say to each other for a long time.

Eleven

"Yeah?" said Maxine into her cell phone, cigarette still in her mouth.

"Maxine Feldman?" said a youngish man's voice she didn't recognize.

"That's me."

"This is Dexter Harris from the *New York Times*. How are you today?"

"Ducky, thanks," said Maxine.

"I wonder if you have time to answer a couple of questions?"

"Of what nature?"

"Concerning," said the young man, "your brother's famous diptych, *Helena and Mercy*."

Maxine clapped the phone shut and pitched it across the room.

It clattered onto her worktable and lay still among the brushes like a dead beetle. She stumped into her bedroom and got dressed. It was eight o'clock on a Saturday morning, for God's sake. She wanted to throttle that Claire St. Cloud with her bare hands. But of course it wasn't Claire who had told; Claire, naturally, wanted to protect Oscar, too. They all did, or so it had seemed. The only people who knew about the painting's real author besides the mousy little man who had hidden Maxine's signature all those years ago were the four of them around that table the other day. And Ethan, of course, assuming he was capable of knowing anything.

And Katerina. Maxine's hands paused on the buttons of her shirt. Well, if Katerina had told, there wasn't much Maxine could say. She couldn't deny that she'd painted *Helena*. Her signature would be easy enough to uncover. She had signed the damn thing because, of course, subconsciously she must have hoped that someday this would happen.

This was just the sort of nice little story that people loved to read about over their breakfasts. "Look here, John, some painter named Maxine Feldman passed off one of her paintings as her brother's and it's in the Met and no one ever knew! It says here it was because of a bet, and she promised him at the end of his life that she would never tell, but someone else told. . . ."

Her cell phone tinkled its lilting little melody again. There was nothing she could say to these people; either she had to lie or break her promise to Oscar. She poured coffee, wandered into her studio, walked over to the window. The phone stopped ringing, but a few minutes later, as she was just finishing her first cup of coffee, it rang again. She ignored it again and rubbed Frago's head; Frago always followed her everywhere in the mornings until he'd been given his walk, which also involved feeding him his breakfast, and then, sated and exercised for the day, he would subside into a comatose sleep under the table or on the couch. He looked up at her, his eyes liquid with yearning.

"I know," she told him in the exaggeratedly gruff voice she always used when she spoke to him. "I know what you want. I read you loud and clear; you are not a mystery to me in any way."

She got out his leash, clipped it to his collar, put her keys and wallet in her pants pocket, and left her cell phone behind.

Outside, the street was completely empty except for a couple of boys in their twenties or early thirties, swaying arm in arm along the sidewalk, looking dreamy, either on their way to brunch after a night of sex or coming home drunk or drugged from a club or party. Their footsteps echoed a little in the hazy morning air. As they passed Maxine, one of them said, "Good morning!"

Unused to being visible to anyone under fifty, surprised, Maxine said, "You, too!" She set off toward the little grassy enclosure near Houston Street where dogs were allowed to run unhindered by leashes. As they walked, she pulled bits of kibble from her trousers pocket and fed them to Frago, who took each piece with undiminished enthusiasm and eagerly resumed his wait for the next one. The kibble was the same crap she'd been feeding him for years, baked nuggets of pulverized meat by-products, cheap grain, preservatives, and God knew what else. Poor mutt, he lived for it. He didn't know any better. Occasionally, he found a chicken bone or a bit of pizza on the sidewalk and managed to swallow it before Maxine could jerk his head away, but other than those windfalls, he never got anything good. Maxine didn't believe in pampering animals. Anyway, he seemed perpetually grateful to receive these dubious tidbits from her hand every morning on their slow rounds.

The dog run near Houston Street was already full of dogs and their owners when Maxine and Frago got there. Maxine scanned the crowd before she let Frago loose. There was no sign of the psychotic German shepherd, so she let him go. Frago immediately shuffled off to the far corner to sniff the anus of his old friend Walter, a dignified beagle of about the same vintage. Walter acquiesced to this greeting with a doleful expression, returned the favor, and then the two old dogs began their usual lope around the fence together, sniffing pee and adding their own elderly dribbles to the mélange. Maxine watched with a smile she was unable to help. She was amused by the way dogs were so insatiably curious about one another, just like people. No wonder the two species got along so symbiotically.

She turned her attention to the human population of the run. She didn't want to admit it, but she was looking for the black-haired girl who looked exactly like Oscar. Of course, she didn't know for certain that this girl really was her niece, but she suspected that she was, and had covertly watched her, wondering whether she also suspected who her aunt was. Maxine sometimes caught the girl watching her curiously and was certain suddenly that she recognized her aunt, but later, at home again, Maxine always dismissed this idea as ridiculous. How would she recognize Maxine? Maxine looked nothing like Oscar; he had taken after their mother, and she took after their father, which was why Oscar had been tall and beautiful and she was squat and ugly. Their father had been a peasanty shtetl Jew, their mother an aristocratic urban Jew, and the siblings had each inherited one parent's evident caste. If the girl noticed her aunt at all, Maxine had always concluded, it was because she was obviously intensely interested in other people. Sometimes Maxine made eye contact with her, and when that happened, the words that almost always rose to her tongue from some ancient genetic instinct were *bubbeleh, shayneh maydeleh, kind,* words she had never, to her memory, spoken aloud in her life.

But the girl who might have been either Ruby or Samantha wasn't here today. Maxine dawdled by one of the benches, debating whether or not to sit down. If she sat down, she would have to get up again. Such were the decisions necessitated by old age. Frago came up and briefly nuzzled her, then ambled off with Walter again. Here at the dog run, he was in his element; she was a visitor.

Maxine lowered herself to the bench seat and allowed her bones to settle there, to rearrange themselves to fit the ninety-degree angle of wood. She leaned back, sighed, wishing she'd had another cup of coffee. As she was lighting a cigarette, the girl who might have been her niece (girl? she was forty or thereabouts, but she looked girlish to Maxine) arrived, looking even more beautiful than usual in a red dress and cowboy boots, bare-legged, her hair loose and wild around her wide, pale face. She was arm in arm with a man who looked much younger than she, a sapling of a boy, lithe and sinewy, with his jeans slung so low that his hipbones showed, a head of hair so lively and self-possessed, it seemed to move independently of his head, like a tiny dog. Samantha/Ruby's dog was enormous, a Russian wolfhound named Svetlana. Svetlana bounded ahead of the two lovers into the run and disrupted a knot of smaller dogs who'd been tangling passionately together. "Svetlana!" yelled the girl in her husky voice.

She and Maxine locked eyes then and both of them looked startled.

Maxine was positive then that the girl was her niece and that she knew Maxine was her aunt. But she had thought this same thing at various times before, and had no proof either way about it.

The girl and her swain went laughing to a bench at the far end and sat there, entwined together, while Svetlana stumbled clumsily but with transparently good intentions into various canine social groups. When she came to Frago, he gave her a benign crotch sniff and nose touch and seemed to be done with her, but she stuck around him, as she sometimes did, loitering hopefully, sensing that he was less snooty than others, less inclined to give her the brush-off. Maxine had a strong feeling that she'd been a rescue dog, abused or abandoned, then brought into a shelter and adopted by this girl as a fully grown dog. She didn't seem properly able to connect with her own kind, for all her pedigree. She was like an inbred duchess, a brain-damaged blue blood.

Frago and Walter exchanged a look: Would they let this weird young beauty into their elderly perambulations? They seemed to agree with a kind of "What the hell" mutual shrug, because Svetlana fell in peaceably enough with them, seemingly calmed by their gentlemanly indifference. The three dogs came toward Maxine's bench, led by Frago, and surrounded her feet in a panting trio of fur and tongues and haunches. She could smell them in the hot morning sun, their doggy muskiness. She had never been this close to Svetlana; leaning down to pet her, she had a sudden urge to read her tag, something people almost never did in the dog run. It was considered a breach of etiquette for humans in here to express too much curiosity about one another's identities. Everyone felt perfectly free to ask the most intimate and nosy questions about one another's dogs' names, habits, funny proclivities, type of food, texture of feces, neuroses, and history, but nobody here revealed their own particulars; it just wasn't done.

Daringly, her heart beating a little faster, under cover of the girl's distraction with her boyfriend, Maxine grabbed Svetlana's tag and looked right at it. Her old eyes, behind thick bifocals, focused on the engraved name and address, and then Svetlana jerked away and began licking her own pink, hairless crotch. Maxine was left with a blurred impression of the name Ruby Feldman, but she wasn't sure. Yet she was sure. The girl looked like a female Oscar, uncannily; even her gestures were Oscar's, the careless way she flung her hands around when she talked, her expansive smile, that self-aware marshaling of her undeniable beauty and charm.

So this was Ruby, then, not Samantha. Maxine had never wanted anything to do with either of them, officially, since the day they'd been born. But having watched this girl—for what, two years now?—here at the dog run struggling with her poor sweet misfit of a dog, Maxine had become inadvertently, instinctively proprietary toward both girl and dog. She'd often itched to give advice to Ruby about Svetlana: "Be firmer with her. Don't let her walk ahead of you. Make her sit before you put her leash on." Auntlike advice, that was what it was; it came out of nowhere, involuntary, completely uncharacteristic, like the words *bubbeleh, shayneh maydeleh, kind.* Maxine's own Tante Esther had dispensed such advice, her mother's older sister, and Maxine had always chafed at it: "Such a pretty girl. You should smile more, maydeleh, wear something flattering, bubbeleh!" Maxine had wanted to smack her, had hated the way she smelled, sharp cologne undergirded with stale chicken fat; it had made her nauseous, and this sort of advice always brought that smell back, cloyingly intimate. . . .

Of course she wouldn't introduce herself to Ruby. What did someone like Ruby need with a decrepit old dyke of an aunt who'd never professed anything more kindly than indifference to her existence for her whole life? It was much too late for any kind of touching familial rapprochement, but here were their two dogs, lying side by side in the wood chips, panting in amicable unison in the summer heat. That was something in and of itself.

It was time to go home. Maxine heaved herself up, clapped her hands to alert Frago to their departure, and gimped toward the exit. As she did so, she caught Ruby's eye again, and looked quickly away; no point in inviting trouble. At the gate, Frago sat without being told and she clipped his leash to his collar, aware that her niece was watching. She thought, You see how he sits? You see how he lets me go out first? That's the way to have a calm and well-adjusted animal. They want you to be the leader; they want you to be strong. She waited for Frago to sit at her left heel, then closed the gate and led him home.

She walked in to the tumbling melody of her cell phone ring. She let Frago off the leash, made sure his water bowl was full, then went to the worktable and picked up the phone and answered it. "What?" she said.

"Maxine Feldman," said that same voice from earlier.

"Yeah," she replied. "You finally got me. I'm amazed you didn't wear out the battery of my phone. I should have turned it off."

"Sorry about that," said the young man. "I'm very sorry to disturb your morning. I just have a couple of questions. It shouldn't take long, five minutes at the most."

Maxine tapped her foot and bided her time, staring out the window at the sky, thinking about what she'd have for lunch. There was a can of chunky chicken noodle soup, some rye crackers. . . . Was there any tuna fish? Maybe there was some tuna fish. She was hungrier than usual; why was that? Then she realized she hadn't had breakfast.

"Hello?" the young man said.

"I was just wondering whether I have any tuna fish," said Maxine.

Dexter Harris laughed.

"Okay," said Maxine, "I give. Ask your questions so I can get to my lunch."

"You're of course familiar with your brother's diptych that hangs in the Met."

"Of course," said Maxine, amused by this polite little game. It reminded her of the matador's tricky dance with the confused, unsuspecting bull. "So who told you?"

"I'm sorry?"

"Oh, come on," said Maxine. "Who told you about *Helena*?"

"I'm not sure I understand what you mean."

"I mean I would love to know who told you the truth about that painting."

"Could you be more specific?"

Maxine looked through her thick lenses at the bright summer sky outside her windows. As her gaze shifted, black motes in both her eyes moved like schools of fat black fish through water. There were so many layers separating her from a pure view of the sky: motes, lenses, glass panes, chicken wire. Maybe she could get that into a painting.

She became aware of the phone, still pressed to her ear. What the hell were they talking about? She was hungry.

"The truth about *Helena*," said Maxine. The hell with it, she thought. He knew, she knew he knew, and if he was going to write some sort of story about it, she couldn't stop him. Well, she'd done her best to keep her promise to her brother, and now she was going to break it; there was no point anymore in keeping it. She went on, "It started when I made a bet with my brother in 1978 in the Washington Square Diner."

She heard him—was his name Dexter?—inhale with predatory relief, an almost sexual sound.

"It started with an argument," she went on, "about abstract versus figurative painting. The whole thing came about because I was a trained artist and he was mostly self-taught. I graduated from art school, and he dropped out after a couple of months. But I always drew, from the beginning, as a little girl. I always doodled and drew. Figures were my first impulse, artistically."

"Your first impulse," Dexter repeated. He was writing all of this down, of course.

"I taught Oscar to draw when we were kids, but that's neither here nor there. What I'm trying to say is, it wasn't a fluke. I always had a real aptitude for figurative art. Portraits were a strength of mine in art school. I studied the various techniques, the history of portraiture. Abstraction came later, after I had absorbed and rejected the more conventional painterly techniques. It seemed to me to be the best and in many ways the only way to describe human experience directly then. It transcended formalization, got at a deeper truth, a more direct relationship between painting and viewer, a direct visceral impression. I always intended my paintings to have a physical impact. Nothing effete or cerebral about them, but Oscar was mocking my work as if it were some prissy schoolgirl imitation. He told me he thought what I did was like mud pies, the easiest thing in the world, so I said, 'I know how to paint a nude woman as well as you do.' He said, 'Oh yeah?' It was like a schoolyard fight. I was mad as hell, and so was he. We bet each other a thousand bucks that we could each paint in the other's style a work good enough to pass off as the other's, the proof being that our dealers would accept them into our next shows. I used Oscar's painting *Mercy,* which he had recently finished, as the template for my imitation of his work, and he borrowed a couple of paintings I had just finished to use as his, and we were off to the races. Helena is Jane Fleming, of course, the art historian. She was my girlfriend at the time. She posed for me. I painted her as if I were Oscar, as if I looked at women the way he did. Oscar painted something so nonsensically bad, I understood that he had no fucking idea what abstraction was about. Just not a single clue. Marks on paper, fairly well organized, but without any aesthetic intent, any painterly intelligence. I have it here in my studio; I kept it for, shall we say, sentimental reasons."

"That is fascinating," said Dexter. "Would you be willing to talk more about the process of painting *Helena* in terms of impersonating your brother?"

Twenty minutes later, Maxine bade him good-bye, then dialed the first of the two numbers she had for Katerina, neither of which was a cell phone. A surly young man answered at the apartment she shared with the young couple. He snarled that Katerina was not in and hung up. The second number was Katerina's studio; it was unlikely she'd be there early on a Saturday morning; more likely, she was at her new lover's, allowing him to manhandle her tiny body and twist it into exotic pretzel shapes and bite her sweet neck with his crooked tobacco-stained teeth. Maxine waited doggedly through four rings, then five. Then, to her surprise, Katerina herself answered.

"Yes?"

"Katerina," Maxine stuttered, thrown off guard.

"Hello, Maxine!" said Katerina.

"I just got a call from the *New York Times,*" said Maxine, touched in spite of herself by the gladness in Katerina's voice.

"Oh, that's great," said Katerina. "What did they want?"

"You mean you don't have any idea?"

Katerina began, trying to put it all together to please Maxine, "Because . . ." She paused, clearly at a loss. "No, why?"

"You didn't tell them about *Helena*?"

"Me!" Katerina cried. "Tell them your secret? I would never."

Maxine blinked. "Well then, who was it? I just gave some five-year-old reporter the interview of his life. I figured there was no point playing footsie. Some Girl Scout at the Met has already uncovered my signature."

"Well, I think that's very exciting," Katerina said. "I wanted to tell, because I thought you deserved credit. I'm glad someone told. I wish it had been me."

"You can read all about it tomorrow," said Maxine, "if you read the *Times.*"

"Not usually," said Katerina, "but tomorrow I will. Congratulations. More papers will call you, of course. This is tremendous for you!"

"I suppose it is," said Maxine. She found that she was fluttering with excitement. Her life had just changed; her fate was made.

"See you Wednesday! I will bring something, to celebrate."

"Yes," said Maxine, bracing herself for more ginger beer, "see you Wednesday."

After she'd called the deli down the street and ordered the ingredients for tuna-salad sandwiches, Maxine clapped the phone's hinged halves together and went to the couch to await the ingredients of her lunch. So who, then? Claire was out; Abigail was out. Lila? Certainly not. None of those three would have told, she would have bet anything in the world.

Then she remembered who else knew and almost hit herself in the forehead. And she *would* tell, too. Running into Maxine the other night had no doubt triggered Jane's long-dormant memory of the whole thing, and then Paula Jabar's spoutings had likewise awakened her feminist instincts; she'd probably gone home full of rancor at the male-dominated art world and had decided to right what she saw as a historical inaccuracy, make sure her old girlfriend Maxine got her long-overdue due. She was an art historian, after all; art history mattered to her. Although she'd taken a number of days to get around to it, maybe that was just because she'd had other things to do, dates with her new boyfriend and whatnot; that was no longer Maxine's concern. Jane Fleming had spilled the beans; of course she had. And since Maxine had brought up the subject that night, she had to admit to herself that maybe she had been hoping this would happen all along. She had hinted to Henry about digging up a scandal, brought *Helena* up with Jane, and also, of course, with Lila and Claire, told Abigail about it, discussed it within earshot of Katerina. Of course she had been hoping this would happen. Her own loose-cannon rant to Ralph, revealing her lifelong jealousy of Oscar, should have tipped her off, as well. Maxine, like most people, had never been fully in control of her own motives and actions, but at least in hindsight she could see where they'd been leading. So it had come to fruition, this seed she had unwittingly planted all over town; she hadn't broken her promise, but she'd made damn sure the truth got out.

She owed Jane one. In the interests of telling her this as soon as possible, she dug out her ancient little phone book and, squinting through her glasses, found a scrawled number in the *F*'s for "Fleming, Jane." It was several decades old, and the black ink was now faded to brown. She punched the numbers into her phone and waited. What were the chances?

The number rang at least; so it was still live, maybe recycled by the phone company for the fourth time since Jane had owned it. One ringy-dingy, then two; on the third ring, someone picked up and said, "Hello?"

"Jane!" said Maxine, shocked.

"Who is this?"

Maxine was silent for an instant—who was she, anyway? Then she remembered. "Maxine Feldman," she said, relieved.

What an odd experience. She had momentarily forgotten her own name. And she was talking to . . . Jane Fleming. Ah.

"Maxine," said Jane. She sounded cautious.

"I owe you a drink, it appears," said Maxine. "I won't pretend I'm not glad you outed me. Or rather, us."

There was a silence. Then Jane said, "How did you know it was me?"

"I ruled out everyone else," said Maxine with a chuckle.

"You're not angry with me?"

"No. Why would I be angry?"

"You asked me not to say anything the other night. But my conscience got the better of me. This is about your artistic legacy, and not only yours. Too many female artists have been overlooked and underestimated for too fucking long. So I called Dexter. He's a young hotshot at the *Times,* their contemporary art writer. I figured he'd do the story justice, and I thought it would be fun to see what happened if just one guy got the story, then everyone else had to scramble to play catch-up."

Maxine laughed. "It was fun to tell the story, finally, I have to admit."

"I'm glad," said Jane.

"Why don't you come down for dinner tonight?" Maxine said. Talking to Jane again felt as if no time had passed and reminded Maxine of how much she'd always liked her. Why had they ever parted ways? What fools they'd been. "I can offer the best tuna sandwich in Christendom and Jewry. And whiskey on the rocks. It's the least I can do, and I would be interested to hear what you've been up to all these years."

Jane said, "I'd love to," but then she hesitated.

"I hear a 'but' hanging somewhere in the air between us."

"No," said Jane. "I had plans, but I can change them. I'd rather do this."

"I'm flattered," said Maxine. "I still live in the same dump. Come whenever you get hungry."

"I'll be there at seven," said Jane.

This left many hours for Maxine to fill. She paced around for a little while. Then her buzzer rang and she let the delivery boy in. Fumbling in her wallet for a couple of bucks to tip him, she went to the door to await his arrival. He came bearing a large box on a dolly, a black kid of about twenty, sweating mightily.

"Thanks!" said Maxine, and shoved some money at him. He departed without changing his expression, without a flicker of either scorn or gratitude at the tip.

A sandwich, a nap, and still the afternoon stretched in front of her. Might as well try to paint the experience of looking through those layers between eyes and sky.

Her buzzer rang at seven o'clock exactly: Jane had always been prompt. She came in bearing a paper cone of flowers and a bottle of something.

"You brought more than I'm providing," said Maxine with mock grumpiness, kissing her on the cheek and noticing as she did so that Jane looked very spiffy, much less mousy than she had the other night. She'd put on some subtle, barely colored lipstick that made her look quietly glamorous, and she wore a blouse with some sort of sparkly stuff on it, sequins maybe. Should I be flattered by this? Maxine wondered. She didn't know, but doubted so very much.

Maxine put the daylilies in a jug of water, then took the bottle out of its liquor-store bag and examined the label. "Hey, nice," she said, although she had no idea about wine. "Pinot noir."

"I wouldn't say no to a glass right this minute," said Jane, seating herself at the table. "The place hasn't changed at all, Max! I remember that curtain from thirty years ago."

"Except now it's caked with dust," said Maxine, trying for lightness, trying for banter. She was nervous, but she hoped it didn't show. "If you touched it, it would probably crumble." She wrested the cork out of the wine and managed to locate a wineglass. Setting it in front of Jane, she added, "I think I bought new dish towels in the eighties."

She sat across from Jane and gently shook her glass of whiskey to hear the ice tinkle.

"To you," said Jane. "The painter of *Helena*."

"And you," said Maxine, "the model."

They clinked glasses. Maxine examined Jane's face closely, in a way she hadn't been able to the other night at Michael Rubinstein's. She had always been interested, visually, in the different ways faces could show age, the way gravity pulled through the years on different features in different people. Jane had puffy, wrinkled, slightly darkened bags under her eyes, but her chin was still taut, the skin around her mouth fairly unlined. Gravity had concentrated its effects in one place for her; she was lucky. She was still sexy in that flyaway, rumpled, academic way Maxine had always liked in her. Her once-brown short hair was half gray now, but still downy and fluffy, like a newly hatched chick.

"Remember," said Jane, smiling. "You painted like a madwoman. You had something to prove. And the thing doesn't look a bit like me."

"It looks exactly like you!"

"That simpering wheat biscuit of a girl?"

"Is that how you see her?"

"How do you see her?" Jane asked.

"She's thoughtful and lovely, yet she's tough. Very much how I saw you at the time."

"Hilarious," said Jane. "Every time I visit that portrait, I marvel that it has anything to do with me."

"It really had more to do with Oscar than with either of us," said Maxine.

Maxine had painted the portrait of Jane by impersonating her brother, looking at Jane through his eyes. It had been more an exercise in identification than a technical challenge. She had reached back to her art-school training for the feints and finesses of making paint look like expression, gesture, living skin. These had come back to her surprisingly easily; the difficult part had been forcing herself to view Jane with Oscar's predatory aggression. In particular, Oscar had had a way of painting women's genitalia; he slightly exaggerated the labia, made the pubic hair just a little more copious than it could possibly have been. "Pussies are like faces," he had once said to Maxine when she'd asked him about this. "No two are alike. I can tell you everything about a woman by looking at her cunt. I could set myself up as a cunt reader at a carnival and make a killing. Some look like little buttocks. Some are flowers. Some are oysters. Some are other things. They're the focal point of every portrait, whether you can tell in the end or not. I start with a woman's cunt and work from there. I hate it when she's got so much hair you can't see anything. Sometimes I ask my models to trim it away. Teddy's an oyster, with long, ruffled inner lips. Abigail is a—"

"Shut the fuck up," Maxine had told him.

According to Oscar's taxonomy, Jane's cunt was a flower; Maxine, impersonating Oscar, exaggerated the plumpness of her petal-like outer labia, emphasized the tiny protrusion of the inner lips, like the flirtatious tip of a tongue, the honey brown quiff of pubic hair that left the lips nearly bare and traveled down her inner thighs. Then she looked at Jane's face as she had examined her genitalia: as representative of the whole woman, assertively idiosyncratic. When the portrait was finished, Maxine had the grimy, unsavory feeling that she understood her brother now better than she had ever wanted to. She'd scrubbed her hands afterward, and had kept scrubbing even after all the paint was gone.

Discussing this on the phone with Dexter earlier, she had, of course, said nothing along these lines; she had talked instead about seeing through Oscar's eyes into the soul of her subject, trying to erase herself and become the woman she was painting. But it was all hogwash; the thing Oscar was famous for, she had discovered, wasn't at all how he went about painting. He metaphorically and, for all she knew, literally raped his models with his brushes and somehow ended up evoking inner strength, an inviolable selfhood. Very odd. She still wasn't sure why that happened, but she knew how he did it as no one else possibly could have.

"Yes, I was amazed that you saw me that way," said Jane. "You seemed to be seeing some better version of me, or so I thought at the time, but then, I was excessively self-conscious when I was younger."

"Did I idealize you back then?" Maxine asked with horror.

"God, I don't know," said Jane. "Honestly, I can't remember back that far. I just know that painting is definitely worthy of Oscar. Brilliant. It's satirical. Such a sly joke, making an über-WASP society girl portrait of a white-trash Southern Baptist like me, and then also passing your own dyke girlfriend off as one of your brother's conquests . . . So clever, Max, just so stunningly smart. Class, gender, stylistic appropriation. And on top of that, by using *Mercy* as the model for *Helena,* in pairing the two paintings, you made both of them about race, as well."

Maxine furrowed her brow.

"Good God!" said Jane. "Don't disillusion me and tell me it was all unintentional."

"I was just trying to win a bet," said Maxine, taking a slug of whiskey. "I don't know about all that other crap. Want a tuna sandwich?"

"In a bit," said Jane. "Let me get a buzz on first."

"Tell me about this boyfriend of yours," said Maxine.

Jane took a sip of wine with the kind of smug, thoughtful little grin people used to attribute to the Cheshire cat from *Alice in Wonderland,* a book that had always given Maxine mental hives.

"All right, then," said Maxine, "don't tell me."

"No no," said Jane, "I like talking about him. It's just that he's very quirky. It's hard to describe him."

"I never knew you were bisexual," said Maxine, trying to sound nonjudgmental, without accusation.

"I'm not," said Jane. "I'm as gay as you are. It's just that . . .."

"What's his name?" Maxine asked, stifling a sigh.

"Sylvester Beely," said Jane. "Syl, he's called."

"What's he like? Sensitive and artistic, or manly and rugged?"

Jane laughed. "Well, he's not . . . artistic, to say the least. Actually, he's far more effeminate than you are. He calls himself a girl with a penis, and in many ways he is."

"Oh," said Maxine.

"But in some ways he's quite rugged," said Jane. "He's not American . . . so his idea of masculinity is more complex and inclusive than that of most men who were born and raised here. He was born in Bombay to a Dutch father and an English mother, raised in India and Africa, schooled in England and at Harvard, where he got an M.B.A., and now he's a self-made millionaire who retired early. He's fifty-seven. A little younger than I am."

"What does he do now that he's retired?" Maxine asked through a welter of frustration.

"He coordinates charitable and humanitarian efforts for AIDS victims in the Third World. And when he's not doing that, he goes white-water kayaking in Canada and studies ancient Greek. He's working his way through Homer's *Odyssey* in the original. He sounds too good to be true, doesn't he? But he's got a lot of mental problems, a lot of fragility, unresolved conflicts, demons. . . . He needs me desperately, which is as much a part of his appeal to me as the rest of it, his success, his intelligence. He's a mess inside. His childhood was hell. His ambitions always kept him from the things he really wanted to do—find love, get married, have a family, emotional stability. . . ."

"And you fulfill all his needs," said Maxine. "You mother him; you fulfill his longing for intimacy."

"No need to be snotty," said Jane. Her tone was light, but her smile was sharp-toothed.

"Yeah," said Maxine. "Well, after I saw you the other night, I kicked myself. I couldn't remember why we broke up, to be honest."

"Give me some more wine," said Jane, holding up her glass.

Maxine poured a good dollop into her glass.

Jane leaned back and fingered the glass's stem, looking up at the ceiling. "I was heartbroken by our affair, Max," she said after a moment. "It took me years to get over you."

"You *were*? It *did*?"

"You didn't know?"

"I had absolutely no idea."

"Oh yes. I was catatonic for a few months after you dumped me."

"I *dumped* you?" Maxine felt as if she'd been plunked down in an alternate universe. She could feel how bug-eyed she looked. She was sick to her stomach with shocked regret.

"Well . . ." said Jane, still not looking at Maxine. "You said you didn't want to see me anymore. I took that to mean I was being dumped. Perhaps I overreacted."

Maxine stared slack-jawed at her hands, which were twisted together on the table.

"You are a tough nut to crack," said Jane. "You mean to say you had no idea that's what happened?"

"I saw it somewhat differently," said Maxine. "It seemed to me we were both unwilling to show our cards. We were both too proud and insecure at once. No one seemed to be willing to fall headlong."

"I fell headlong!" Jane said, half laughing, half angry. "Never before or since did I give or have I given of myself so completely. I felt you couldn't handle my intensity. I felt you were put off by it. Whenever we would start to get close, you would back off, shut the door, say you had a lot of work to do. I mean, hell, it only lasted a few months. But it devastated me. It's amazing how very brief affairs can go so deep, cut to the bone, so it takes years to get over what lasted only hours."

Maxine felt weak, ashen, befuddled. "I didn't know," she said. "Truly, Jane. I had no idea. I would have loved to be with you for a long time, to be with you still. I feel awful. I mean this. I was very sorry to see you go."

" 'Very sorry to see me go,' " said Jane. "Sounds like you didn't suffer too much."

"I can't very well take a lie-detector test about this," said Maxine. "But Jane, I never knew how you felt about me; I had not the slightest idea. This whole conversation has me feeling as if you and I were in two different affairs. I wanted to fall in love with you but felt somehow blocked. I don't know why."

Maxine and Jane looked at each other.

"I thought you were such a coward," said Jane.

"I thought you were remote," said Maxine. "I wanted to know you better, but I had no idea how to get there."

Their mutual gaze deepened a little.

"I'm glad you've found love," said Maxine.

"Well, thanks," said Jane. "I wish you had found it, too."

"I'm horrified that you felt the way you did and I never knew it."

"I never really saw what I had to offer you," Jane replied. "You were so interesting and famous and all that. I was this boring academic type."

"What?" Maxine said.

"You were so exciting. You had such strong opinions about everything. I loved being with you. It made me feel bohemian and unconventional, corny as it sounds, instead of a kid from a trailer park masquerading as an academic, which is what I am. You were the kind of woman I had hoped to meet all my life."

"Why the hell couldn't you show me you felt like that?"

"I did show you," said Jane.

"Hell no," said Maxine. "You did not. This is not all my fucking fault. I was not the villain here. If you had felt so passionately about me, don't you think I should have had an inkling of that? I am not stupid. And I had no frigging idea."

"Well then, I don't know what the problem was," said Jane.

"You should have told me," said Maxine. "The problem was that you didn't tell me."

Jane was silent, twisting her glass by the stem, biting her lower lip.

"You were too proud and insecure to tell me," Maxine went on. "Just like I was too proud and insecure to admit I was falling for a woman so much younger than me. We both screwed up, Jane."

"All right," said Jane. "We both screwed up."

"Well, I'm glad that now you have the worldly, rich, white-water-kayaking, humanitarian Syl Beely to shower you with feelings and open his heart to you. I'm sorry to sound so bitter."

Jane reached across the table and put her cool, dry hand over Maxine's hot, hard one. "Maxine," she said, "I wish things had been different."

Maxine felt herself stiffen at the unexpected touch, so dearly welcome, so deeply threatening. As she had when Katerina had taken her hand, she willed her own to lie inert, for fear of scaring Jane's hand away.

"And you should know," Jane went on, "that you were loved. I loved you."

Maxine, with an effort that rivaled all the great efforts of her life, forced herself to turn her own hand so it was holding Jane's as Jane's was holding hers. She looked into Jane's sharp, plain, intelligent face. "Time for dinner?" she said.

"I love how it's always time for dinner once a day," Jane said, "no matter what human tragedies are going on; even in places where sometimes there is no dinner, as Syl would point out, there's still that time in the evening when you hunker down with your fellow humans and try to keep warm."

Maxine managed to hold back, all at once, a sharp comment about the bromides of politically correct Syl, an affection-deflecting remark about how this hand-holding was too little, too late, and a self-deprecating joke about her own dinners, which were almost always solitary, totally devoid of warm fellow humans. Instead, she briefly tightened her hand around Jane's—she hoped not too awkwardly—and smiled—she hoped warmly—then got up to assemble the sandwiches.

Twelve

When Abigail saw the story about *Helena* in the *Times* the next day, she reached for her phone and immediately called Maxine. "They quote you here," she said right away to Maxine when she answered, not bothering with pleasantries. "You told the whole story. Why did you do that?"

"Because they were going to run the story with or without my side of it."

"Well, Lila Scofield told them 'No comment,'" said Abigail. She was sitting with Ethan in the breakfast nook, feeding him two soft-boiled eggs with a piece of buttered wheat toast torn up and soaked in the soft yolks. "She didn't say a word!"

"They uncovered my signature," said Maxine. "Jane Fleming is the one who told them. The model. My old girlfriend. I hadn't reckoned with her."

"I bet you've been getting calls all day."

"Everyone seems quite excited, the people at the Met not least of all."

"What a headline," said Abigail, looking at the first page of the "Arts and Leisure" section. " 'After More Than Thirty Years, Truth Revealed: Met Masterpiece Painted by Artist's Sister.' All the feminists will be having a party, assuming there are any left anymore."

"There must still be three or four hairy-legged trolls around here somewhere," Maxine said through a mouthful of something. She swallowed. "Sorry, I'm in the middle of a tuna fish sandwich."

Abigail cleared her throat. "You broke your promise to Oscar!"

"The story was out," said Maxine.

"You didn't have to add to it."

"Well, I know that, but since they were going to write it anyway, I figured they might as well get it right the first time around. I didn't want them to screw it up and then I'd have to be setting the story straight for months. It's a big story, and I figured it ought to come out right the first time, and I'm the only one who could tell it."

"Okay," said Abigail, slightly mollified. "Anyway, you must be very glad it's finally out."

"Honestly," said Maxine, "how could I not be. I got a call from Michael Rubinstein, my dealer, and he's talking about having a retrospective as soon as we can get one together. He's hoping the Met will lend *Helena* to his gallery."

"Oh," said Abigail. "That's marvelous."

"Isn't it," said Maxine. "Meanwhile, Jane Fleming came for dinner last night. She's pitching an interview with me to *Art in*

America. And here's the real twist in the story. I just got a call from an editor at *Artforum.* They want to do a piece, as they call it, on me and my nemesis, Paula Jabar, a woman I cannot personally or professionally tolerate. They want me to paint a nude portrait of her in the style of *Helena* and *Mercy* while she interviews me. But how can I say no to *that*?" Maxine laughed, a rich chuckle Abigail hadn't heard from her before.

"Ironic," said Abigail. "But wonderful."

"I'm disgusted by having to associate with Paula," said Maxine with gusto and, Abigail suspected, a large dollop of disingenuousness. "Anyway, they're probably just trying to get me to prove I really can paint a portrait, that *Helena* wasn't a fluke, which it may well have been. Why can't the piece just be about my real work?"

"You're complaining about the premise of an *Artforum* piece about you?"

"I'm hardly complaining," said Maxine.

There was a pause as both of them realized there was no more either of them wanted to say on the topic, at least for now.

"Guess who I'm having over for lunch today?" Abigail offered.

"I'm sure I can't," said Maxine.

"Teddy's daughter and her two children," said Abigail. "Samantha. She wants to come and meet her half brother. She called the other day, very shy and apologetic, wondering if I'd mind. I said, 'No, of course not. Come up for lunch, but be forewarned: He's not able to converse or make interpersonal contact.' She said she knew that; she just wants to see him."

"I think I see her sister at the dog run," said Maxine. "Ruby."

"How do you know it's her?"

"She looks exactly like Oscar, and she's the right age, and her dog is registered to Ruby Feldman."

"Gosh," said Abigail. "Why don't you say something to her?"

"Because that's not my style," said Maxine. "Meanwhile, that's all very modern and convivial, Teddy's spawn having lunch with you."

Abigail thought Maxine sounded uncommonly mellow today, but that made perfect sense. Long-thwarted ambitious people tended to be suddenly much nicer when they got the attention they felt they deserved. Oscar had been exactly the same way. So Maxine was at peace now; Abigail felt nothing but happiness for her.

After they hung up, she resumed feeding Ethan. "I wonder," she muttered to him, wiping egg off his chin, "whether Maxine somehow engineered this. I just wonder. I wouldn't put it past her. . . ."

The phone rang again. Abigail put the spoon down and answered it. It was Ralph.

"Have you read today's *Times*?" he asked, sounding aggrieved.

"I just got off the phone with Maxine," said Abigail. "She's being interviewed for *Artforum* by Paula Jabar and *Art in America* by Jane Fleming. Her dealer is talking about a retrospective. And I'm sure that's just the beginning. This is the best art scandal of the year. She's on her way to superstardom."

"But what about Oscar?" Ralph said. "Assuming I took you up on your offer, how would I make this look good for him in any way?"

"I do not see how this detracts from Oscar's achievements or his greatness. So he lost a bet with his sister! Big deal! He painted *Mercy*, didn't he? The answer is yes, because I was there; I watched him. It's as great as *Helena*, if not greater. And this sudden bright light shining on Maxine will certainly be refracted or reflected, or whatever the word is, onto Oscar. This notoriety is only good for your book."

" 'All publicity is good publicity,' " Ralph quoted in a tone that suggested he didn't altogether buy it. "Sure."

Abigail, hearing the anguish in his voice, said with compassion, "You shouldn't idealize Oscar, Ralph. It's not realistic. He was flawed in so many ways."

"I know that," said Ralph. "I have criticized him several times. I don't idealize him, I don't think."

"Maybe that was the wrong word," said Abigail. "I meant you shouldn't be too disappointed as new truths about him come to light."

"Maxine painted *Helena*," said Ralph. "I don't believe it. That diptych changed my life. And one of the reasons it affected me so deeply was the actual juxtaposition of *Mercy* to *Helena*, a painting of a black woman and a painting of a white one. I was amazed at how one white male American painter was able to transcend race, paint a black woman the same way he painted a white one, without condescending or fetishizing. If he didn't paint *Helena*, then how am I to interpret *Mercy*?"

"I guess you could look at it as a portrait of my housekeeper," said Abigail. "Not a bad one, either."

Ralph was silent.

"Can you explain exactly why this upsets you so much?" Abigail asked.

"In the European tradition," Ralph said, as if he hadn't heard her, "black women in paintings are servants who kneel or stand behind the white women, holding their jewels or the trains of their robes—but also providing contrast, to show up the fair purity of their mistresses. You may be aware of the quote by Ruskin that goes, 'I always think the main purpose for which Negroes must have been made was to be painted by Van Dyke and Veronese.' "

"I wasn't aware of that quote, no," said Abigail. "Well, what about Gauguin?"

"What about him?"

"His paintings of Polynesian women."

"Sexual fantasies. Fetishizing. Pure romanticization of the *femme sauvage*. They're about his own ego, his own damn self."

"If you say so," said Abigail. "But they're beautiful."

"*Mercy* is about the woman herself. It's about a Woman, capital *W*—not a black woman."

Abigail could hear him inhale self-importantly through his nostrils and waited with half-annoyed trepidation to hear what he would say next.

"Oscar accorded her the same selfhood he accorded his white portraits," Ralph went on when she didn't say anything. "There is no self-congratulation in the painting, nor is there either lust or a sense of Other. That is remarkable."

"But Oscar did paint *Mercy*," Abigail pointed out.

"But now it's all changed."

She smiled; he sounded so earnestly perturbed, like a child. "Why has this affected your opinion of *Mercy*? Oscar painted *Mercy*; that hasn't changed."

"I was under the impression that he had painted *Mercy* and *Helena* as a diptych," Ralph answered. "The brush strokes in both paintings are a departure from Oscar's other work. They are bolder, more primitive. The colors are blockier, jazzier. The woman in *Mercy* is a nightclub singer: Did he employ this technique because it's more, quote/unquote, negroid? No! Because look, he painted his blue-blooded society butterfly with exactly the same vivid, aggressive style, the same jazzy palette, the same reds and mauves and absinthe undertones." He paused. "Except he didn't. Maxine did."

He stopped talking, but he wasn't waiting for Abigail to contribute anything to this conversation; he was gathering his thoughts. Abigail noticed that her telephone mouthpiece smelled weirdly of broccoli. Had she been eating too many cruciferous vegetables?

"Both women represent stereotypes, but Oscar transcends these clichés of debutante and chanteuse by imbuing each one with an independent character that seems to break away from the artist's brush and possess her own soul. I thought, seeing those paintings for the first time, that *Mercy* represented a real breakthrough in the representation of black women in mainstream, which is to say white male, art. I couldn't put into words what I thought at the time; I was simply awestruck by the power I felt emanating from the juxtaposition of two women whose lives would hardly, in real life, touch each other."

"Well," said Abigail, "maybe you're right, and *Mercy* has turned out to be as racially dubious a painting as anything Gauguin ever did, and *Helena* was just a stylistic imitation by another painter trying to win a bet. But maybe you also need to see Oscar clearly instead of needing him to be some great racial equalizer. He was as far from a racist as anyone I've ever met. Take it from me. I wouldn't lie to you."

"I believe you . . ." said Ralph with gloomy resignation.

Abigail reassured him again that this would all be to the good, then got him off the phone.

She went to her computer, put on her glasses, and checked her E-mail. Abigail loved the computer; the chatty immediacy of E-mail, the instant gratification of Google, the Internet's global intimacy. It made her feel less lonely to play on-line Scrabble with live people and chat with them late at night sometimes when she couldn't sleep. She loved looking at gossip Web sites, on-line newspapers, young people's startlingly intimate blogs. This plastic box contained the entire world, allowed access to the goings-on of so many people without having to expose herself. Often, when she was on-line, whole swaths of time went by. She found this both alarming and unavoidable.

She had three E-mails, two of which were spam, one of which was from Ralph.

"I Give Up," the header said. The message read in its entirety: "Dear Abigail, we have a deal! Ralph."

Well! That was fast; they had just hung up the phone a few moments before. Then she saw that it had been sent just before midnight the night before, when he hadn't seen the article about *Helena* yet.

Abigail thought about this for a moment. Then she hit the reply icon and wrote back craftily, taking his E-mail at face value despite all the new information: "Dear Ralph, I am very glad to hear it. We will hammer out the details later. Abigail."

Then she went to the Google page and typed in "Nicoise salad recipe," found one that looked plausible, and printed it out. Then she typed in "Chilled cantaloupe soup recipe," looked at several, chose one, and printed that out, too. She felt a surge of rare domestic inspiration, an unfamiliar excitement at being about to prepare from scratch a good meal for important strangers.

The moment Marcus arrived, Abigail put her shopping list into her purse and went out to the elevator. When she came out of her cool, dark building onto the street, the morning air was already staggeringly hot. She blinked a few times with the shock of it, then made her way over to Broadway, feeling like a slow, lumbering, half-blind rhinoceros. In the grocery store, nothing looked familiar to her. Had everything been replaced with new brands? She saw strange fruits and vegetables that seemed to have just been invented. She filled her cart and paid for everything, then started back to her apartment. The bags were almost too heavy to carry; she hadn't thought about how much a cantaloupè weighed. She thought about getting a cab, but the whole thing seemed like so much trouble, it daunted her just to contemplate hailing one. The sunlight glinting off windshields and metal and broken glass hurt her eyes. On West End Avenue, she set the bags down on a stoop for a moment and sat; it was undignified and unlike her to do this, but she was sweating and her arms were tired. She should have thought ahead, should have ordered from FreshDirect. Oh well.

She wiped her forehead on the back of her hand, sat there until the hot pulse calmed in her wrists and temples. Then she pulled herself to her feet and managed to get herself and all her groceries home. The cool, dim air of her apartment felt welcoming and safe; she was so glad to be home, and she felt as if her jaunt to the store had been a metaphorical pilgrimage, a difficult journey with some high, imperative meaning. She hoisted the bags onto the kitchen counter, then went to see how things were going with Ethan and Marcus.

She found them in Ethan's room. Ethan lay on a mat, and Marcus was helping him through his leg lifts. Abigail was always amazed at how rigorous these exercises were and how well Ethan was able to do them. Marcus was a big believer in the therapeutic benefits of exercise, and he had convinced Abigail several years ago in her initial interview with him that this would help Ethan more than anything else. And he had been right: Ethan's mood swings had stabilized; his sleep was better.

"How is everything, boys?" she asked with a cheer she didn't feel.

"He's in a good mood today," said Marcus, who always seemed

to be able to divine things going on in Ethan that even his mother couldn't. Marcus was a large, sweet black man who had told Abigail he had eight children at home. He seemed much too young to her to have any, but she knew that the older she got, the younger everyone else seemed. Marcus's head was large and round, and his face gleamed with sweat and goodwill. He didn't seem entirely human.

"Glad to hear it," said Abigail. She backed out of Ethan's room and went to her quiet, dark bedroom to lie down for a little while. Her bed was broad and comfortable; she lay on top of the bedspread with her shoes on. She intended to lie there for five minutes, then get up and make lunch, but when she awoke, her pillow was soaked with sweat, her hair was damp, and her mouth was dry. She sat up, befuddled. The clock said it was nearly noon. She had been asleep for two hours. She leapt up and, patting her head to smooth her hair, rushed to the kitchen. She stood there blinking for a moment, trying to orient herself, then sat down in the breakfast nook and pored over the recipes, trying to get her mind around how she would do all those things in time for Samantha's arrival in half an hour. Picturing herself from an aerial perspective, she had an image of herself as a rumpled old woman in a dull apartment with a weird son, mussed hair, and nothing good to eat. Meanwhile, Samantha's mother cooked exciting food, always looked glamorous, and lived in an interesting house; Abigail had always suspected this. She started to weep with self-pity. This was extremely unlike her. She shook herself, dried her eyes on a napkin. Of course this was just silly, irrational anxiety. She was nervous. That was all. There was nothing to be afraid of: This was Oscar's daughter, after all, Oscar, whom Abigail had known as well as she knew herself.

When the doorman called to say that Samantha was on her way

up, Abigail had managed to cut the cantaloupe in half and get the scrubbed potatoes in some simmering water. She wiped her brow with the back of her hand and went to the door.

"Hello," she said, opening it, squinting at the figures in the brightly lit hallway. "I'm Abigail Feldman. Please come in!"

"Thank you," came a woman's voice. "Come on, Buster, let's go."

Abigail led them back to the kitchen and gestured to the breakfast nook. "Please sit down," she said. "Oh, shoot! What do I have to offer your kids to drink?"

"Oh, I brought stuff for the kids, don't worry," said Samantha. She stood in the center of the room, a tall, rather ungainly young woman with flyaway dark hair and a baby riding on her hip, a little boy clinging possessively to her legs. She looked like a less remarkable, more pragmatic version of Teddy. She was painfully thin and seemed harried and tense.

"It's really so nice to meet you finally," said Abigail, oddly at ease now that she saw who Samantha was.

"Oh," said Samantha, "thanks for inviting us. We can't stay too long, don't worry."

"I was just in the middle of cooking lunch," said Abigail. "Sit down. Would you like . . ." She regarded her, thought for an instant. "A beer? I think I have one or two bottles in the icebox."

"Would I like a beer," said Samantha with a longing little laugh. "God, would I. But I'm breast-feeding, so I better not."

"I've read on-line that a little beer is good for breast milk," Abigail said, feeling protective toward this gaunt, unhappy creature. "It's got B vitamins or something."

"My husband would kill me." Samantha sat on the breakfast-nook bench, settled the little boy next to her, rummaged around in her enormous bag, and produced a small box of apple juice with a miniature straw protruding from it, which he began sucking on aggressively. "Can I help you cook?" she asked then, looking up at Abigail, suddenly bright-eyed.

Abigail handed her the cold bottle of Tecate she'd opened. "Oh gosh," she said. "I don't know. I was going to make an elaborate feast, but I . . . fell asleep."

Samantha laughed. "I do that all the time. Big plans, then I conk out the minute these two go down."

"I have no such excuse," said Abigail.

The little boy squealed and slapped his baby sister, who smiled and blinked. He gave a wild-eyed grin to no one in particular. He looked like an evil little elf. He was about three years old, pale and thin, with bluish circles under his eyes and a fragile neck, but Abigail could see the potential for explosiveness in the manic corners of his mouth, his eyes darting to adults' faces to gauge their reaction to him, the kinetic restlessness of his limbs. His baby sister was, by way of contrast, fat, placid, and unassuming.

"Buster, no," said Samantha. "That's uncalled for."

Buster laughed at his mother, his whole face perverse and gleeful.

"Hey, Buster," Abigail said, "I bet you can't count backward from ten."

He looked up at her. "Yeah I can."

Abigail sat at the other end of the bench. "Come here and sit in my lap and prove it to me."

Buster climbed into Abigail's lap. "Ten nine seven," he shouted, nestling against her. "Five three four one."

"That is very good!" Abigail said, smiling at Samantha, who didn't smile back. "I think you might have missed a few, though. Want to try one more time?"

He leapt off her lap and went over to the refrigerator, where he began making smeary palm prints on the shiny whiteness.

Abigail produced her two recipes. "I was going to make these. I got as far as boiling the potatoes."

Samantha took them from her and looked them over. "Oh, how nice. But so much trouble! We could just have boiled potatoes and sliced cantaloupe."

"You could use a good meal, looks like," Abigail blurted. "Oh, gosh, I'm sorry."

Samantha looked at Abigail. Then she took a slug of beer. "I'm too thin," she said.

"Well, compared to me, anyone would be," said Abigail.

"Since the kids were born, I just run around all the time."

"Drink your beer. Put your feet up. I'm going to make this salad. Maxine was talking about tuna fish this morning and she got me craving it. What's your little girl's name?"

"Josephine," said Samantha. "We named her after my husband's grandmother. My husband is Ivan Sandusky. He's a research scientist. He's the smart one. I used to be a painter, but I gave it up when I had kids. I was into watercolor still lifes. Nothing like my father's work at all. I was never going to set the art world on fire, so it's no great loss, but I do miss it sometimes."

"You should take it up again," said Abigail.

"Maybe someday," said Samantha. "For now, I want to concentrate on the kids. They grow up and leave before you know it. I don't want to miss out."

"*Some* of them grow up and leave," said Abigail, smiling.

"Oh!" said Samantha.

"Gallows humor," said Abigail. She got up and rinsed the green beans in a colander. Then she sat down again and began to snap their noses and tails off.

"Oh, I can do that," said Samantha with beery enthusiasm. She took the colander of beans from Abigail and began snapping them.

Abigail got up and pulled things from the shopping bag. "Let's see," she said, peering at the recipe. "A simple vinaigrette with shallots. Shouldn't be too hard."

"Want me to chop the shallots?" Samantha asked. "I wear contact lenses. I don't cry when I cut oniony things; I think the lenses protect me."

Abigail handed her the shallots, a knife, and a cutting board. She had been silently taking the measure of this daughter of her husband, assessing her. She was slightly nonplussed by how daughterly she was, how easily she had fallen into the role of younger, subservient, agreeable girl with a strange older woman; her affable chattiness didn't match her drawn face. No wonder she was under so much stress; it must have taken a great deal of energy and work to constantly have to manufacture such an impenetrable shield.

"Are you close to your mother?" Abigail asked, whisking olive oil and vinegar together.

"This is weird, isn't it?" said Samantha. "I mean, given the relationship between you and my mother, it's weird that I'm sitting here. I asked Ruby to come with me, but she didn't want to."

"Ah," said Abigail. "I can imagine she must feel loyal to your mother."

"Actually, it's our father she's loyal to," said Samantha. "She's probably jealous of you, for seeing so much of him."

"I didn't see much more of him than you did," said Abigail. She tasted the dressing and whisked in the shallots Samantha had minced. Cooking was easy once you got into the swing of it; it was just getting up the nerve to start something she'd always had trouble with.

"To answer your question, yes, I am close to my mother," said Samantha. "I got the parent who was there all the time; Ruby got the parent who almost never was. So she's freer than I am, in a way. Sometimes I resent her for it. So paradoxical. Because I couldn't be happier with the way my own life has turned out, and I really don't envy her at all, being single, with no kids, and having to work every day."

Abigail began to assemble the salad, without the green beans, which Samantha had taken proprietary charge of and which Abigail had relinquished to her with some internal amusement; the heap of beans sat at Samantha's elbow now, forgotten.

"Of course," Samantha went on—Abigail noticed that her beer was nearly gone already—"I know that not every mother has the luxury of choosing to stay home with her children. But for all I always loved and respected my mother, I worked very hard not to end up like her. I chose a good provider for a mate. I chose to be a wife and mother, and not to work at all, not even to paint. I pour all my energy into my family. Ivan works just as hard to support us, and he comes home for dinner almost every night and puts the kids to bed. He couldn't be less like my father. I don't regret my choice: I saw how my mother worried about money, how hard it was for her to raise us alone. I always sensed my mother's struggles through all her independent bravado, and although I was always extremely close to her, I swore never to turn into her. I have a feeling, although we have never talked about this, that Ruby did the same thing, but in the opposite direction, for a different reason."

"Ah," said Abigail, running cold water over the hot potatoes and hard-boiled eggs.

"Rube and I were so close when we were younger. And maybe we still would be if she were married now and had a baby or two.

We would have so much to talk about. Also, if she had kids, Ruby might have learned to be more sensitive to others. She's always stepping on people's toes, hurting their feelings, my mother's most of all. And all she seems interested in are things I, quite frankly, had hoped she would have outgrown by now. Boyfriends, drinking, traveling. Writing *poetry.*"

"Some people write poetry well into their nineties," said Abigail. "And travel and drink, for that matter. As for boyfriends . . ."

"We're almost forty, for God's sake. Ruby is stuck in her late twenties. She dresses like she's in graduate school. She says she's happy, but how can she be, really? And whenever I try to talk to her about my own life, my children and marriage, she acts bored, superior even, in a way I find galling and ignorant. She has no idea how motherhood makes you a different, really a better, person— more selfless, more giving, more mature. You know what I mean?"

"I'm not sure how mature it made me," said Abigail, dumping the canned Italian tuna on the salad platter.

"And the love you feel for your children is so deep, really so soulful and gut-wrenching, how could you choose to miss out on that? And having children aside! Marriage itself is . . . well, a 'people-growing machine,' as one of the self-help books calls it. You can't be in a good, strong marriage and be immature or selfish. The two are totally incompatible."

Abigail turned to her and said, "To be honest, I wonder about my own choices sometimes, which I suppose were in many ways like yours. I gave myself to my husband and son instead of finding my own place independently of anyone else. There's so much I never learned about myself. Not to mention the world. I would guess that Ruby knows things you don't, just as you know things she doesn't."

Samantha looked surprised, as if she'd anticipated an ally and found an adversary instead. "Maybe," she said. "Don't get me wrong—as kids, we were inseparable. We thought it was the best luck, having a twin sister for a best friend. But something changed between us after I married Ivan. I think Ruby got jealous. She thinks Ivan is overly possessive and controlling of me and I'm an overly involved mother, both of which are completely ridiculous notions. That's marriage! That's motherhood! I belong to other people now, and Ruby can't come first with me anymore. If that hurts her feelings, well, too bad. This is just the way things go when you grow up."

Abigail set the table with plates, silverware, napkins. The little boy, Buster, or Peter, whatever his name was, had nestled against his mother on the bench and fallen asleep, his lips parted. Asleep, he looked angelic. Abigail, with unconscious yearning, remembered the recent warm heft of him in her lap, the whiff of yeasty crackers on his breath, his hot, clammy hand alighting briefly on her clavicle.

"I have thought, through the years, in my more charitable moments, about how hard it must have been for your mother," Abigail said. "I know Oscar never supported you. I am sorry for that. He and I never discussed you girls directly, so I never took steps to ensure you were properly cared for financially by him. That was my own pettiness. Of course it was because I resented you, but that was childish of me."

"How amazing of you to say that," said Samantha.

"And I know you hardly ever saw your father," Abigail went on.

"Right," said Samantha. "And when we did, he and my mother demanded each other's full attention."

"Yes," said Abigail. She drizzled the vinaigrette over the salad and looked at it for a moment. She had forgotten all about the cantaloupe soup. Impressing this girl no longer mattered to her, and anyway, Samantha clearly wouldn't have cared if she had served a pile of shredded Kleenex; food was obviously not among her passions.

"About Ruby," Samantha said. "You know, I didn't mean to imply that her poetry is bad or anything. It's actually pretty good. She even publishes it in literary magazines. . . ."

Clearly, Samantha was itching to say more about Ruby, but Abigail knew from having sisters herself that this itch could never be scratched. The love and rivalry were too intertwined to ever satisfactorily express either. She imagined that Samantha was feeling guilty for her earlier remarks and now wanted to acknowledge the positive side of the sisterly equation, and she smiled inwardly at how well she knew this dynamic, how it never went away no matter how old you got. She was still exactly the same way with both of her sisters, even though one of them was dead now.

Abigail set the salad on the table. Marcus brought Ethan in then, freshly bathed and dressed in clean clothing, his wet hair combed, his face clean-shaven. Samantha stared at the sight of her half brother, tall and beautiful and impassive and pale, being led into the kitchen by an enormous, gentle black man.

"Here he is," said Marcus. "Ready for his lunch." He sat Ethan down next to Samantha and said to Abigail, as if no one else were in the kitchen, "See you the day after tomorrow, Mrs. Feldman." He vanished without another word.

"This is Ethan," said Abigail to Samantha. She set a plate of sliced cantaloupe on the table.

"Hello, Ethan," said Samantha.

Ethan didn't look at her, but his expression looked quizzical to Abigail.

"Ethan," she said, sitting across from them, "this is your half sister, Samantha, and these are her children, Peter and Josephine."

Ethan twiddled his left ear with his right hand.

"I think he knows you're here," said Abigail, spooning Niçoise salad onto her plate. "Is Buster hungry?"

"He'll wake up when he's ready," said Samantha, smiling down at her son. "He's very self-directed. He has a genius IQ, like Ivan, by the way."

"Ah," said Abigail. "So we both have special sons."

Samantha plucked one wizened black olive from the tray. She put it into her mouth and chewed it as if it were medicine, then said, as if Abigail hadn't spoken, "We don't know officially, of course, since it's too early to test him, but it's obvious." She kissed the top of her placid daughter's head. "Jo will probably take after me. Mediocre in all things."

"You never know," Abigail said, fighting an urge to slap her. "Josephine might turn out to be the smartest of you all."

Samantha dropped her olive pit into her empty beer bottle and said, "Thank you for inviting us over. What a delicious lunch."

"But," said Abigail with a mock Jewish-mother inflection, "you're not eating anything."

"I'll eat when Buster wakes up," said Samantha. She looked over at Ethan. "Ethan," she said. She spoke a little too loudly for him, Abigail thought. "I'm glad to meet you finally. I always knew I had a brother, all my life, and I was always so curious about you. You look a lot like our father and my twin sister, Ruby. She's your half sister, too."

Abigail reached across the table and held a forkful of fish and potato to Ethan's mouth with a napkin underneath to catch any spillage. He took the food, chewed briefly, and swallowed, his right hand still touching his left ear.

"When I was a little girl," said Samantha, "I used to dream about you. You were very strong. In one dream, you picked up a Volkswagen Beetle and carried it down the street. And in another dream, you moved all my mother's furniture around her house. She came home and saw you and said, 'Ethan! What are you doing?' and you smiled at her and walked out of the house; then she looked at what you had done and said to Ruby and me, 'It actually looks better this way.' "

Abigail looked in consternation at Samantha. It had never once occurred to her that Teddy's daughters had, as children, known about their father's other child, but of course Oscar would have told the girls about Ethan, and of course they must have been strongly curious about him; she herself would have been insatiably curious about an unknown brother. "What an amazing dream," she said.

"Ethan was my secret hero when I was little," said Samantha, more softly now, to Abigail. "I know it sounds ridiculous. I used to daydream about him coming to rescue me when I got teased by another kid or was worried about a test. I pretended Ethan would come and beat up the other kid or take my test for me."

Abigail shook her head. "My gosh," she said. "Do you hear that, Ethan? Your little sister thought you would protect her."

Ethan made a low thrumming noise in the back of his throat.

"He understands," Abigail said with certainty.

"Really?" said Samantha.

"Of course he does," said Abigail, holding more food to Ethan's mouth. He ate it immediately. "He's hungry today," she added. "Physical therapy always works up his appetite."

"So what does he make of all this?" Samantha asked. "My being here."

"I have no idea," said Abigail, giving Ethan another bite. "I don't know what he makes of anything."

"Is it lonely, living here with him?"

"It depends on what you mean by 'lonely,'" said Abigail.

"Was he always like this?"

"He seemed normal for the first couple of years. Then suddenly we noticed that he didn't seem as responsive and emotional as other kids. He was diagnosed when he was Peter's age. Buster."

Samantha tightened her arm around her sleeping little boy and looked down at him. "Dad said Ethan didn't talk but that he had a strong presence. I knew it annoyed him, how loud Ruby and I were, so I thought that meant he loved Ethan more."

"He wasn't much of a father to any of you," said Abigail. "Around here, he ignored Ethan. I think he was a little afraid of him."

"I always thought Dad was a selfish brat," said Samantha. "The way he had to have my mother's undivided attention. And I guess I also judged him for having two families. That seemed selfish, too."

"He was the most selfish man who ever lived," said Abigail.

"Did you love him?"

"Is your husband selfish?"

Samantha looked startled. Then she said slowly, "Well, yes. He is extremely possessive of me and demanding of my time and attention." She hesitated, still thinking, then said, "But it feels different, being the one whose attention he wants, rather than the one whose attention he can't deal with. Being the center of *his* attention rather than being pushed away by him."

"Now you see," said Abigail.

"Well, the difference is that my kids won't have to grow up hat-ing their father for never being around and for monopolizing me whenever he is."

"They can hate him for other reasons," said Abigail with a little laugh.

Samantha shook her head, surprised.

Thirteen

Lewis disembarked from the far side of his car like an astronaut on the moon emerging from his spaceship, leery of the inhospitable atmosphere, uncertain of the effects on his movements of a radically different gravitational field. Teddy watched through her front window as he came around the car and moved gingerly toward her house. He carried a briefcase. He was wearing brown trousers and a blue button-down shirt. His bald head gleamed in the bright sun. He looked trim and handsome. She could hardly breathe. It was so odd; she had known him so well for so long, but he seemed to her now, on her homey Brooklyn street, full of mystery and potential, as new as Adam freshly made.

She had invited him over for some sort of meal, but she hadn't cooked anything, and she couldn't even remember whether there was anything much to eat in the kitchen. She hadn't been hungry in several days. She felt a nauseated elation that prevented her from eating. She had lain awake the past several nights, too excited to sleep. When she looked in the mirror, she was amazed by how young and flushed she looked, how alive. Talking to Lila on the phone earlier, they had laughed together about how they were both in the same state. It reminded them of Vassar, freshman year, when they'd both fallen in love over the same weekend with a pair of Brooklyn boys they'd met on the Staten Island ferry during a daring overnight jaunt—Teddy's idea—to New York City.

Teddy had insisted that they buy a bag of pears and apples and ride the Staten Island ferry all night in honor of Edna St. Vincent Millay's poem "Recuerdo," which went, "We were very tired, we were very merry—/We had gone back and forth all night on the ferry." But the notion of buying Millay's apples and pears had fallen by the wayside and turned into a bottle of scotch instead. Teddy and Lila had sipped it from the bottle in a brown paper bag, feeling very daring, wrapped in their merino wool coats, sitting on a bench looking out at Manhattan.

Tom and Albert were inside the ferry, where the rows of benches were, playing jazz with an upturned hat at their feet. Tom played trumpet, Albert trombone. Teddy and Lila had wandered tipsily in to watch them play and had, of course, caught their eyes. During a break, the boys approached the girls and began chatting them up. They were not much older than Teddy and Lila, but they seemed decades older in terms of worldliness and experience. They were from Bay Ridge, but they shared an apartment now in Greenwich Village and played in a jazz combo. Teddy had staked a claim right away on Tom, the rougher, older, more profane and aggressive of the two, so Lila had gotten Albert, his younger and milder brother. The foursome had sat outside on the deck all night long, drinking, talking, and, finally, necking in their Teddy-ordained pairs, till the sun came up "dripping, a bucketful of gold." Then the boys escorted the girls by subway up to Grand Central Station, treated them to breakfast at an Automat, and then Teddy and Lila had caught an early train back to Poughkeepsie and sat cuddled together, staring dreamily out the window at the gentle pink-and-blue morning river, the trees flashing by.

For a week or two afterward, Teddy and Lila had been in this same state of jittery, euphoric exhaustion, waiting for the dormitory telephone to ring. It never did, but by the time they realized it wouldn't, they'd moved on to other youthful obsessions.

Teddy opened the door before Lewis could ring the doorbell. "Welcome to Oz," she said, laughing at him. She pulled him into her house. In the living room, he set his briefcase on the coffee table and took a deep breath.

"Want a tour?" she asked.

"All I can see right now is you," he said. "Sorry." They exchanged dazed, elated looks; then she melted against him.

"I am so excited," she said into his mouth, her voice rippling with laughter.

"I have been on fire since you left my house," he said.

"So have I."

"Can this happen to people as old as we are?"

"I had no idea."

"I had a slight idea."

She pulled back to look him right in the eye. "What's in the briefcase, Lewis? Surely you're not planning to work while you're here."

He released her reluctantly and opened the briefcase. "Do you have a record player?"

He handed her a few albums in their original battered cardboard covers. "I brought music."

She took them, chuckling, and looked through them. "The Lovin' Spoonful!" she said. "Oh! The Stones. That skinny little English boy sounds just like an old black man in the Delta."

She took *Beggars' Banquet* out of its sleeve and set it on the turntable. This she did with some difficulty; she hadn't operated a record player for years, since Oscar was alive, but more importantly, she was dying to touch Lewis again. The music started: "Please allow me to introduce myself . . ." Teddy was swamped by a memory of how hot and raw and alive everything had seemed back then.

"I must have been in my mid-thirties when this came out," she said.

"Remember when I took you to that Stones show at the Academy of Music? I got those tickets from a musician client who thought I would pass them along to someone younger . . ." Lewis laughed. "We were the oldest people there."

"By far," said Teddy. "Back then, being in your thirties was middle-aged, remember?"

Lewis moved toward her as if through heavy warm water, slid one arm around her waist, and took her hand in his.

"Why don't we just go to bed," she said. "And fuck."

"I want to torture you first," he said.

She burrowed her face into the crook of his neck and they moved around her living room, their thighs and groins pressed together, moving with raunchy intent, breathing in unison. They had both stopped laughing. Teddy was swooning against him, liquid. They were like two wax figures joining together in the heat.

She had felt so different with Oscar. His body had been bulkier and more solid. Sex with him had been like wrestling with a big, hungry bear; she had always felt very small and fragile with him. Oscar had been blunt and carnal and boyish in bed. Lewis was built exactly like Teddy, aerodynamically sinewy; being with him felt incestuously kinky. He was inventive, ardent, almost feminine in the dexterous subtlety of his hands on her flesh, but the way he moved inside her was not feminine at all.

Remembering that now, craving it again, she stumbled a little in their dance. "To bed," she said, her words half plead, half command.

"What's wrong with right here?" he asked her. He let her go and, bending down, took off his shoes and socks, stepped out of his trousers, unbuttoned his shirt and took that off, too. Then he stripped Teddy's dress off. She wasn't wearing anything underneath it. She was barefoot. They were just about the same height; he was possibly an inch taller than she was. His hard-on pressed against her pelvic bone. She reached down and felt it and her eyes closed; her hand tightened around it.

"Even better than last time," she said, breathless, trying to joke, strangely embarrassed by her own lust. "Have you been taking those pills?"

"No," he said, "just the result of years of anticipation."

He put his hands on her hips and held them still while he entered her, bending his knees slightly until he was inside her, then straightening up to his full height. She felt herself expand to take him in, then enfold him tightly.

"We fit perfectly," he said, his eyes blazing blue, inches from her own.

She was speechless. They swayed to the music, rocking, arms around each other.

"I have no food," she said.

"But you invited me for lunch." He lifted her with a small grunt, her thighs in his hands, her feet crossed behind his back, and carried her over to the green velvet couch. Still holding her, he slowly sat and lay back on the couch so she was straddling him. "I may never eat again," he said with his mouth on hers.

She was suddenly nervous about this new position, the shift he'd made so impetuously in their connection, suddenly protective of him in case it didn't work. "Let's just stay like this till we starve and they find us skeletons overgrown with cobwebs," she chattered. "Actually, Benny might knock on the door sometime tonight if you don't go out and send him home."

"I drove myself," said Lewis. He didn't seem nervous at all, which thrilled her. "Benny is far away."

She stretched along the length of him and felt the rasp of his body hair on her skin. Their bellies were pressed together; they both breathed for a moment, getting used to this.

"Mmm," he said. "Now this I like."

"Remember when I worked for you?"

"You were a slave driver."

"I still am," she said, driving him deeper into herself and resting her open mouth on his shoulder. Many pulses went by as they fucked each other hard.

"Aggh," she said. "If I had only known before what this would be *like* . . ."

His voice was as easy as ever, right in her ear. "Oh ye of little faith."

"Will you spend the night?"

"Fuck it," said Lewis, "I'll stay here till I die of sexual exhaustion."

"Don't talk about death," she said.

More pulses went by in silence. Then she felt him shaking with laughter underneath her.

"What?" she asked, pulling back to look down at him.

"Death," said Lewis. "What a joke."

Teddy convulsed with a completely unexpected orgasm, which left her gasping with a residue of tears against his chest. She watched his slack-jawed, helpless face as he came.

They looked at each other.

"Look how perfectly beautiful you are," he said. "You look about twenty-five years old."

"I'm so hungry," she said.

"You're hungry?"

"I'm starving."

"What should we eat?"

"I know you came expecting a home-cooked meal," she said. "But I can't move. There's a new Peruvian place that just opened nearby; they left a delivery menu on my stoop yesterday."

"I have a bottle of champagne in that briefcase, too. I meant to put it on ice before we got carried away. Should we call now and order up a feast?"

"Use your cell phone," said Teddy. "I can't possibly lift that heavy receiver right now."

"Helpless thing," he said.

She looked at him suspiciously.

"Just the way I like you," he added, and got up. While he ordered food and opened the champagne, Teddy lay on the ancient bottle green couch and inhaled its decades of smells. How extremely odd, to be madly in love with Lewis. How extremely odd, to be lying here naked, inhaling the smell of her old couch and luxuriating in the memory of babies' diapers changed, Oscar's sweat, Samantha's childhood vomit, Ruby's high-school incense and pot, fur and dander from a succession of cats. How odd, to be calling out for Peruvian food. What was Peruvian food, anyway? And Teddy didn't normally drink champagne, but right now she craved it. She was zooming inside, her brain zipping and popping. Funny, she had fallen in love this way twice in her life, and both times the experience was intensified by the knowledge that this could never be a whole love. The barrier with Oscar had been circumstantial, but the one with Lewis was temporal, and that was much harder to bear. If she'd made a different decision, she and Lewis might have had a long life together of fellowship and adventure. . . . Well, at least it wasn't over quite yet. At least they had this now. There was no point to regret.

Lewis sauntered in naked with two glasses of champagne. She gazed at him through the pearly summer light.

"Hello, old boy," she said.

"Drink your champagne, old girl," he replied. "I hope you like steak with eight different kinds of starch."

"I've never heard of anything so perfect in my life," she said. "I'll answer the door when they come; I've got a bathrobe somewhere."

"They'll think you're a senile old shut-in."

"They'll think I'm somebody's abandoned great-grand-mother."

He landed next to her on the couch. They floated together in the sea of her living room, drinking and eating, talking and listening to music, until much later, when they resurfaced and found themselves cross-legged, naked, looking at each other in the dim yellow light from the streetlamp outside.

"Your house is crammed as full of stuff as mine is," said Lewis, surprised, looking around him as if for the first time.

"I was hoping you'd never notice."

"Do you ever find yourself perversely thrilled by accumulating so much junk?"

"No! It's just been this way since Oscar died. I haven't had the energy to keep on top of it all. Frankly, I'm horrified at myself for it."

"It comforts me," said Lewis. "As death approaches . . ."

"You're obsessed with death!"

He smiled. "Not anymore. Suddenly not."

"Well, you talk about it an awful lot."

"Yes, but now I feel it there in the abstract. Until recently, it was ever present and painful as an open wound. Now it seems far off and unreal."

"What's made the difference?"

"You," he said. "My fixation with death was caused by loneliness."

"Even though you had Ellen," said Teddy slyly.

"Teddy, you are evil. I have never felt less lonely in my life. Let's go to Tuscany and rent a big house with no stuff in it and live there in sexual bliss for a while. Will you? Or anywhere else you want."

"Oh, yes, why not, a villa in Tuscany will do," said Teddy, feeling joy rising in her gorge like a bubble of helium gas. "Although Tuscany is such a cliché. Let's leave all these piles of old magazines behind and just . . . run off together."

"I can hardly believe it," said Lewis. "I can hardly grasp my luck. I never thought this would happen."

"Yes you did," said Teddy. "You never gave up for a second, and that's why we're here. I owe you one."

"You can never repay me," he said, "but I look forward to seeing you try."

Lila and Abigail met for lunch at an old bistro in the West Village where Lila had often eaten with her first husband. They settled into their booth under the high ceiling in the cool air.

"I hate summer," said Lila. "The older I get, the more I hate it. It just gets so *hot.*"

"What about winter? Winter is no better."

"Winter is brutal," said Lila.

"I never thought I'd get old in New York. I always planned to move south somewhere."

"But then you don't," said Lila. "I know. Because everyone you know is here."

"Seeing you and Teddy in the same room the other day," said Abigail, "I was surprised it wasn't more dramatic."

"Of course," said Lila, "we hadn't known you'd be there, so we weren't prepared. Maybe that was why it wasn't as horrible as it might have been."

"Maxine insisted. She's very bossy, and I can't say no to her."

"Maxine strikes me as lonely," said Lila.

Abigail rolled her eyes. "By choice," she said. "Anyway, I have to confess that I didn't expect to admire Teddy, but I did. I admire her."

"I've admired her for about a thousand years," said Lila. "It's impossible not to."

"On another note," said Abigail as two bubbling glasses of prosecco arrived, "how's your love affair going?"

Lila ducked her head and looked at Abigail through her eyelashes with a coy little smile. Abigail found this expression slightly irritating and wished Lila wouldn't make it. It was what the Victorian novelists used to call a "moue." She had never liked it in fictional characters, and she didn't like it in real people. More than anything else, she felt disappointment. She had dressed as carefully for this lunch as if she were meeting a lover. The prospect of this new friendship had caused her so much hopeful excitement, she had hardly been able to sleep the night before.

Lila said through demurely pursed lips, "Very well."

Something in Lila's face alerted Abigail then to a deeper possibility. She said, "Really?" with as much polite skepticism as she could muster.

Lila hesitated. Then she said, "Well, I like him a lot."

"But you're not excited about him?"

"I don't know," said Lila in a different tone, natural and plaintive. "I feel as if I ought to be. He's very nice, and attentive, and, you know, good at sex and all that. And at my age, to find a man like Rex . . ."

"But?" said Abigail.

"It's just that . . ." Lila paused to consider what she was about to say. "For some reason, I seem to be reluctant to go through this whole rigmarole again. After my second husband died, I found myself alone, kids grown, and I was afraid I would go nuts, but it turned out that I loved being alone after two husbands, three kids, all needing my constant attention."

Abigail thought of her long-ago affair with Edward. It had felt so separate from her domestic life, even though he had visited her at her apartment. He had needed nothing from her except what she most wanted to give him. When he had visited her, they had been sealed off in a bubble of sensual pleasures: a bowl of ripe fruit or briny olives, a bottle of good wine, music playing, usually Schubert or Bach, and, of course, poetry—they had read aloud to each other. The sex had been almost, but of course not really, secondary.

"But isn't this different?" she said. "He's not living in your house. You only see him for dates. You don't have to take care of him."

"I know, but I change when there's a man around," said Lila. "I diminish myself. I can feel it happening even now at this late date with Rex. I get all kittenish and seductive and stupid."

"I think I know what you mean," said Abigail. "I had an extra-marital affair with Ethan's doctor. With him, I felt not myself at all, or rather, I felt I was a different person, a different part of myself, than I'd ever been before. But he made me feel better than anyone ever had before, or has since. Once, he actually told me I looked like Botticelli's Venus. I felt purely sexual with him, and I saw that as a good thing. I felt like a red-haired seductress. Such luxury, I had never known, the freedom to be that way and no other way with someone. Can you imagine, me?"

Lila looked closely at her. Abigail quailed a little under the direct scrutiny, imagining what she must have seen. "Well yes," Lila said after a moment, "why not? But with Rex, I don't know, it's not secretive or illicit. I feel a familiar pressure to please him, to put him above me somehow, as if he would shatter if he knew how smart and powerful I really was, not that I am; it's just that whatever powers I have, I squelch. At my age, it's ridiculous, but maybe some things never change."

"Well, you should just stop doing that and see what would happen if you didn't play dumb."

Lila considered this with a mildly defensive expression. "Maybe so," she said. "I'm not sure it's worth the trouble. I think I've had enough romance for one lifetime. I think I'd like to live out the rest of my life in peace and quiet. My grandchildren give me all the passion I require. It would be fine with me if no one ever had to look at my old naked self again."

"Gosh," said Abigail, thinking she wouldn't mind one more tryst with Edward. She wondered briefly where he was now. "How did you manage to diminish yourself all those years with two different husbands and not just . . . explode?"

"I think, in fact, looking back now, that I was quite strong as a wife. Both my husbands were passive men who looked to me for direction and impetus. But I never did become a novelist. What I think in retrospect is that I held myself back in order to push them to succeed."

"Like me with Oscar," said Abigail.

"But Oscar was a great man. My husbands were both mediocre."

The oysters arrived. Abigail looked at them in polite consternation.

"Oh hell," said Lila, "they're not kosher, are they? You should have said something!"

"I'm conflicted," said Abigail. "I love oysters."

"I won't tell," said Lila, squeezing lemon over all twelve.

"Remember the old days?" said Abigail. "I'm not even sure what I mean by that. Which days and what I remember about them."

"There were a lot of old days. I find that the older I get, the more sharply and clearly I remember being very young. Twenty, mostly. I remember college so well, better than any other time in my life. I went to Vassar with Teddy . . . until she had to drop out when her father lost all his money. The fifties . . . we had such adventures. We'd take the train down to the city and get into as much trouble as we could. Teddy was the ringleader, and I went along with anything whatsoever. We went to hear a lot of jazz."

"Back in the late forties, when I was in college," said Abigail, "Oscar used to take me to jazz clubs up in Harlem and in the Village. I would go because I loved Oscar, but I hated jazz. It was so squawky and honking, such a lot of posturing, I thought. Oh boy, though, did I love Oscar. I couldn't believe it when he asked me to marry him, I really couldn't. I was his pal."

"You were so lucky," said Lila.

Abigail considered her, liking her immensely now that she'd admitted her new romance wasn't as thrilling as she'd been intimating. Abigail hadn't had a close female friend since Maribelle had died. Maxine, of course, didn't count. "Are you shocked that I had an affair with Ethan's doctor?" she asked.

"No," said Lila hesitantly. "After all, Oscar . . . I mean, you were even."

"Did you ever?" Abigail asked. She had been wondering. "With Oscar."

Lila's eyes flared. "Me, no, I was Teddy's best friend. I would never have, even if he'd shown any interest, which he never did."

"Oscar seduced his best friend's wife."

"Well, Oscar," said Lila indulgently.

Abigail poured a little vinegar-and-shallot dressing on an oyster and slurped it down with pleasure. "It ruined Moe's life," she said. "He threw his wife out and divorced her, and she died of an overdose. Oscar was such a schmuck. You know, he barely acknowledged his own son. He would just go around the apartment pretending Ethan wasn't there."

Lila laughed. "Horrible," she said.

"Yes, I know, we all just laugh and go on adoring him. How did Oscar get away with everything? Even this flap over *Helena* is bolstering his reputation. No matter what, he can't be tarnished."

"Some people are golden," said Lila. "Blessed by the gods, allowed to do as they please without any repercussions."

"Well, he still had to die," said Abigail. "But he died exactly as he had wanted to. A little ahead of schedule, but in his sleep, comfortably, of a heart attack. I'm sorry I didn't call Teddy to tell her. I didn't know her number; that's the truth."

"She suffered a lot," said Lila. "She still mourns him."

"To tell you the truth, I think she was far more in love with him than I was. But their love affair was always illicit. I know from my own how sexy that is. It never got old with Edward. I never tired of him, and I always felt passionately toward him."

"How long did your affair last?"

"Three years!" said Abigail. The thought now astonished her, that that handsome young man had maintained his interest in her for so long. "It only ended because he moved away when his wife got sick, to Arizona, for her lungs. Oh, I was heartbroken. It's funny how heartbreak fades gradually. When he left, I truly thought I couldn't go on. I loved that man, but after a few years, I woke up one morning and found that I wasn't pining anymore. Life went on with Oscar."

The waiter took away the oyster tray and empty glasses, smirking.

"Did Oscar know about your affair?" Lila asked.

"I doubt it," said Abigail, "but if he had, he wouldn't have cared at all."

"I don't believe you," said Lila.

"It's true."

"I bet he would have been devastated."

"No," said Abigail, thoughtfully. "Maybe at first, but he would have gotten over it."

Lila let it drop, although it was clear she disagreed. "The old days," she said. "I remember one night over at Teddy's when Oscar was there, a party they were having. Does it bother you to hear about this?"

"After all this time, I'm well past anything but curiosity," said Abigail.

"Well, they had on some sort of wild music, as usual. I always loved jazz, unlike you. And candles lit, a fire in the fireplace; it was magical and bohemian. Teddy was making something, probably a big paella, in the kitchen. Oscar was sketching a young dancer who must have been about his daughters' age, twenty or thereabouts. Samantha and Ruby had both left home by then. The young girl was so smitten with him. I watched from a couch. . . . Oscar must have been in his early sixties then, which made him more than three times her age. She was sprawled on Teddy's couch . . . long legs draped over one arm. Big brown eyes, hair messy in that seductive way, her limbs all sprawling. He drew her as if . . . you know. I remember watching her seduce Oscar, waiting to feel envious, and feeling only curiosity. It was then that I must have realized that I wasn't pining for Oscar anymore. I watched her and admired her as if I were him."

"Oh yes, I remember when young girls looked so delectable to me suddenly," said Abigail. "It wasn't a sexual thing, I don't think; it was just getting on to the next phase of life. If we'd lived in a primitive sort of tribe or something, we'd have been elevated to wise old crone status, helping the young girls mate and raise their young. There must be a biological component to that feeling. It's like lust, in that it's a kind of sensual fascination, but it isn't lust. But it makes us love to watch them all the same."

"All right, I have to know something," said Lila. The wine had arrived, and they were now well into their first glasses. The color in Lila's soft cheeks was high. Her eyes sparkled. Abigail was smitten anew; Lila looked so much like Emily Robinson, the pretty blond girl she'd admired in her class at Brooklyn College. Emily had been sexily plump like Lila, with that same endearing, beguiling combination of earnestness and intelligence.

"Okay, what?" said Abigail.

"I can't ask Teddy, for some reason," said Lila. "All right, here it is. What was Oscar like in bed?"

Abigail burst into a guffaw. "Oh my!" she said. "What a question."

"Sorry," said Lila. "I hope you're not offended."

"Not at all," said Abigail. She lifted her wineglass and took a sip. Then she put her glass down and said, "He didn't interest me at all that way. We didn't have great chemistry, I guess. I preferred Edward. Edward was sensitive and gentle, thoughtful. Oscar didn't care about anything but his own pleasure. Like a big dog."

Lila's eyes turned inward, as if she were picturing this. "That's what I thought," she said. Abigail could almost see her mouth watering. "My husbands were both so irritatingly sensitive and gentle, I sometimes wanted to shake them. You know . . . not at the same time, of course. But somehow I always ended up with those poetic types. I really would have preferred a big dog."

"Well, you should have shtupped Oscar! Everyone else got to."

"My friend's lover?"

"I agree, it would have been very bad form."

"Anyway, he wasn't interested in me."

"Oh, sure he was."

"I swear he wasn't."

"I don't see how he possibly couldn't have been," said Abigail.

"I am sure that the only reason you never went to bed with him was that you were loyal to Teddy. If you hadn't been . . ."

Abigail and Lila both laughed.

"That's funny," said Lila, "you, reassuring me that your husband really did desire me."

"I guess that's just the kind of man Oscar was," said Abigail.

"Actually, I think it's more that that's the kind of woman you are," said Lila.

"That I'll take as a compliment," said Abigail, "although I don't know why."

"Yes you do," said Lila.

Maxine had a sour taste in the back of her throat from all the smoking she'd been doing lately. It was incredible that she had avoided getting even a smoker's hack, let alone emphysema or lung cancer. The only bad effect seemed to be this foul taste in her gullet. Maybe back in the dim, unremembered dawn of her life, she had made a pact with some devil or minor demon for consequence-free smoking in exchange for her mortal soul. What did she need with a mortal soul? She needed to smoke.

Lighting another cigarette, she said to Paula Jabar, "Well, I'm just about done. How are you coming along?"

For the past three hours, Paula had been asking Maxine questions, standing there naked in her studio while Maxine painted her in the style of *Mercy* and *Helena*. Some whiz kid at *Artforum* had decided that this would be a great idea, for Maxine to be interviewed by Paula while she painted Paula's portrait, then to run a reproduction of the portrait alongside an edited transcription of the interview. Maxine didn't like to talk while she painted. It felt unnatural.

Her brain wasn't made that way. Compounding her exhaustion was the fact that she wanted very badly to sound brilliant, unpretentious, original, and fascinating, and she wanted the portrait to be all of those things, too, as well as do justice to Paula's beauty. And even worse, she had become aware of an increasing attraction to Paula, intensifying the longer they talked, the longer she was forced to stare at that lush young body and reproduce it in paint, the sexiest of substances. But the most complicated factor of all for Maxine during these past hours had been a definite, inescapable sinking feeling of humble hats-off respect for her once-despised nemesis. The girl was smart. She was warm, too, and funny. Her self-conscious ghetto patois was almost nowhere in evidence. Her questions were knowledgeable and provocative. In fact, she had enchanted and seduced Maxine from the instant she'd arrived, in a cloud of tropical scent, a shimmering, dusky vision in greens and blues, and slid out of her dress and underthings without an instant's self-consciousness. Even if this had been little more than a carefully calculated ploy to disarm a hostile party, it had worked on an old tortoise as crusty and suspicious as Maxine, who had to admit to herself that Paula Jabar deserved every shred of her fame, fortune, critical success, and popular adulation. Admitting this to herself in the grip of all her simultaneous and equal desires was costing her a good deal of her limited energy.

"Just a few more questions, if you can hack it," said Paula. "You've said a lot of tremendous things already, though, so if you want to stop . . ."

"No," said Maxine with a burst of determination. "I spent eighty-four years waiting for this, I don't want it to end an instant too soon."

"Well then," said Paula. "We've spent three hours discussing your influences and your techniques and your history and all that, so let's get down to some brass tacks here."

"Okay," said Maxine, as if she were heading into a blizzard with an umbrella and a book of matches. "Shoot."

"I was not exactly on my A game the other night, but I liked your bluntness. I get so much admiration and praise, it's satisfying for someone I respect so much to take me to task. You made me think."

"I thought you handled it perfectly," said Maxine, feeling icy winds begin to shriek around her. She squinted at Paula through the smoke from the cigarette clamped between her teeth. Paula was standing in front of a bare white wall at the edge of the studio in full daylight from the windows. She stood with her arms at her sides, her legs slightly apart, looking directly at Maxine. It was a strong stance, simple and natural. Her muscular haunches were in alluring disproportion to her narrow torso. Her breasts were small and firm and tipped with brown nipples. Her biceps bulged; her skin was a glossy and perfectly consistent shade of half-French, half-Algerian caramel.

Paula smiled. "I handled it *okay,*" she said, as if that hadn't been the point, to have Maxine reassure her. "But now I want to know, between you and me and your dog and the readership of *Artforum*; I want to hear you let fly about the current art world, what's going on now with us kids. I imagine your statement the other night was only the tip of the iceberg. I bet you hate a lot of what you see out there. I bet it drives you up a wall."

"I'm not sure I have anything to add to what I said that night," said Maxine. She paused for a while as she added tiny dabs of acid green to Paula's breastbone and lips and the deep reddish gloss of her hair. The portrait wasn't entirely satisfactory. Something was off in Paula's expression; Maxine hadn't quite caught the brutal, cool, uncompromising ambition that lay just underneath her sexy warmth. She had painted a gorgeous young woman, not an artist.

She stepped back a moment to study Paula's eyes as she had painted them, then looked up at her real eyes. She looked at her genitals, then at the genitals she'd painted. Paula's black pubic hair had been waxed into a narrow vertical band, in which her cunt was set and displayed like a jewel. Her dark eyes were impermeable, tough, knowing. These were the key to getting Paula, her extreme lack of vulnerability, her self-possession. Her sexuality was marshaled by artifice and contained by her watchfulness. Oscar would have done something extreme to make eyes and labia pop out of the picture, but what? How the hell was she supposed to know how to do this? Why the fuck had she agreed to this silly exercise? Maybe *Helena* had been a fluke.

In a fit of intuitive irritation, she stabbed a daub of dark purple on each eyelid, a pointillist darkening, then duplicated it on Paula's labia; then did the same with light jabs of pure white paint, the only pure white in the entire painting. That was it; that was the right direction. Suddenly, Paula's eyes and cunt jumped out at the viewer, highlighted with equal menacing force. It gave the painting, Maxine thought, a startling focus. Eyes and cunt were connected to each other now in a way that both repelled and intrigued. That was Paula.

Maxine said in a confiding rush loosened by the sense of relief this gave her, "I don't get out much to galleries. I'm not very interested in what you kids are up to now, frankly. The art world is no longer relevant. The only reason I've kept painting, speaking for myself, is that I have nothing better to do, and because people still buy them occasionally, so I can pay the electric bill."

"You think no one cares about art anymore?"

"I think very few people care about art anymore, if by 'art' you mean painting."

"Well, they ought to."

"No, they shouldn't," said Maxine. "It's been supplanted by more 'exciting' things. Conceptual hoo-ha and technical wizardry. Art is primarily special effects and marketing schemes. Beauty is apparently considered limp-wristed and useless now."

Paula laughed, and didn't deny this. "What do you think of these younger male artists who use their semen instead of paint?"

Maxine picked up a bigger brush and jabbed it repeatedly and lightly into a slick of a smoky, soft black, her favorite, to coat the tips of the bristles. "There's nothing new under the sun."

Paula smiled with a glint of aggression. "You objected to my ghetto boxes; don't you have anything to say about these art-star boys who come all over their work and sell it for half a million dollars? Semen!"

"I think," said Maxine, jabbing the brush here and there on the canvas to create the spongy texture of shadows on the wall behind Paula, "it's a great racket."

"I expected you to rant about the aesthetic poverty of it all."

"I might," said Maxine, "in a different mood." She said nothing more for a few minutes, concentrating on getting the subtle shadows right on Paula's collarbone, under her lower lip. The bitter taste in the back of her throat was worse. She put the cigarette out in the ashtray by her elbow and looked at the portrait from about two feet away, then four, then six, then immediately touched the tips of the brush again very lightly to Paula's clavicle. This thing was almost finished. The shocking white on the eyelids and labia had been a stroke of genius, or at least a stroke of inspiration brought on by desperation, which was often the same thing, in Maxine's experience.

"To change the subject, what do you most regret doing or not doing in your life?" Paula asked.

"I regret," said Maxine, "and you can print this, that I let the love of my life, Jane Fleming, get away about thirty years ago. My second-greatest regret is that I wasn't more famous during my lifetime. I wish I had seized and pursued and hunted down the two things I most wanted and failed to secure for myself. Self-denial is pointless. Niceness is ridiculous. You're a very smart young woman, to know this already."

"You think I'm not nice?" Paula asked, dimples flashing.

"I think you're perfectly nice, when you want to be. But if someone gets in your way, I imagine you would not stop to worry about anyone's tender feelings. If something is in your way, it has to be gotten out of your way. You want to be famous, and that's what it takes. There is no other way."

"I'm not so sure about that," said Paula.

"You live where? New Jersey?"

"Yes," said Paula.

"In Montclair, I understand," said Maxine. "Nice town. And you're married?"

"Yes," said Paula.

"To a white academic, am I correct?"

"My husband teaches philosophy at Rutgers, yes," said Paula. "And he is white. But Irish." She laughed. "The niggas of Europe."

"Oh," said Maxine, "Europe has many different kinds of niggers. So you're married; I hope happily on the whole, and if so, I would say, hold on to him no matter what, because when you're old, you'll be glad you did. It is unnatural to grow old alone. I envy those lucky people who have longtime mates who remember them when they were young, remember them through the years." She took a deep breath, put a hand on her chest. "Speaking of old age, my dear. We have taken up enough of each other's time. In other words, I need to lie down now."

Paula reached over and turned off the tape recorder and, without asking permission, went over to look at the portrait. She stood just behind Maxine, gazing. Maxine stiffened, suddenly worried.

"Oh my God," Paula whispered into Maxine's ear. "Girl, you are good."

Maxine felt herself melt a little, felt her heart warm and tender in her own chest, almost like an ache. "Thank you," she said.

"This is great, Maxine. I feel honored. . . ." Paula kissed Maxine's cheek, cupped her other cheek in one hand, and bumped her head briefly against Maxine's. Maxine sighed like a small child being caressed by her mother, except this was Paula Jabar, and she was naked.

"I'll get dressed and go now," said Paula, "and let you rest. . . ."

When Paula had dressed and gone, taking her perfume with her, her bright brown eyes, her flowing gestures and shimmering outfit, Maxine went in search of Katerina. She found her crouched over a box of drawings at the back of the studio.

"Did I say everything all right?" Maxine asked her.

Katerina looked up from the box. There was a smudge of dust on her chin. "I didn't listen to everything," she said apologetically. "But I could tell you were brilliant."

"Katerina," said Maxine, "I told you a while ago, you are the executor—or should I say executrix—of my will."

"I know," said Katerina. "When you die, I have to make sure your will is honored, and call your lawyer, and see that your ashes are thrown into New York harbor."

"But what you don't know is that I've left you everything," said Maxine. "All of my paintings, my dog, this loft, and the money in my bank account. You can have all of it, and my paints, and my journals, and everything else. All I ask is that you walk Frago twice a day and make sure my retrospective is done right. Work closely with Michael Rubinstein. You know more than anyone else the work I'm most proud of."

Katerina had stood up during this little speech, and now she grasped Maxine's hand and said, "Are you going to die?"

"Yes," said Maxine, then added through her bone-weary muzziness, "eventually I am, so I wanted you to know all of this from me before I go. You've been an absolute angel to me these past few years, and I can't think of anyone else I'd rather leave it all to."

"What about the tefillin?" Katerina asked.

"Give them to Abigail. Let her decide whether or not that little kid should get them. Everything else, all my crap, what little money I have, you keep. You can live here or sell the place and move somewhere more interesting. I don't care."

Katerina said, "I don't deserve this."

"Now I'm going to go lie down," said Maxine, letting her hand go. "If I'm not up by the time you leave, don't forget to come and wake me."

"I won't forget," said Katerina, looking dazed.

In her bedroom, Maxine kicked off her shoes and flopped onto her bed with a grunt of relief. She lay on her back and looked up at her ceiling. Several things flitted through her mind at once—regret about a few of the things she'd said to Paula this afternoon, which sounded fatuous when she replayed them in her memory; an image of her niece Ruby at the dog run, looking so much like Oscar; a sudden craving for vanilla ice cream; a brief memory of Oscar as a young man walking down Broadway snapping pictures of a young Maxine, who was thirsty and hot and out of sorts; a momentary fear that Frago needed to go out and was suffering from an overfull bladder; a sudden recollection of the newsstand on Houston Street her father had always taken her to every morning, where the old Armenian always cackled at little Maxine as he handed her father his newspapers, one in Yiddish, one in English. The Armenian had lost his front teeth and half his fingers; his cheeks were bristled with black whiskers like spiders' legs. Every morning, he had given Maxine a lollipop. He was like the troll who lived under the bridge in the old story. With the image of the Armenian handing over the lollipop, eyes bulging with frightening goodwill, as vivid in her mind as if it were happening right that moment, Maxine drifted into a deep and dream-filled sleep.

Epilogue

Henry Burke and Ralph Washington stood alone together at Maxine's retrospective with glasses of red wine. They were the only ones in the broad hallway of the Michael Rubinstein Gallery, where *Helena* hung next to *Paula*. People were just starting to arrive; a few early birds milled about, examining Maxine's new series of black-and-white abstracts in the main gallery. Upstairs in the smaller galleries was a selection of the best of her older works.

Both men wore tuxedos. Henry's was rented and fit him imperfectly; Ralph had recently bought his, and wore it with dapper enjoyment. Henry looked peaked and ill at ease; he had lost a good deal of weight over the past months. Ralph, on the other hand, had gained a few pounds, and had achieved a courtly, gleaming plumpness, which oddly became him.

"Well," said Henry, not looking Ralph in the eye. "Maxine's work looks good, all hung up like this. I had wondered how it would be, in the aggregate. And these two portraits are great in their own right."

"How's your book?" Ralph asked.

"It's coming along," said Henry, not altogether honestly. "There's so much rich material to mine."

In truth, he was flummoxed by the richness of the material he'd amassed. And distracting him from writing the book was the fact that he had somehow managed to fall into a sexually passionate love affair with Ruby Feldman. Adultery was exhausting, he found; he didn't have the stomach for it. He was on the verge of mental collapse at the moment. His wife, Melanie, was wandering around in the main gallery. Soon, she and his mistress would be in the same room. He thought he might faint, throw up, or both at once.

"That's for sure," said Ralph, chuckling. He had cut off his devil's horn dreadlocks and now sported a close Afro, a neat cap of hair. "It was an honor to get to know all these women in his life. I have become especially close to his widow, Abigail."

Henry stared at him. "When I started out," he said with a tinge of bitterness, "I thought Oscar was the most enviable man in human history. I thought he was the guy who had it all." He took a gingerly sip of wine. He was drinking it to help himself relax, but every acidic sip brought him closer to vomiting, so it was a careful balancing act. "Now, after talking to all the people who knew him best, I see him very differently. I see him as a very lonely man. Very isolated among all these devoted women. I learned a lot from my research, you could say."

"I'm sorry to hear that," said Ralph with preacherly consolation. His lips gleamed redly with the wine. "I had the opposite experience. I discovered how truly lucky Oscar was, how blessed. I had originally thought of him as a sort of outsider, isolated, as you say, by his own self-imposed limitations. Now I see that he created his own inside. He was always true to himself."

Henry stared at him again, formulating a question. "I wonder," he said after a moment, "what you make of his two households. It strikes me that he needed to have a toehold in both places to avoid real intimacy."

Ralph laughed, throwing his head back. Henry blinked, surprised at the force of the other man's amusement. "Oh ho ho," Ralph said, laughing. "Oscar would think it was funny to hear you say that."

"Maybe," said Henry. He scratched his chin. "I'm sure he would."

"What would Maxine make of all this hoopla if she were alive to see it?" Ralph asked, looking around. The Metropolitan Museum of Art had loaned *Helena* to the gallery. Out of gratitude, Michael Rubinstein had offered in return to host, instead of the usual free opening for all the riffraff in street clothes, an invitation-only black-tie party to raise money for the museum. "They called her a feminist art pioneer in the *Voice* yesterday."

"Maxine would have choked on her own tongue before she would have had anything to do with the word *feminist*," said Henry. "She said she thought feminism was boring and didactic."

Ralph looked up at the portrait of Paula. "Do you think these are as good as Oscar's portraits, the way a lot of people are saying?"

Henry peered first at one portrait and then the other, as if he had never thought much about the question before and was considering it for the first time. Maybe it was just his mood, but the painting of the younger Jane Fleming seemed just slightly self-conscious, and the new one, of Paula Jabar, seemed a little unbalanced, overly vivid. He contrasted them in his memory's eye to *Mercy*, which he recalled was jazzy without being garish, joyful and full of life.

"No," said Henry. "Frankly, I think *Mercy* is by far the best of the three. Do you think these are as good?"

"I'm afraid I do," said Ralph. "I wish I didn't. I feel disloyal to Oscar."

"Maybe I'm seeing them differently, knowing they're imitations of Oscar by Maxine and not really genuinely her own artistic vision," said Henry.

"Could be," said Ralph. "Knowing that changed everything for me. I tried not to let it."

Just then, a group of five women entered from the street, coming in at the far end of the gallery, chattering, patting and smoothing their hair to repair the ravages of the windy evening outside: Teddy and her two daughters, her friend Lila, and Oscar's widow, Abigail, dressed in evening gowns, all in striking colors. They appeared to be laughing together at something Teddy was saying.

Henry's heart constricted at the sight of Ruby. Where was Melanie? Ruby was wearing a strapless green dress and had her hair piled on top of her head. She looked breathtakingly glamorous; Henry couldn't imagine how he had managed to win her, assuming she could ever be won. He had fallen madly, adolescently in love with her, and now felt that he couldn't live without her. This had not been part of his plan. He had only meant to follow Teddy's advice to have an innocent but passionate affair of the heart so his wife would sleep with him again. He had never meant for it to get so out of hand. He wished Melanie would magically vanish off the face of the earth so he could marry Ruby. He would never have either the nerve or the heartlessness to leave Melanie; for the sake of his son, he would have to give Ruby up before Melanie found out about the whole thing and his life exploded. But the thought of going on for the rest of his life without Ruby, now that he knew what it was like to be with her, felt like being locked in a stone tower with no windows. But if Melanie found out . . . He swallowed hard to tamp down a rising tide of nausea.

"What's Abigail doing with Teddy and her little coterie?" he asked.

"Oh, they're all very friendly with one another now," said Ralph.

"Why?"

"Why not?" said Ralph. "No reason not to be, anymore."

Surrounding the group of five women, escorting one or more of them apiece, were three men. Henry recognized Samantha's tall, gangly, exceedingly dorky husband, Ivan Sandusky, with his thatch of white hair and potbelly, and he had a feeling the bald, slender old man was Teddy's old friend and new beau; she had mentioned him the week before when they'd talked on the telephone. But he had no idea who the slouching young man was, his hand hovering near Ruby's elbow, his hair unnecessarily copious. All Henry knew was that he didn't like the way Ruby leaned her shoulder against that boy's so intimately. The idea that she might have other lovers besides himself had never occurred to Henry before, and now that it had, he found himself violently jealous, on top of all the other terrible things he was already feeling.

The deejay suddenly got his act together; music leapt from the speakers. After a moment, Henry recognized Stravinsky's *Rite of Spring*.

Michael Rubinstein came bustling through the hall. Behind him scuttled an officious-looking, glamorous young black woman.

"Hello," he said to the two biographers, and dove into the gathering crowd.

"Get something to drink if you like," said the assistant just before she vanished behind her employer.

"We are drinking," said Henry to Ralph.

Ralph nodded at Henry. "I've been looking forward to this evening," he said. "I imagine you have, too."

"Oh, God no," said Henry.

"Why not?"

Henry looked at Ralph. "I barely know you," he said. "But I have no one else to tell this to. I'm having an affair with Oscar's daughter Ruby. My wife is here tonight, too; wild horses and five armies couldn't have kept her away. They're both here. We couldn't get a baby-sitter for Maxine's memorial service, so she stayed home that day; I was hoping the same thing would happen tonight, but no such luck. I'm terrified one of them will make a scene. My wife will smell it out the minute she sees Ruby and me together; she'll just *know*. And Ruby won't back down if Melanie comes at her; she has no sentimental ideals about the sanctity of marriage. She thinks it's absurd for people to be one another's property or to impose the unnatural restrictions of monogamy on human nature."

Ralph looked at Henry with dawning empathy. Then he burst out laughing.

"What's so funny?" Henry asked.

"Oscar would *love* that," said Ralph. "He would love it! Relax, man. They're not going to make a scene, not here. Just enjoy yourself. Ruby? Well done. She's a lovely girl. She doesn't seem the type to be confrontational or dramatic. You should just enjoy yourself."

"She brought a date," said Henry.

"Pretend you're Oscar for one night. Enjoy yourself, drink up, and get that look off your face like you're about to pass out on the floor."

"Fuck," said Henry. He put his hand on Ralph's shoulder to steady himself and finished his wine.

Ralph said, "Come on, let's join the party."

Two Portraits of the Artist as a Bad Boy

OSCAR FELDMAN
A Life in Paint.
By Ralph Washington.
445 pp. W.W. Norton & Company. $34.95.

AN EYE FOR WOMEN
The Life of Oscar Feldman.
By Henry Burke.
398 pp. Yale University Press. $29.95.

By **PENNY HIGHTOWER-JONES**

WHENEVER two biographies of the same subject come out at roughly the same time, it goes without saying that it's impossible not to read them comparatively. And when these biographies are as radically different in approach and tone as "Oscar Feldman" and "An Eye for Women," a reviewer might be forgiven for having, as it were, a field day.

Biographical subjects don't get much juicier than Oscar Feldman, who was a notorious womanizer and a figurative painter during the Abstract Expressionists' ironclad rule of downtown New York. Born on the Lower East Side in 1923, the son of a Jewish butcher, a graduate of Brooklyn College, and a dropout from New York's Art Students League, Oscar Feldman was a largely self-taught painter who disdained his contemporaries and separated himself from the New York School of painters. His only subject, his obsession in both life and work, was the female nude. "Women are the mystery of life," he once wrote.

This lusty contrarian denied himself no pleasure he deemed worthy of pursuing, whether booze, sex, artistic success, or controversy. Where most men might have found one wife, household and set of offspring more than enough, Oscar Feldman managed to have two, simultaneously, for many decades: the Riverside Drive apartment owned by his wife, Abigail Feldman, mother of his autistic son, Ethan; and the house in Greenpoint, Brooklyn, owned by his mistress of more than forty years, Claire St. Cloud, familiarly known as "Teddy," the mother of his illegitimate twin daughters, Ruby and Samantha, who bear the name Feldman. In addition, Feldman kept a studio on the Bowery, where he painted, and, by all accounts, bedded, a long succession of models.

"Oscar Feldman" and "An Eye for Women" both succeed well enough in terms of organizing Feldman's daily life and integrating his work; Washington and Burke are both adept chroniclers and proficient, if workmanlike, writers, and both have a solid grasp of Mr. Feldman's legacy as an artist.

Where the quality of the two books diverges, and where one can be said to succeed and the other to laboriously fail, is in capturing the magnificently selfish ebullience of Feldman's life and relating this appetitive nature to his paintings. Where Mr. Burke is unsparing, almost gimlet-eyed, in his approach to Mr. Feldman's excesses and peccadilloes, Mr. Washington seems to be blowing soap bubbles and air kisses at him.

For example, when broaching the topic of Lily McGovern Santangelo, the model for the 1988 portrait "Gina" (Feldman always gave his portraits a name other than the model's in order, he said, to distinguish art from life), Mr. Burke writes, "Oscar took her to bed without a second thought, despite the fact that she was eighteen years old, a virgin, and at the time seriously contemplating becoming a Franciscan nun.

" 'I met him at my father's birthday party and agreed to model for him because he completely bamboozled me,' " Burke quotes Mrs. Santangelo, now a devout Catholic housewife and mother of three in Rye, New York, as saying. " 'Somehow I could not say no to him. He was very forceful. I was ashamed for years about it. I said many prayers that my sin should be erased and that I could find it in my heart to forgive him.' "

Mr. Washington, on the other hand, apparently either declined to interview Mrs. Santangelo or decided to disregard her side of the story. He chooses instead to drop a rosy, almost romantic veil over his subject's near rape of a girl young enough to be his granddaughter. He writes: "When the lovely, haunting portrait he called *Gina* was completed, having immortalized her in paint, Oscar took the girl to bed and deflowered her."

Washington then quotes from Feldman's daily journal on the subject (a passage one suspects was written with swaggering irony, although Washington presents the entry with a straight face): " 'She was like a newborn suckling fawn, still wet with amniotic fluid.' "

Burke and Washington have equally divergent approaches to the recent, highly publicized revelation that the "Helena" half of Mr. Feldman's famous 1978 diptych, "Mercy and Helena," which had hung for almost thirty years in a place no less illustrious than the Met, was in actuality painted by Mr. Feldman's sister, Maxine, a well-known abstract painter in her own right, in order to win a bet: Each was to paint a work in the style of the other and pass it off as the other's.

Mr. Burke writes, "After Maxine painted *Helena* and Oscar painted what Maxine later described as 'a complete mess without a clue about abstraction,' Oscar must have been forced to admit, if only privately to himself, that his sister was a far more technically accomplished painter than he was."

He goes on to quote the model for "Helena," the art historian Jane Fleming, who revealed that Maxine had painted it, as saying: " 'I thought it was long past time that the art world saw Maxine for the genius she is. The irony is that Oscar's reputation hasn't been tarnished at all; this just brought him more attention. Typical.' "

Mr. Washington, on the other hand, lamely and euphemistically writes, "The ensuing media storm served not only to deservedly enhance Maxine Feldman's reputation as a painter but also to establish beyond a doubt that Oscar Feldman was too great an artist to be injured by the revelation that only one of his many, many paintings was not, after all, by him. If imitation can be said to be the sincerest form of flattery, then *Helena* stands as an ironic but undeniable testament to his greatness."

If these two written portraits of Oscar Feldman were put on canvas and displayed side by side as a diptych, Burke's would be bright, complex and bold. Burke treats Feldman with all due respect, but also with a light-handed, almost fraternal forbearance, as if his subject were an interesting, garrulous, self-revelatory specimen he'd met in a bar. His is a clear, honest, unsparing portrait of the kind of larger-than-life, amoral artist who seemingly doesn't exist anymore: hard-drinking, prodigious, idiosyncratic, charismatic, possessing an intensely visceral gusto more than any other quality, be it genius, originality, or integrity.

Ralph Washington's Oscar Feldman is executed in the primary colors of a Disney cartoon, didactically outlined and regularly featured, and finished with a good gloss of whitewash.

One thing the two biographers completely agree on, however, is that Oscar Feldman had either the good fortune or the good sense to be surrounded by women as interesting as he was. Abigail Feldman, the late Maxine Feldman, and Teddy St. Cloud emerge in both biographies as fascinating subjects in their own right, so fascinating that this female reviewer couldn't help wishing Mr. Feldman had moved over and given his real-life women a little more room.

Penny Hightower-Jones is a professor of art history at Rutgers.

ALSO BY KATE CHRISTENSEN

THE EPICURE'S LAMENT

Afflicted with a rare disease that will be fatal unless he quits smoking, wily misanthrope Hugo Whittier retreats to his family's dilapidated mansion, determined to smoke himself to death. To his chagrin, his sanctimonious older brother moves in, closely followed by Hugo's estranged wife, their alleged daughter, and his gay uncle. Infuriated at the violation of his sanctum, Hugo devises perverse ploys to send the intruders packing. Yet, the unexpected consequences of his schemes keep forcing him to reconsider love and life itself.

Fiction/978-0-385-72098-4

JEREMY THRANE

Jeremy Thrane seems to have everything. As the boyfriend of the handsome (but closeted) movie star Ted Masterson, he lives in Ted's beautiful apartment and has an easy job that gives him time to read books and write his novel. When a gossip columnist overhears Jeremy talking about Ted, Jeremy's perfect world begins to crumble, and Ted asks him to leave. Jeremy finds that he needs to reconnect with the eccentric family whose love he has taken for granted and determine which of his friends truly have his well-being in mind. In a dizzying world of art galleries, casual sex, dry wit, and drier martinis, Jeremy Thrane must finally figure out what it means to grow up and fall in love.

Fiction/978-0-385-72034-2

IN THE DRINK

At the age of twenty-nine Claudia Steiner finds herself serving as secretary to an insane socialite who barks orders from her toilet and expects Claudia to ghostwrite her novels. For this she is paid enough to keep her in overpriced cocktails and cabs, but not enough to cover the rent on her roach-infested apartment. She's hopelessly in love with her best friend, William, who may or may not be gay, and she's still pursued by her ex-lover, an unpublished epic poet married to a Romanian stripper. Claudia's wry sense of humor and keen appreciation for whiskey keep the demons at bay, but what keeps her going is her persistent little flame of belief in herself.

Fiction/978-0-385-72021-2

ANCHOR BOOKS
Available at your local bookstore, or
visit www.randomhouse.com